Jeremiah unfolded, drawing hi

been wearing the coat, any onlooker, mortal or otherwise,
would have seen the m

From the wrist up, runn
of mortal labor and yea
Summer's Court, ran ink
mistake them for tribal
daggered fingers, sending
The knotwork, vaguely tribal or vaguely Celtic, shifted with
his mood.

Those who remembered his tenure at Court would have
heard the whispers. *A dwarven-inked lance—they crossed him,
though, and did not expect him to survive.*

He lived, did the Armormaster, and Finnion's clan is no more.

Bannon & Clare

"Saintcrow scores a hit with this terrific steampunk series that rockets through a Britain-that-wasn't with magic and industrial mayhem with a firm nod to Holmes. Genius and a rocking good time."
—Patricia Briggs

"Saintcrow melds a complex magic system with a subtle but effective steampunk society, adds fully fleshed and complicated characters, and delivers a clever and highly engaging mystery that kept me turning pages, fascinated to the very end."
—Laura Anne Gilman

"Innovative world-building, powerful steampunk, master storyteller at her best. Don't miss this one.... She's fabulous."
—Christine Feehan

"Lilith Saintcrow spins a world of deadly magic, grand adventure, and fast-paced intrigue through the clattering streets of a maze-like mechanized Londonium. *The Iron Wyrm Affair* is a fantastic mix of action, steam, and mystery dredged in dark magic with a hint of romance. Loved it! Do not miss this wonderful addition to the steampunk genre."
—Devon Monk

"Lilith Saintcrow's foray into steampunk plunges the reader into a Victorian England rife with magic and menace, where clockwork horses pace the cobbled streets, dragons rule the ironworks, and it will take a sorceress's discipline and a logician's powers of deduction to unravel a bloody conspiracy."
—Jacqueline Carey

BY LILITH SAINTCROW

Blood Call

GALLOW AND RAGGED
Trailer Park Fae
Roadside Magic
Wasteland King

BANNON & CLARE
The Iron Wyrm Affair
The Red Plague Affair
The Ripper Affair

DANTE VALENTINE NOVELS
Working for the Devil
Dead Man Rising
The Devil's Right Hand
Saint City Sinners
To Hell and Back
Dante Valentine (omnibus)

JILL KISMET NOVELS
Night Shift
Hunter's Prayer
Redemption Alley
Flesh Circus
Heaven's Spite
Angel Town
Jill Kismet (omnibus)

A ROMANCE OF ARQUITAINE NOVELS
The Hedgewitch Queen
The Bandit King

AS LILI ST. CROW

THE STRANGE ANGELS SERIES
Strange Angels
Betrayals
Jealousy
Defiance
Reckoning

ROADSIDE MAGIC

Gallow and Ragged:
BOOK TWO

LILITH SAINTCROW

www.orbitbooks.net

Copyright © 2016 by Lilith Saintcrow
Excerpt from *Wasteland King* copyright © 2016
by Lilith Saintcrow
Excerpt from *Blood Call* copyright © 2015 by Lilith Saintcrow

Orbit
Hachette Book Group
1290 Avenue of the Americas
New York, NY 10104
www.orbitbooks.net

Printed in the United States of America

RRD-C

First edition: January 2016

10 9 8 7 6 5 4 3 2 1

Orbit is an imprint of Hachette Book Group.
The Orbit name and logo are trademarks of Little, Brown Book Group Limited.

The Hachette Speakers Bureau provides a wide range of authors for speaking events. To find out more, go to www.hachettespeakersbureau.com or call (866) 376-6591.

The publisher is not responsible for websites (or their content) that are not owned by the publisher.

Library of Congress Cataloging-in-Publication Data
Saintcrow, Lilith.
  Roadside magic / Lilith Saintcrow.—First edition.
      pages ; cm.—(Gallow and ragged ; Book 2)
  ISBN 978-0-316-27787-7 (paperback)—ISBN
978-1-4789-6083-6 (audio book downloadable)—ISBN
978-0-316-27786-0 (ebook)   1. Fairies—Fiction.   I. Title.
  PS3619.A3984R63 2016
  813'.6—dc23
                                                    2015030107

For L.I, again, as promised.

Hark, hark, the dogs all bark,
The beggars are coming to town,
Some in rags, and some in jags,
And one in a velvet gown.
—MOTHER GOOSE

VENGEANCE

1

*S*he waited, perched next to a stone gargoyle's leering, watching the rubies of brakelights, the diamonds of headlights. Smelling exhaust and cold iron, a breath of damp from the river. A hint of crackling ozone—lightning about to strike. The faint good aroma of a soft spring rain approaching.

He did not keep her waiting long.

"Oh, my darling. What fine merriment we have had." Goodfellow melded out of the darkness, his boyface alight with glee. "You are the best of children, delighting your sire's heart so ful—"

The song hit him squarely, fueled by Robin's calm, controlled breathing, and knocked the Fatherless to the ground. She was on her feet in an instant, the stolen crowbar burning in her palms as she lifted, brought it down with a convulsive crunch. Iron smoked on sidhe flesh, and by the time she ran out of breath and the song died, thick blue blood spattered the rooftop, smoking and sizzling.

"You," she hissed between her teeth. "You killed her. You pixie-led her car. You killed Sean. You *did* it."

Amazingly, Puck Goodfellow began to laugh. "Aye!" he shouted, spitting broken teeth. They gleamed, sharp ivory, chiming against the roof. "Robin, Robin Ragged, I will kill all those close to thy *heart,* I will have thy voice!*" He slashed upward with his venom-tip dagger, but Robin was ready and skipped aside.*

Not today. *She didn't say it. She'd finished her inhale, and the song burst out again, given free rein.*

Smoke, blood, iron, the crowbar stamping time as the razor-edged music descended on the Fatherless. Some whispered that he was the oldest of the sidhe, some said he remembered what had caused the Sundering. Others sometimes hinted he was the cause of the division in the Children of Danu, the Little Folk, the Blessed.

When the song faded, Robin dropped the crowbar. It clattered on the roof.

The thing lying before her was no longer sidhe. Full-Twisted and misshapen it writhed; its piping little cries struck the ear foully.

She bent, swiftly, and her quick fingers had the pipes and the dagger, Puck Goodfellow's treasures. The Twisted thing with its hornlike turtle-shell swiped at her with a clawed, malformed hand, and its voice was now a growl, warning.

Her breath came high and hard, her ribs flickering. The dagger went into her pocket, its sheath of supple leaf-stamped leather blackened and too finely grained to be animal hide. The pipes—she almost shuddered with revulsion as she poked a finger in each one, and near the bottom, where they were thicker, she touched glass thrice.

Three glass ampoules, like the ones she had bargained Mac-Donnell's kin into making. Decoys within decoys, but these held a sludge that moved grudgingly against its chantment-sealed container. A true cure. Like her, he had decided the only safe place to hide such a thing was in his own pocket.

The Twisted, back-broken thing that had been Puck Goodfellow struggled to rise. Morning would probably find it here, too malformed to speak or walk. It might starve to death, it might cripple out the rest of its existence like Parsifleur Pidge, though she had Twisted it far past that poor woodwight's ill-luck. Robin looked down at it, tucking the pipes in her other pocket.

They were powerful, and there was no better time to learn their use.

"For Daisy," she said quietly, "and for Sean."

The thing writhed again, trying to rise, the thick shell of bone on its corkscrewed back scraping the roof. Robin turned away. Full night was falling, and she had only one thought now.

I must find a place to hide.

THE SAVOIGH LIMITED

2

All through that long day, the thing on the rooftop smoked, rocking back and forth belly-up on its bony shell. Its flaccid limbs flopped uselessly; cloudy spring sunshine striped it with steaming weals. It made tiny, unmusical sounds, lost in the noise of traffic below. Horns blared, engines gunned, the murmur of crowds enfolded it. The sun was cruel, for all it was weak, and the thing's eyes were runnels of black tar pouring down its wasted cheeks. Once proud and capering, it was now a Twisted wreck, its wounds still seeping. She had been thorough, the avenging child.

As thorough as he would be, soon. But first, he had to survive the assault of the mortal sun; iron-poisoned and Twist-wounded as he was, it burned as if he were one of Unwinter's dark-creeping legions. The heavy-misting rain was no balm, full of poisonous city fumes and the stinking effluvia of the metal the foolish salt-sweet mortals used to scar every piece of free soil they found.

Had it been summer, their sun might have finished the work the daughter had begun.

Below, the Savoigh Limited throbbed. Once its stone facade

and plaster walls, ornate fixtures and heavy-framed mirrors had been new, then outdated, then seedy, and now refurbished. The winds of urban gentrification blew erratic but inexorable, and the Savoigh, with its uniformed doormen and its high-rent offices, its tiny cold-water studios for the bohemians and its ancient, growling boiler in the basement, had become that most terrible of structures: a fashionable heap.

Rocking steadily, the rhythm of the thing's shell quickened as it threatened to topple. Its piping sounds became more intense, tiny, malformed cries of effort. They soaked through the rooftop's rough surface, burrowing down.

Afterward, if the residents of the Savoigh Limited remembered that chill spring day at all, they remembered an endless string of bad luck. Printers jamming, coffeemakers sputtering, milk and creamer clotted and sour even before their sell-by dates. A scented candle shattered on the fifth floor, spilling hot wax across important paperwork and almost catching the drapes on fire. Plaster sagged. Stray cats wandered in, yowling, and didn't leave until the aroma of their urine soaked the entire building. The boiler sputtered and creaked, moaning, its displeasure felt through wooden floors. Fingers jammed in doors and drawers, toasters overheating, electrical outlets sparking when the cords were jiggled, four fender-benders out front, and the doormen decrying the paucity of tips. Toes catching on carpets, stairs missed and neckbreaking tumbles barely averted, papers scattered and microwaves either not heating anything or scorch-burning it to the container, two mini fridges inexplicably ceasing to work, and more.

All through this, the rocking continued, the creature gaining inches across the roof. Lunchtime came and went, and it became obvious what the thing was aiming for—a pool of shadow in the lee of an HVAC hood, ink-shadow lengthening as the sun tipped past its zenith.

The ill-luck below crested, and one or two of the artists in the studios—their windows facing blank brick walls, their floors humped and buckled as the building settled into gracious decay—saw tiny darts of light in their peripheral vision, gone as soon as they turned their heads. One thought he was having hallucinations and began to furiously paint the two canvases that would make him world-famous before he slid into a hole of madness and alcohol. The other, her recording equipment suddenly functioning, began to play cascades of melody on her electric piano, and for the rest of her life never played from sheet music again. Her compositions were said to cause visions, and she retreated from the world years later to a drafty farmhouse in Maine.

Rocking again. Tipping on the horn-thick edge of the bony shell, sliding into blessed coolness for a moment as the shade swallowed it, back the other way, teetering on the opposite edge, a sharp whistling cry as it pitched back into the shadow, hesitated on the brink...

...and toppled over, landing with a flat chiming sound, out of the killing daylight.

Stillness. Below, paint splashed, music floated down an empty hall, printers suddenly rebooted, the two mini fridges just as inexplicably started working again. A hush descended on the Savoigh Limited, and as the sun-scarred creature huddled under its shell in its dark almost-hole, a rumble of thunder sounded in the distance.

The spring storms were on their way.

A STRANGER'S BED

3

Robin Ragged's throat burned. So did her eyes, every tear she had dammed behind a blank expression threatening to spill free in a bitter flood. There was a joy in solitude, certainly—no bright avid gazes, no crimson lips sneering or whispering hurtful gossip behind scented fans—but it meant she had no reason to keep her face a mask, or her heart a stone.

So she walked alongside the weed-flanked road, a slim, bareshouldered woman in a blue dress, her black heels making crisp little sounds on cracked paving. Despite the tangled glory of her redgold curls, no gaze caught on her, no catcalls pierced her sphere of numbness. Of course, any mortal sensitive enough to see her would no doubt be wise enough to keep his foolish mouth shut, unless he was of the mad or feytouched.

If he was, she would have to find some means of making certain her presence wasn't babbled about. The thought filled her with exhausted revulsion, even if she did have a knife now.

A leafbladed curve in a finely grained, age-blackened sheath hung from a stolen belt low on her hips, chantment-knotted leather attaching it securely, and every time her hand brushed the bone hilt, a queasy thrill sank through her. She was no knight or assassin; death did not delight her as it did some.

Oh, come now, Robin. There is a certain death that would delight you.

That was a useless, dangerous thought, so long practice swept it neatly under a mental carpet. Such a habit, born of long years at Court, was convenient enough.

Especially if you sought to hide a truth from yourself.

It would have been best to leave the city. No realm, sideways or mortal, would hide you forever if both Summer and Unwinter wanted to find you badly enough. The easiest entrances to Summer moved slowly, sometimes on one continent, sometimes another—but Unwinter could find a way through anywhere, its borders only ever a step away, its blood-freshened thresholds losing their vigor only slowly over centuries. Still... the mortal world was weary and gray, but it was also wide, and she could lead a merry chase before she was inevitably brought down. Was it worth it?

Worry about that later. There was one last debt to be paid before Robin could strike out into the mortal world and leave the sidhe to their plague. Now that Summer's borders had been broken, the infection was very likely to spread.

It's what she *deserves.*

Well, yes, but all the other sidhe, especially the lesser who sickened so quickly? Even the ones she'd never met, or the elf-horses, or...

Robin found herself, as the sun reached nooning and tried to pierce a veil of damp-misting cloud, in almost-familiar territory. Thin metal walls, squatting trailers and mobiles, weeds forcing up between cracks in the paving, broken-down fences and trashwood behind the huddled backs of every small squatting domicile. She blinked, pushing her hair back from her forehead, brought back to full, uncomfortable alertness.

She was not grief-mazed enough to wander into the trailer park that had recently held the Queen's prized human pet, the scientist who had mixed the black boils of plague in his little glass bottles and whirling machineries under the benign glow of his computer. She could not step there again for many long mortal lifetimes, not if she wished to remain breathing. The Unseelie had gone a-hunting through that particular mortal space, though now she knew Jacob Henzler's death hadn't been of their making.

No, they had only ridden in the Goodfellow's wake, and though she had struck Puck down in vengeance, she had not added Henzler's name to the list of those she was avenging. Perhaps she should have.

Too late. Look about you now, and plan.

This was another sad little collection of tin cans masquerading as homes clinging to a neglected slice of the city, but there was a certain comfort to be found in its familiarity. Faded paint and rusting walls, the cars up on concrete blocks threaded through with tall weeds, the ramshackle fences and sun-bleached children's toys scattered and overgrown, the trampolines—three of them in this park alone—sitting proudly, like the status symbols they were.

There *were* nice parks, she supposed, with mortals who chose to live in such structures and cared for them. Once, her mother had even received a catalog—BRAND-NEW HOMES! EASY LIVING! Smiling faces, a family grouped around a grill on a patio, all airbrushed until they looked almost like sidhe. Bright smiles, clear skin, but without the sharp, glossy sheen of the sideways realms. Instead, theirs was a purely mortal beauty, interchangeable and brief. Young Robin, not knowing anything about the sideways realms, had thought that the only kind of loveliness once, and a good one, too. Something to be yearned for.

She and her sister had played the game so often. *When I have my own trailer I'm gonna*... Choosing features, deciding about drapes and carpets, the height of luxury a big television and a man whose job kept him gone most of the time. *And all the magazines*, Daisy would whisper. *I'll cut out them pitchers and make them murals, Rob. You see if I don't.*

Stone and Throne, but Daisy had loved her magazines. She could escape into anything sent monthly—Robin would steal them from the drugstore or the supermarket, neighbors' houses or doctors' offices, her technique practiced and sure. It didn't matter what they were about—racing, hunting and fishing, fashion, cooking, anything—Daisy perused them all with the same grave attention, a small line between her childish eyebrows and her redgold hair, paler than Robin's own, falling forward in sleek curls.

Not knowing what had killed her baby sister was bad enough, but to find out she had been pixie-led into a car accident by Puck himself, and then the biggest lie of all... or was it truth?

Dearest Robin, who did *you think you were named for?*

Robin almost staggered. Noon, and she had not yet found a hole to hide in. She needed rest, and milk if she could find it. Half-n-half, sun-yellow butter, even the falsity of flavored, sugar-drenched creamer would do. Anything.

At the end of the street, a brown-and-white trailer slumped. Instinct drew Robin toward it, but before she went any further she turned thrice widdershins, against the direction of the sun. She also touched the matted lock of hair tied carefully with blue silken ribbon on the left side of her head, under the longer sweep of her curls. Next to it, the bone comb nestled, and two long pins, well secured. She needed none of them at the moment, but the elflock was reassuring. You could always tell a Half—or really, any mortal with a tinge of sidhe blood—by the little things. A seam left unraveling, a habit of turning in a complete circle, a single item of clothing worn inside out. Such things had been known to fox pursuit ever since mortals appeared.

Nowadays, simple unbelief sometimes worked, but that was a luxury the Ragged did not have. Long ago, she might have been able to knock at a door and beg a cup of milk and leave a small chantment of spite were she refused, or gratitude if not. It might have even been the best kind, warm from an udder grass-fed and sun-sweetened, not pale and processed. It was more difficult to steal fresh cream these days, with cold iron fencing miserable cows in lots full of refuse and excrement.

Her chosen trailer was old but neat and trim, the postage stamp of a yard edged. Three newspapers sat soggy on the trailer's porch, and the top one looked fresh. She could have checked the dates, but why bother? She had only the foggiest remembrance of how the mortals counted time anymore. There was Summer's half of the year, and Unwinter's. More did not concern a sidhe, especially at Court. The mortal world changed, fickle as the sidhe themselves, and the mortals dragged cold iron from the earth's halls to poison every living bit of green. Sooner or later, though, their machines would fail, their cities would crumble, field and forest would return.

Or so some of the sidhe said, affecting at prophecy.

Robin climbed the rickety porch steps, ignoring the stuffed-full mailbox. No screen, the porch light still burning, and the trashcan, empty, sat at the end of the gently hillocked gravel

13

driveway. The door was locked, of course, but almost any mortal lock was glad to help a sidhe along. This one was a little happier than most, and she nipped quickly through.

It was close and fusty inside, and Robin halted as a cat hissed from atop a humpbacked couch in a darkened living room. It was a sleek beast, a black pelt with white collar and cuffs, its wide green eyes lambent in the shuttered gloom. The kitchen was poor but clean, she saw with a glance, and while the place smelled close, it did not reek of dank neglect. Any sidhe seeking shelter here would find it agreeable. In the old days, a slatternly kitchen would be left stuffed full of ill-luck and maddened pixies.

The cat, catching a breath of sidhe, hopped off her perch and trotted to make acquaintance, forgetting her initial shock. Half sideways themselves, felines were always a good omen, even if they did sometimes hunt scatterbrained pixies and small liggots. Robin bent to scratch behind the ears, smooth the fur along the spine, and whisper a thread of chantment. No mortal in the house that she could hear, and she could be gone in a moment should one arrive. The little catkin here would serve as a handsome sentinel.

Properly introduced, the cat stropped her ankles as she cautiously tried the kitchen. A plastic container of dry cat food, cunningly designed so that it would measure out more as the cat ate, and a burbling fountain full of clear water set on the floor for the cat's delectation, its tank only half full. She could smell a litter box, but not very strongly. There was half a carton of milk in the fridge, and it had not spoiled. Robin drank it all, her throat moving with long, hasty swallows, strangely naked without her locket. Gallow had kept that...

She had not wanted to think of him.

Fortunately, she was tired enough there was little sting to

the memory, even fresh and new as it was. The former Armor-master had seemed almost willing to let her stay, draw trouble and yet more violence to him—*if,* that is, she could be as blithe and bonny as her dead sister.

Daisy.

Jeremiah Gallow's wife.

The trailer's narrow hall held no pictures. She pushed the bedroom door open slowly and found a monk's narrow bed, a closet full of blue overalls with EDDIE neatly embroidered on the left pocket flap, three pairs of workboots ranged below. Cold iron and engine grease, and the smell of a dark-haired male; Robin sniffed a little more deeply. Nobody had slept here for a few days. Perhaps he would be gone tonight, too.

Eddie's dressertop held a jewelry box that played a tinkling tune when opened and a white card stitched with silver tinsel. A wedding invitation. Perhaps he was a-visiting. When he returned, hopefully he would find good fortune awaiting him, and not a smoking ruin reeking of Unwinter.

Robin Ragged fell onto a stranger's bed and did not dream.

BIRTH

4

The storm, stalking the city all through morning and half the afternoon, finally leapt on its quarry with a gush of warm spring rain and a rattle of heavenly artillery. Fat, heavy droplets drummed across the rooftops and washed away frost-rimes from the last hard chill as the wind veered and became sweeter. The Gates of Seelie were open, and lion-maned spring roared forth. Surprised mortals scurried through the downpour, newspapers and grocery bags became soaked, drips started through some ceilings, street drains still blocked from last year's fallen leaves, pine needles, or mortal refuse gurgled and foamed.

Atop the Savoigh, water beaded on the thing's hard, hornlike shell, each drop softening its semi-translucent barrier. The metal hood shielded it from stinging wind, and lightning flashed along whorls and rings decorating its hunched, unlovely carapace. Faint shadows played underneath, something inside twisting and turning, angles pulsing and shimmers of green-yellow.

Thinning, like a snail's curled home soaked in honey or a tortoise's in simmering oils, the hard surface slowly collapsing. It settled, a sheet of hardened leather now instead of a shell, over a small, curled form. Knees drawn up, its vague approximation of a head far too large for the rest of it, spines along its back flexing but unable to pierce through.

Little spatters of foxfire began, flickering around the collapsed shell. It pulsed, a low punky glow, and the pixies solidified as they always did where the Veil was thinning, clotted, or disturbed. Each one a dot of chiming light, their excited wing-clatters lost in the thunder—blue, red, gold, green, each burst of color passing through a pixie's neighbors and giving way to the next, a semaphore of feverish joy. The braver ones swooped down to almost touch the pulsating shape, and each time one did it flushed yellowgreen and darted away, buzzing a little high-pitched squeal. Excitement or trepidation, who could tell? They were probably indistinguishable to the little naked, glowing forms with their gossamer wings.

Lightning again, bleaching the rooftop. In the moment afterward, the tough, thick, elastic covering showed an odd protuberance, almost as if a small fist had struck it from inside.

The pixies flittered, fluttered, but now they observed from a safe distance. Scatterbrained and hummingbird as they were, they knew enough to stay out of reach. Some forgot but were pulled back by the agitated chiming of their brethren.

The spines along its unseen back flexed, not quite piercing the tough almost-leather, membranous as a turtle's egg. The thing, bigger now, rolled across the top of the roof, fists and feet flailing. The rain thinned its covering even more. The pixies, dodging raindrops and turning white each time lightning flashed, followed. The Veil thinned afresh, reverberating with whatever event was rising to the surface of *now*.

A snap. A crunch. A shower of wet saltsmell, spines now piercing the thinned membrane. The thing, on all fours, shook and twisted, the toothy projections from its back scraping and rending. Clear fluid bubbled free, the drumming rain mixing opalescent, steaming slugsheen onto the roof. The Savoigh Limited's ragged, carved gargoyles couldn't bear to watch; they gazed at the river-streets below instead.

Thunder boomed. The thing tore free of the membrane and tumbled free, wet and naked on a gush of smoking birthfluid that stain-scorched the roof's grit-crunching top. Rain spattered, each drop striking twice from the violence of impact. Extra-jointed hands flailing, a scream tearing from a wet *O* of a mouth, yellowgreen irises flashing before the black of the pupils swallowed them whole, the creature steamed. It was clawed both hand and foot; the membrane that had held it dissolved under steady pounding water.

They called him *Eldest*, and *Fatherless*. It pleased him to allow it, sometimes, and surely no other sidhe could do *this*.

The pixies fluttered nearer, nearer, then scattered as its hands and feet shot out again, grasping as if to tear. The newborn thing howled, and the pixies burned yellowgreen to match its eyes before settling on a throbbing, stinging crimson cloud. More and more of them came, flocking to the disturbance in the Veil, climbing out of small holes between the real and the more-than-real.

It collapsed and lay under stinging water-needles. For now, it was content simply to cough the fluid out of its lungs, vomiting jets of rubbery acid foam that etched complex patterns into the mortal roof.

Its belly was hunger-distended, though. Soon, it would need to eat. The pixies were too quick for it to catch in its weakened state.

It didn't matter. Once the rain stopped, prey would creep out to see what the rain had washed up or exposed. Mortals would be best, certainly, but they were large and it was small, no matter that its teeth were sharp.

But...rats. Pigeons. Even in this concrete hell, the mortals kept pets. Cats. Dogs.

A veritable buffet. Its teeth champed, thinking about it. It caught a mouthful of the exhaust-tinged rain, not satisfying in any way, but its warmth helped. An aperitif, you could say.

The reborn thing dozed, curled around its hunger, waiting for the rain to pass.

A VERY THIN SHIELD

5

D usk turned to dark well before true nightfall as the storm's wing passed over a small trailer park on Guayahoya Avenue. The sun, as it sank, peered underneath the clouds, turning the west to a furnace of gold and blood. The last streakflashes of crimson and yellow faded to indigo dusk. Quiet fell, broken only by cars grinding to a halt and quick bursts of supper-scent puffing out before trailer doors slammed. Evening thickened, swirling under trees whose wet branches now had hard little green nubs, spring overflowing forth all at once.

A soft breeze rattled droplets from bough and bush. Night tiptoed over the city, thief instead of grande dame.

A feline hiss brought Robin into wakefulness with a terrified jolt, a taste of bitter almonds on her tongue and every nerve taut-prickling. The cat, her formal black and white disarranged by the puffing of her fur, hissed again, and Robin was off the bed in a flash, instinct driving her toward the closet before she halted, her skirt swinging.

No. Be canny, Ragged.

They were not close, not yet. She shut her eyes, listening,

taut as a bard's lutestring, the mortal house a very thin shield indeed.

There. A silver buzz against the nerves, a faraway ultrasonic thrilling most mortals wouldn't hear. They would *feel* it, though—a cold brush up their backs, a sudden uneasiness.

Huntwhistles. Unwinter's knights rode tonight, perhaps even Unwinter himself. She was no longer stumbling-weary; milk and rest had soothed her aches. She had two pins, the bone comb, her wits, and the music below her thoughts—the massive noise that could kill if she let it loose for long enough. Not to mention the knife at her belt and the pipes tucked in her secret skirt pocket—a collection of age-blackened and use-lacquered reeds, lashed together with tendons too fine to be animal.

Puck's treasures, now hers.

But it was night, and only spring instead of the full season of glory. Even though Summer had opened the Gates, Unwinter could still ride dusk to dawn if he chose. Slipping into Summer to rest might have been an attractive option, save for the thought of some sidhe remarking on her and carrying tales to the Queen. Robin did not wish to face *her* again so soon, either.

Did Summer know who had invited the lord of the Hunt into her lands? Could she guess? Goodfellow perhaps had not told her, but Robin could not trust as much. Then there was Sean.

All the stars of Summer's dusk ground into shattered amber dust, the child she had cared for gone into whatever awaited mortals after death.

No, when she saw Summer again, Robin wished to be thoroughly prepared.

First, though, she had to survive the night. The silver huntwhistles were far away, but the cat began to growl low in her chest, an amazingly deep noise from such a small animal.

Robin kept breathing. Four in, four out, you could not sing if you could not breathe, and though her hand wrapped itself about the cold hilt of the loathsome dagger, the song was still her best weapon.

A scratching. Much closer than the huntwhistles. The knights were coursing abroad, probably hoping to find any prey at all, a net she might be able to elude. It was the silent hunters she would have to worry about.

More scritch-scratching, and a desire to laugh rose in Robin's throat, killed a-borning by the discipline of breath. The music under her thoughts took on a sonorous dissonance. *Who is that nibbling at my house?*

Only the wind, she replied silently, *the child of heaven.* Mortals never realized how much truth was in the old tales. Sometimes they slipped through into the sideways realms—mostly children, but also adults who had not lost the habit of seeing. Usually a swift death awaited them, or a return to the mortal world full of slow, lingering illness, not realizing what they pined for. A few survived somewhat unscathed, and their stories passed into myth and child's tale, warning and dream.

Her gaze traveled across the bedroom, to the neat dresser and the invitation-card with its tinsel. She ghosted across cheap carpet, still listening to the scratches. Mortals did not bury iron under their doorsteps anymore, or nail up horseshoes to bar ill-wishing. There was salt in the kitchen; she could have poured thin lines over every windowsill and doorstep, but that would simply tell any passerby that someone wished to guard something of value.

Sidhe were a curious, curious folk. Always peering and poking, prying and noticing.

Soft padding footsteps. More scratching. How many of them? Why had they not broken in already to lay waste to flesh and trailer alike? She was an ill guest indeed, bringing destruction to such a neat, humble home.

The wedding invitation was heavy paper, and inside, written with purple ink under the printed date and time, was a round childish hand: *Uncle Eddie, you'd better be there to give me away! Love, Kara.* The moonglow tinsel on the card unraveled under Robin's quick fingers, whispered chantment dropping from her lips. The Old Language slipped and slithered between the strands, the pins and needles of Realmaking spreading into her palms.

Realmaking was precious, but it required something to begin with. She could not simply spin chantment out of empty air; that was a fullblood's trick. When given something, though, she could make something *else*, something that wouldn't fade into leaf and twig come daybreak. It was strange that a tinge of perishable mortal in one's blood was necessary for Realmaking. They were rare, those architects of the fully real, and no fullblood, highborn or low, had ever been among their number.

A flick of the wrist, another, silver glitters attaching to her fingertips. A full complement of ten, and a swift lance of pain through her temples as a jolting impact crashed into the side of the trailer, rocking it on its foundations.

What in Stone's name is that? She skipped down the hall, past the tiny scrubbed-clean bathroom with its strangely unsmelly litter box. Her shoes lightened, their chantments waking, too, as she called upon speed and lightfoot, and by the time the living room window shattered she was in the kitchen, her fingernails throwing hard, sharp darts of hungry moonlight as she tweezed open the cabinet near the oven. A blue canister of salt was tucked behind other spices. Her hand darted in and the small bottles and cans holding pepper, garlic, onion salt, oregano, thyme, all swept out in a jumbled mass, falling like rain, shattering and spilling their fragrant cargo. She whirled, and it was not as bad as it could have been.

Not barrow-wights, with their subtly wrong, noseless faces and their strangler's fingers dripping with gold leached of its daylight luster. Not fullborn knights, either, or Unwinter's narrow-nosed, leaping dogs with their needle-teeth. Instead, it was two lean, graceful drow and a woodwight, accompanied by a looming silver-necklaced shadow that chilled her clear through until she realized it was a stonctroll on a moonfire leash, making a low, unhappy grumbling sound as one of the drow poked it with a silvertipped stick.

None of them were familiar from song or rumor, or known to her. They piled pell-mell into the mortal living room, one of the raven-haired drow leaping atop the couch and hissing, his handsome face distorted as the teeth elongated, rows of serrated pearls. The woodwight swelled, his lean brown frame crackle-heaving between treeshape and biped, living green sprouting from his long, knobbed fingers. Serrated leaves, a dark trunk—an elm, a bad-tempered tree indeed.

The troll heaved forward again, widening the hole in the side of the trailer. Glass shattered, cheap metal buckled and bent, and Robin flicked her right pinkie fingernail with the pad of her thumb.

A silver dart crackled into being, splashing against the woodwight and scoring deep. Golden, resinous sapblood sprayed, and the wight's knothole mouth opened bellow-wide. A furious scream made of creaking, snapping, thick-groaning branches poured out.

The troll halted, its tiny close-set eyes blinking in confusion. It withdrew slightly, and the second raven-haired drow peered

25

over its shoulder, poking at it afresh with the silvertip stick. Robin flicked her right middle and ring fingers, one dart catching in the woodwight's branches and tangling, the other flying true and striking at the troll's eyes. Index finger, another dart made a high keening noise as it streaked for the first drow, who batted it away with contemptuous ease. The spray of sapblood from the woodwight eased, and the thing hissed a malediction at her, a black-winged curse flapping, ungainly, through the close confines.

The troll howled, the noise and its stinking breath fluttering Robin's skirt, cracking the screen on the ancient television, and batting the flying curse aside. It lashed out, horselike, with each limb in turn, the first its left hindleg, catching the second drow with a crack audible even through the uproar. The first drow leapt forward, shaking out something that glittered gold with flashes of ruby, and Robin's skin chilled all over.

Is that what I think it is?

She flicked her thumbnail now, and a high piercing whistle burst between her lips. Ruddy orange flashed, the dart becoming a whip of flame, and it kissed the edge of the woodwight's trunk.

Golden sapblood kindled, and a new layer of noise intruded. Robin ignored it, skipping aside with the canister of salt now in her right hand. *A fine time to wish I had cold iron*, she thought pointlessly, and dodged, for the gold-and-ruby glimmer in the first drow's hands was a net, hair-fine metallic strands with red droplets at their junctures, supple-straining as it sensed its holder's quarry. It retreated with a cheated hiss, and the drow snarled at her again.

So *someone* wished her taken alive. Unwinter had sworn to Puck Goodfellow that he would not hunt her, but drow were not of Summer unless they were half something else, whether mortal or another manner of sidhe, and in any case it did not matter.

The Ragged did not mean to let these suitors, or any other, press their attentions *too* closely upon her. The curse, flapping in the living room, vanished under a sheet of flame. Robin's whistle ended, and she whooped in a fresh breath, bringing her left hand forward.

The sinister hand. These darts would be more brittle...but far more powerfully malefic.

The troll, fire-maddened and half-blinded, heaved. The entire trailer lifted, foundation to roof, buckling and breaking. The woodwight, screaming and completely alight by now, blundered into the couch, thrusting itself straight into the troll's face as well. The poor creature—stonetrolls were not known for their intelligence—was hopelessly entangled with the side of the trailer, insulation and sharp metal ribboning around its hard hide. It heaved again, and the drow with the net slip-stumbled between carpet and linoleum, his dark, liquid eyes widening as footing became treacherous.

Robin jabbed her left hand forward and the drow dodged aside, crashing into a flimsy closet door—but she hadn't released the darts, and now she flicked them all, fanwise and deadly, a baking draft scouring her from top to toe and her eyes slitted against the blast. Smoke billowed; it would make the air unbreathable after a few more moments. The back door was behind her; she fumbled with her left hand for the knob, her right hand sweeping in a semicircle, scattering salt in an arc that would not halt Unwinter's minion.

But it would delay him, and salt could be fashioned into other things. There was the song, too, her loosening throat scorched with smoke-tang, and just as the drow with the net shook himself free of the ruins of the coat closet and the troll heaved again, the knob turned under her fingers and she half-fell backward, saving herself with a wrenching fishlike jump as the wet wooden steps outside splintered.

The troll heaved yet again, dragging his leash-holder with him, breaking through the remainder of the wall and, instead of backing away from the inferno, plunged forward, crashing entirely through the other side of the trailer. The noise was incredible, mortals would soon take notice, her heels clattered on a narrow strip of damp pavement. The mortal whose home they had just destroyed had a charcoal grill set here, all rust carefully scrubbed from its legs and black bowl. It went flying as Robin's hip bumped it, clattering and striking gonglike as it rolled.

Did I strike him, please tell me I did—

The net-bearing drow bulleted out of the burning trailer. The wight's scream and flapping curse had vanished into a snap and crackle of flame, a burst of hot air lifting smoke and sparks heavenward as the fire could now suck on the night air outside the shattered home, window-glass shivered into breaking. Robin kept backing up over the small concrete patio, light, shuffling skips, and the urge to cough tickled mercilessly at the back of her palate. She denied it, saw she had, indeed, managed to hit the net-bearer. Thick yellowgreenish ichor threaded with crimson stained his side, his face was a ruin of scratches and soot, his hair full of burning sparks, and one of his feet was tangled with a mass of glittering spikes, fading quickly as they burrowed through his boots, seeking the flesh underneath.

The song burst free of Robin's throat, a low, throbbing orchestral noise. It smashed into the net-bearer head-on, and he flew backward into the fire, which took another deep breath, finding fresh fuel, and grunted a mass of sparks and blackening smoke skyward. A wet, heavy breeze full of spring-smell and the good greenness of more rain approaching whisked it into a curtain of burning.

Robin halted, her sides heaving. The stonetroll, truly maddened now, dragged the other drow away into the damp night, its grinding shrieks interspersed with the dark sidhe's screams. It would not be calmed until it had exhausted itself.

She struggled to control her breathing, staring at the flames. *The cat. Stone and Throne, the cat. Is she still inside?*

Sirens in the distance. Some mortal had noticed this, and Robin did not wish to be here when they swarmed. Still, she darted along the back of the house, searching for any unburnt portion. *I am sorry. I am so sorry. I did not mean for this to happen.*

What else had she expected? She was a Half, mortal and sidhe in equal measure, a faithless sidhe bitch possibly sired by a monstrous ancient, the cause of more trouble and sorrow than any mortal could ever hope to be.

There was no sign of the cat, and Robin, smoke-tarnished, fled before anyone else arrived.

A GODDAMN GOOD BIT OF LUCK

6

*E*ddie Sharnahan returned that morning from his niece's wedding to find his trailer gone, but that was all right because he
had insurance and Juniper, her black-and-white fur reeking of
smoke, was unharmed. He held her in the soft morning drizzle
while he surveyed the smoking ruins, and none of the emergency
personnel noticed that the cat's frenzied rubbing against her master's face lent a faint dusty glitter to him. They didn't notice the
malformed curse lingering in the wreckage, either, or when it
blindly scented something familiar from the burning it had been
trapped in and crawled toward Eddie, shivering and Twisted from
the sap-fueled flames.

Sharnahan's work buddy Clyde, a wide-set foreman with a
seamed brown bullet head and a fine wide white mustache, let
Eddie stay at his house while the insurance paperwork was processed. A week afterward, Eddie bought a lotto ticket at the Kwik-
Ease during their morning coffee run. It turned out to be worth
a cool ten million, which was a goddamn good bit of luck, he
remarked to his buddy.

Clyde just grunted and asked if that meant he'd be quitting on *the spot or would give him two weeks. Sharnahan did the latter, then retired after a beer-soaked party at Clyde's.*

Unfortunately, Eddie was dead within six months of a bone cancer spurred by a black flapping curse's last fading breath. He left half the money to the animal shelter he'd gotten Juniper from, and Juniper and the remaining half to his niece, who had married rich, divorced richer, and finally moved to San Francisco with Juniper, who lived longer than any feline had a right to. The niece became the Crazy Cat Lady of Holt Hill and often was heard to remark that cats were lucky. They brought the good fairies.

Her beloved uncle had always told her so.

BRAVADO
7

*H*unting *Unseelie again.* Midnight found Jeremiah Gallow crouched easily on the edge of a rooftop, surveying the terrain. *Feels fucking familiar, doesn't it?*

The city wheeled below him, waves of traffic on concrete shores, tang of cold iron and the fog of exhaust, garbage in alleys and a faint note of burning on a chill spring wind. The breeze had lost winter's bite—Summer's Gates were open now, both her realm and the mortal world turned toward renewal— and its broad back carried other, darker scents. Rain blurred and softened the air, a tang of ozone from the afternoon's lightning and a heavy, spicy expectancy.

The sidhe are out tonight. Close your windows, hide your cows, and above all else, bar your doorways with iron.

He closed his eyes, a lean man with a heavy dun coat, its side mended with needle-chantment and its leather patches scuffed and scarred, his dark hair cut military-short to hug his skull. Mortal gazes would slide right over him, maybe pausing briefly at the breadth of his shoulders or a flash of the light, the piercing green of his irises. On a jobsite he was close to invisible, just another construction worker, young enough not to have run to fat but old enough that a career other than backbreaking labor was a vanishing prospect. He showed up on time, traded dirty jokes, ate his lunch, had a beer or two or went home, everyone's buddy and nobody's friend.

There. Silver threads pierced the sound of traffic, stitching through the dark fabric of mortal night. The huntwhistles were far away and to the south—they had noticed the burning of his mortal trailer and knew he would not be weary or stupid enough to burrow himself near it. They hoped to find his trail near the ashes, now.

The Unseelie were no doubt hunting a woman tonight, too.

Robin Ragged would be using every trick she could beg, win, or steal to confuse her trail, but Jeremiah had the locket that had rested next to her skin and now throbbed against his own as he thought about its owner. Simple chantment would lead him to her—it had, in fact, brought him to this wreck of a building downtown, an Art Deco leftover with gargoyles watching the street, sandwiched between two high-rises. There was a lot of cold iron in its construction, and a curious slick patch on the roof that reeked of sidhe. If it was spoor, it was nothing he'd encountered in the sideways realms or the mortal world, and its presence here was troubling, to say the least. Given the way Gallow's skin crawled when he approached it, a death had been meted out.

It hadn't been hers, though. That was all he cared to ascertain, before his nape prickled uneasily. He had left that particular building hurriedly, following Robin's trail, and it was good that he had.

Otherwise they might have caught him before he was ready, on another much more modern rooftop in the financial district.

Jeremiah unfolded, drawing himself up, and if he hadn't

been wearing the coat, any onlooker, mortal or otherwise, would have seen the marks on his arms begin to writhe. From the wrist up, running over muscle hardened from years of mortal labor and years before that as the Armormaster of Summer's Court, ran ink-dark, thorny tendrils. Mortals would mistake them for tribal tattoos, cupping his shoulders with daggered fingers, sending branches down his chest and back. The knotwork, vaguely tribal or vaguely Celtic, shifted with his mood.

Those who remembered his tenure at Court would have heard the whispers. *A dwarven-inked lance—they crossed him, though, and did not expect him to survive.*

He lived, did the Armormaster, and Finnion's clan is no more.

Jeremiah turned, his workboot soles gripping just enough, and the shadows gathering at the far end of the rooftop showed gleams of pale gold worn at throat, wrist, fingers. Pallid, noseless faces floated on the darkness, sharp, pointed chins and wide, generous cheekbones.

In certain lights, you might even call a barrow-wight attractive. Right before their sharp silver blades rent your flesh.

Three he could see, and behind them more tiny glimmers. His nostrils flared slightly, and he caught the crusted salt and wetwood scent of drow. The tinge of heavy, low-burning incense meant not just any of the Lightless, but the Red Clan.

The Unclean.

His arms ran with familiar pins and needles. The lance resolved into being, dappled moonlight along its edges, its haft suddenly solid against his palms. Its blade lengthened, the leafshape becoming a wicked almost-curve, thickening near the end. The haft lengthened, too, its tasseled end dripping moonfire—the more distance he could gain, the better. One-against-many on open ground, with a sharp drop to his back, wasn't the worst situation.

Unless, of course, there were harpies to flank him. One problem at a time.

"*Gallow*," one of the barrow-wights breathed, a rasp of scales against the cold weeping walls of a burrow.

Jeremiah inhaled, and the lance finished resolving, the blade shimmering with more moonfire before it flushed, its edge a wicked red gleam.

Cold iron, that most mortal of metals.

"As you see me, Unwinter filth." A thin, unamused smile accompanied the words. He'd fallen back into the sidhe way of speaking, with its curious mix of insult and circumlocution. "Either give a name or withdraw." Pure bravado—the cold weight at his chest, the medallion on its silver chain, was a reminder of just how badly they would want him dead.

Unwinter's Horn, wrenched from the extra-jointed, mailed grasp of the lord of the Hunt himself, would earn its bearer a rich reward, presented along with Gallow's head. You did not send drow and wights to simply *capture*; you sent them when you wished your prey to suffer before he choked his last.

Chasing Robin, or him? Both?

Who cared? All that mattered now was the killing. The ice of the Horn and the warmth of Robin's locket faded against the certainty of combat.

It was a relief to finally have a clear-cut problem in front of him.

The lance's blade whistled, a low, ominous, sweet noise, as one of the drow darted forward. The rasp of blades leaving sheaths—daggers, of course, the drow fought with little else, but the wights had silver sickle-blades, alive with pallid glow and wicked sharp all along their crescent edges. The horn hilts were shaped especially for their strangler's hands, and if they had survived long enough to earn such blades, they were quick and brutal.

36

Perhaps even cunning.

The lance vibrated in his hands, communicating in its silent, hungry way. The battle unreeled inside his head, present and immediate future interlocking. Fairly straightforward, a tangle of action and reaction flexing and splitting as he took a single step to the side, the weapon lifted slightly, playing through the first move in the sequence that would end with the first barrow-wight sheared in half, greenish ichor splatting dully—but they spread out, evidently cautious, so he halted, the tangles taking on a cast he didn't quite like.

Then attack.

Faraway thunder rumbled; Gallow *moved*. The cursed sidhe speed was still with him, the mortal rooftop a drum his soles whisked over light as a kitten's tail brushing against a wall. The lance's blade made a low, sweet sound as it clove chill night air, the drawn-out note dropping at the end as sharp iron tore sidhe flesh. An arc of green ichor, droplets hanging in the air as the lancehaft socked itself against the fulcrum of his hip, the remaining wights scattering and two of the drow leaping, an HVAC unit's casing creak-buckling as their glove-shod feet *pushed* against it. Angles shifted, the tangle becoming a braided snarl, and he had enough time if he could just gain enough height. Muscles screaming as he leapt as well, mortal world rippling as the Veil snapped like pennons in a high breeze above Summer's castle upon the green hills.

The haft scraped his palms; he'd largely lost the protective calluses. Construction wasn't the same as combat; a cramp seized his left side with clawed fingers.

Just where Unwinter's poisoned blade had struck him.

Gallow ignored it, the lance spinning as it shortened, the blade flushing red as he stabbed with a *crunch* through drow skull. The lance keened, a jolt of warmth up his arms as it sucked a death into its hungry core, and the splatter of sponge-rotted bone and blood and brain was still hanging in the air when he landed, spinning on the ball of his right foot.

The lance flicked once, twice, lizard-tongue darts. Four drow left, three wights, the terrain was open enough that he could dance. They sought to ring him, the wights hissing and the drow thrumming in their peculiar subvocal almost-language. Their caverns, under forest or mountain, were always full of that grumble, as well as the soft, slippery phosphorescence of their excrescences, clinging in barb-arrowed trails very much like the markings on his own body.

Every sidhe art had its pattern.

A short rush forward, the lance singing to itself, warmed and loosened. A drow folding down as the blade punched through its middle, twisting with a savage jerk and bursting free with hungry serrated teeth. To rip and gouge, to whistle and slice, a sleepy warmth replacing its hunger as it gulped another death into its core. He was no more than a bow upon an instrument's strings, drawing back and forth to sing a cacophony of shattered bone and split flesh, sidhe blood and ichor spattering in unholy flowers. One of the wights had the presence of mind to spit a blackwing curse or two, but Jeremiah skipped aside, past caring about cramps or muscle-tearing, adrenaline-sparks tearing through his bloodstream. Turning, the lance bending impossibly as he leaned back, avoiding the solid silver arc of a bone-hilted blade, too close *too goddamn close*, his knee flashing up to sink into the juncture of the wight's legs.

They didn't breed like mortals, or even like other sidhe, but there was still a nerve-bundle there that could hurt them plenty, if you hit hard enough.

A long, ear-tearing howl threatened to deafen him, but he was already past the wight as the lanceblade sank in and cut deep, Gallow's body airborne and spinning, his axis almost parallel to the rooftop as the Veil bunched and shivered. Landing, still spinning, the lance a propeller now, the last wight baring its yellowed fangs and hissing. Another curse, this one hurried and malformed, hurtled flapping for Gallow's eyes, but his own spat phrase of the Old Language batted it aside, a dart of moonglow shredding the black wings.

Skidding, heels digging in and his breath coming harsh-tearing, he jolted to a stop with the lance's haft behind his back, its blade pointing down from his right hand, left hand outflung for balance and his head down. Tiny black flowers bloomed in his vision, his lungs heaving.

One of the drow was still alive, flopping weakly. The wights, rotting into brackish iron-poisoned slime, sent up thin curls of noisome steam. The one he'd kneed twitched slightly before its open mouth runneled with decay, its face collapsing.

Jeremiah paced to the survivor, wincing as his body reminded him he was out of practice. He would harden soon enough—nothing like true combat to wring the softness out of a man, even a sidhe.

The drow, its arm severed, clutched its remaining hand to the gushing wound. It hissed in the Old Language, syllables dropping like rain. Not a curse, but no gentle love-words, either.

Gallow shrugged as its tortured gaze lit on him. "It will take more than the Red Clan to bring me to bay."

More of the sidhe tongue, the Veil resonating uneasily between mortal and sideways realms. Death and the tongue of chantment and curse both warped at that fabric, and Jeremiah, when younger, had wondered at the implied relationships.

Not very often, or very deeply, though. His concerns, like his talents, were not . . . philosophical.

The drow spat two more words and laughed, writhing on

39

a mortal rooftop, and Jeremiah's skin turned cold. The lance struck, ringing as its tip punched through spongy ribs and sank into the roof beneath, a hot knife into butter.

One final death, sucked into the weapon's ever-aching, ever-hungry core. Gallow yanked it free, his arms tingling as he forced it into insubstantiality. The locket, nestling safely against the top of his breastbone, was warm against his fingertips, he drew it out and watched it spin lazily on its hair-fine chain as those final words still echoed.

Robin Ragged.

"I'll find her first," he muttered, and surveyed his work afresh. It was barely a skirmish, not really a victory. There would be more of Unwinter abroad tonight. His side ached, and the thought that perhaps the poison had not been drawn entirely from the knife-wound was not comforting in the least.

He hopped easily onto the waist-high barrier at the roof's edge. Not so long ago he had gazed down at mortals from the shell of a half-finished building and thought of letting himself fall. Odd that a few days, just a handful of mortal hours, could change a man's outlook so completely.

Moments later the rooftop was empty, and in another part of the city the silver huntwhistles rose afresh over a roil of distant thunder.

The prey had been sighted.

DIN R
8

The truck stop on Highway 4, at the very edge of the city, burned with electric light, soaked itself in diesel fumes, and was full of enough cold iron to deter any sidhe with less than at least a half share of mortal blood. Robin hopped nimbly onto a Dumpster's slick lid, leapt to catch the rung of a rusting ladder, and hung for a moment before a whispered chantment boosted her up just enough to brace one of her feet on an odd, protruding brick. Why there was only half a ladder didn't concern her as much as its sudden wobbling and rocking, but she reached the roof without further disaster.

Inside would have been better, but the place was stuffed full of mortals, mostly wide-shouldered men hunched over plates of fried grease. Everything in Robin shuddered at the thought of actually speaking to one of the worn, bleached-dry waitresses, or holding enough of a glamour to keep from being eyed by the men. Even the thought of creeping in to steal butter or a carton of milk made her stomach twist.

Besides, the less she rubbed shoulders with mortals, the better. For them, *and* for her.

Up here, the breeze had turned sharp, and curls of steam rose from her bare shoulders. The temperature didn't bother her much; nothing short of stonecracking steppe-freeze could trouble a Half who had learned the warming breath. She still clasped her elbows in her palms, hugging herself. Huge metal letters—DIN R, the E missing and the stumps of its support struts sheared and rusted—made low, uneasy sounds, singing as moving air mouthed them and the building below throbbed, a wasp-nest waking.

She turned in a full circle sunwise, then the other way, rubbed the smoke-tarnish from her eyes, felt at her collarbone before she remembered her locket was gone. Touched the pins and the bone comb nestled in her hair next to the matted elflock, touched the knife's cold hilt.

The east was lightening into gray; Night had turned its last corner and shambled wearily for her own bed. In Summer, the Home on the Hill would be almost silent, only the kitchens full of susurration as the brughnies and merrimegs woke and began tending the ovens. While the Gates were open, sometimes Summer Herself would wake at dawn, but rarely before, and never during Unwinter's half of the year.

Still turning aimlessly, Robin shut her eyes. Her heels scraped as she moved, once twice thrice widdershins, once twice deosil, her skirt swinging and the motion inadequate to stave off crowding thoughts.

Everything inside her skin was whirling, too.

A clatter from below stopped her, redgold curls bouncing as she froze. Golden light flooded the rear of the restaurant, and she crouched before she realized it was just the diner's back door. A crunch and a slam was a bag of garbage tossed into the Dumpster she'd climbed on, and the light faded to a dim glow.

Curious, she straightened slowly and crept to the edge of the roof.

A lean young man propped himself against the chain-link fence separating the diner's back from a wide expanse of cracked paving full of the shining beetles of trucks, a quick red flash illuminating his aquiline face and dark hair as he lit a cigarette. The brughnies called them *nagsticks*; they smelled awful and tasted worse. Still, they were stolen sometimes, often by pixies, either to fox a mortal or to use as currency at one of the sidhe markets. Goblins and trolls sometimes liked them, eating as many as a dozen at a time and falling down in a foam-mouth stupor, seeing whatever passed for visions, to them. A mortal poison, less fatal than cold iron.

Robin watched. He was young, merely a boy, with no shadow of down upon his cheeks yet. Why was he puffing on one of those awful things? His dark head was segmented, a hairnet pressing the hair into geometric sections. His eyes glimmered a little as he half-lidded them, obviously enjoying his stolen moment.

She stepped back, carefully. Again. The letters presented a brave front to the world, but behind them on the roof, the supports were a jungle of rust and damp. She had slept deeply in the trailer, but everything in her still ached a bit. Weariness and pain, both mortal sensations. At least the highborn affected not to feel them. Not until close to death.

She settled where the E had been, propping her back against a wide, rusted beam. It itched a little, though her mortal half insulated her from cold iron's poisoning.

Robin had never thought she'd be grateful for mortal blood. How long had she spent at Court, wondering if any of the knights there had spent a summer with Mama? To find out, instead, that she was the child of a monster...

43

You did it! The crowbar, smashing time and again as the shape below her writhed and flung up its malformed hands. Her mortal stepfather would have been proud of how coldly she had caused pain. Daddy Snowe, always full of stories about how he'd gotten back at someone who had disrespected him, or looked at him sidelong, or any of a hundred insults.

I'd almost rather be mortal. It was a lie, though. Anything was better than their brief, gray, meaningless lives. Wasn't it?

Robin lifted her hand, examining her palm. No bubbling rash from cold iron, no tinge of smoke left on her since turning had whisked it away, no bruising from gripping the crowbar so tightly. Her skin was whole, unmarked by bruise or plague.

The aching was *inside*. Mortal enough for that, at least.

"The poor cat," she whispered, and pulled her knees up, tucking her skirt around her legs. Behind the diner, the door slammed again, the mortal boy going back to whatever tasks awaited him. Once, Robin might have spoken to him, given a simple chantment to ease weariness or take the nagstick craving from him.

Any kindness she could offer would only bring disaster in its wake. Had she finally learned her lesson? Sean, trapped in amber by a vengeful queen, shattered on a cold, uncaring sidhe floor. A pawn in a game he could never have understood, removed from the board and broken into glass-sharp amber fragments.

Robin rested her chin on her knees, fixed her gaze on the horizon. The gray was strengthening. When the sun finally breached that faraway shore, she would be ready.

In the meantime, she sat and brooded and did her best not to think on what Gallow might be doing, if his house had been visited by Unseelie in search of her, or if he had the sense to flee, take himself back to Summer to become Armormaster again. That would be safest for him, indeed.

He had, after all, challenged Unwinter himself. Perhaps it was only because Robin looked like Daisy, and he felt…what? *Stop it, Robin.*

But oh, she wondered, and the wait for true dawn was long.

SUMMERHOME
9

Summerhome stretched green and white upon the Hill, its towers bare of pennants or flags. A red dawn had arisen, black smoke rising from fleecy drifts of blossom in the orchard as the bodies of both Unseelie and the lesser casualties of Summer's folk were burned, woodwights and brughnies tending the flames with nets of chantment. Their high-beaked masks, the noses stuffed full of merrywell and other helpful herbs, floated above dark, motheaten robes—the heavy blue velvet had not been used for many a long year, tarnished silver thread alive with chantment to shield the wearer from spark or vapor.

The highborn sidhe fallen in Unwinter's treacherous raid upon the heart of Seelie were already interred in the Moaning Caves, and the Half-mortal or above, corpses barely tinged with the quickrot that accompanied most sidhe upon their death, would be torched on pyres along the Dreaming Sea. Summer's will had restored her lands; the smoke was the only sign of the violation. That, and a certain...paleness. Perhaps the air was not as rich as it once had been. Perhaps the greensward was not quite as fragrant.

"Such a waste." A soft, bell-clear murmur, and she drew her

heavy mantle higher about her milk-white shoulders. Golden hair tumbled down in heavy ripples. A particularly acute observer might have noticed the beginning of tangles under the sleek waves.

A *wise* observer would know not to comment upon them, to pretend not to notice.

"And yet." The Queen sighed, the Jewel on her forehead dark as it had not been for long, long years as well. A single spark of green revolved in its depths, burning bright and steady as hatred. "The ashes will nourish the trees, the mourning will pass, and we shall once again be merry."

She turned, but not far, showing only a slice of her pale cheek and a single glimmer of a black, black eye. Behind her, shadows and heavy draperies filled the private bower. Summer was a creature of light and air, but this close, secret room held little of either. Even the candleflames were low and reddened, bruised pinprick-eyes.

In the precise center of plain, mellow-burnished wooden floor, he knelt as was polite when called before *her*. Broad-shouldered, he would be tall when he rose, and his armor, though dull leather instead of a fullblood knight's polish and glimmering metal, was well made and chased with chantment beside. He was no high Seelie knight, but the two hilts rising behind his fine shoulders were fluid-curved, dwarven work. His hair was much too long to be currently Court-fashionable, and its color—rich chestnut, but with a tinge of green, as if moss had crept among the strands—bespoke some dryad in his lineage. Curtaining his face, brushing his shoulders, it shielded his features from the faint candlelight.

He stared at the floor, unmoving, and after a short while Summer laughed. "There is a task I would set thee, Crenn."

The Half knight—for such he was, a fullblood dam and a

mortal sire ensnared under a whitethorn tree—did not move. His tone matched hers, almost a whisper. "Then I shall perform it."

Maybe, for a moment, he had considered giving another answer, one less politic and, hence, less wise.

Summer did not seem to care. "Very well. There is a creature I wish hunted, trapped, and brought to me without so much as a feather disturbed."

A long pause. "That is not... usual."

"Is it beyond your abilities, Half?"

No movement broke his perfect stillness. Yet he remained silent.

"I thought not." Summer moved, a flicker of her pale fingers. A pair of drow-sharp eyes might have noticed a shadow on the back of one, perhaps a spot of age—but it had to be a trick of the dim lighting. Summer never withered, eternal and beautiful...

...or so all the songs said, and of course the bards who sang of her grace would not lie.

Alastair Crenn remained still. His boots were of mortal make, sturdy leather. The rest of him was sidhe-dressed, except for the earring in his left ear, a hoop of cold, dull iron. Precious few, even Half, would wear such a thing so flagrantly.

Finally, Summer spoke again, her tone not so dulcet. Instead, each word was edged, crisp, and cold. "Bring me Robin Ragged, whole and well, no matter where she has rambled."

Crenn considered this. "I have heard her life belongs to Gallow, the former Queensglass."

"I do not recall releasing him from service. Just as I do not recall asking you for gossip, Half."

His head dropped a fraction. That was all.

"Gallow-my-glass claimed her life as a boon, and I granted

it." The Seelie Queen turned back to the window. Did a tremor go through her, rustling the great velvet mantle figured with the constellations of Summer's evening sky? "Your task is to bring her to me, Crenn. Whole and well, without a bruise or a scratch."

"And if she is unwilling?"

"That," Summer said softly, "has never halted your course before, huntsman. Take yourself from my sight, and execute your errand."

"As Summer commands." He rose with a quick habitual shake of his shaggy head.

She let him reach the heavy oaken door before the hook was sweetened with bait. "Crenn."

He halted between one step and the next.

"Bring her to me, and I will make you beautiful again."

His shoulders stiffened. He made no answer, and Summer's mocking laughter, a knife-edge hidden under velvet, followed him out the door and down the narrow, winding stone steps, their centers hollowed by many feet. The North Tower had not been used in a long while, but it was here Summer had retreated after Unwinter and his cursed minions broke the borders and ravaged her holdings.

At the bottom of the staircase, another knight paused. Braghn Moran the dark-haired, once the lover of another highborn sidhe lady, now high in Summer's favor and forgetful of his former paramour, bared his sharp teeth at Crenn. The highblood's pristine, sun-chased armor threw back torchlight with a vengeance, a glamour of light and air moving with him.

His mailed fist clasped the thin arm of a vacant-eyed changeling, its cornsilk hair disarranged and its homely, freckled face blank as a well's eye. It wore a colorless shift, and the cloying spoilfruit smell of a drugging chantment lingered around it. Tiny jewels of drool swelled at the corners of its generous mouth, and since it was no longer holding a visitor's place in the mortal world, the high, cartilaginous points of its ears poked up through its hair, almost meeting behind its head.

"Such a little thing," Crenn said by way of greeting. An indirect insult, to not address a fullborn properly, and yet he avoided the impoliteness of sullying the Moran's title with his half-mortal mouth.

The Feathersalt's former lover did not curl his lip. "Undeserving but lucky, to have an audience with such an august personage." Faint disdain colored the words, but only that.

"No doubt." Crenn strode past. Above, there would be a hungry smile, and the flash of a flint-bladed knife. It was the third changeling he had witnessed brought back to Summer's tender mercies just this morn, as he arrived at Summerhome to answer a summons in the form of a graceful white bird.

The dove had struck into the heart of his swamps and called him away from his tedious, comforting solitude.

Unwinter had indeed struck deep, as well. All Summer's subjects fumed at his treachery, to strike as the Gates were opened, after a revel to welcome renewal from the Queen's white hands and green Jewel, the fount of all Seelie.

Still, Alastair Crenn, the Huntsman of Marrowdowne's deep tangled fens, found much to wonder at. How had Unwinter found the means to break the borders? How many changelings would be called home to Summer's hunger and the flint knife? Why would Summer send *him*, a Half knight turned assassin, after the Ragged, whose voice could kill and whose shuttling to the mortal world, erranding for Summer herself, had been much remarked upon of late?

I will make you beautiful again.

His face twitched, once, and he restrained the urge to touch the seamed and runneled flesh. He strode through the Great Hall, noting the black streaks on the map of Summer's dominions burned into glossy marble, the paling at the edges. Cor's Heart was suspiciously faded, the Far End nearly vanished, and Marrowdowne itself frayed near the delta-mouth, where the Dreaming Sea swallowed both sand and fresh water from the Marrow's winding, fern-choked flow.

The glassine steps before the great door were faded, cracked, and dull, too, and all Summer trembled for a moment. Crenn's sharp ears prickled, and he heard the sound of a blade cleaving air, and a single soft, choked cry echoing from the northmost tower.

One less changeling in the world.

His pace quickened. Dawn was near, and he was about to visit the mortal world for the first time in a very long while.

A SMALL KINDNESS
10

Jeremiah was beginning to wish he hadn't left his truck behind. The cold iron in it would have interfered with his tracking, but it would have thrown off Unwinter's minions, too. It might have even confused Robin's looping, wandering trail.

Instead, Gallow fought a running battle across the city, from rooftop to park, drow and barrow-wights swarming along the faint marks of her flight. Two of the hunting-bands had cullaugh-nets, meant to bring down fine, feathered prey without damage.

So they wanted Robin taken alive. Of course, since Puck had extracted a vow from Unwinter himself not to harm her, and since the lord of that gray and ash-choked land might think the Ragged still had the cure for the plague felling sidhe left and right, it made sense. He wondered if she sensed the pursuit, if she guessed he was at her heels as well.

A little past 5 a.m. found him at the edge of a trailer park in Northside, his entire body cold as he watched emergency personnel pour water on a fire that refused to be tamed. The smoke reeked of drow and the pine-resin of spilled woodwight sapblood, but Robin's trail led away—as well as a wide, stinking path of stonetroll, splattering black-smoking blood that petrified the edges of any living green it found. Traceries of stone, howling into the night.

She was a canny wench, indeed. Had he ever thought Robin helpless? Of course, there was her voice—and had there been a mortal in that trailer?

He didn't want to think about that.

He *also* didn't want to consider that he hadn't thought about Daisy much, if at all, for the whole damn night.

She's been dead five years, Jer. Focus on the present.

Just like a faithless fucking sidhe. Memory, like grief, was a mortal game. They died, it was what mortals *did*, brief blossomings and quick declines. Even a scatterbrained, evanescent pixie was likely to last longer than any of those mired in the gray, chill-mortal world.

The lance hummed, prickling in his arms, down his back. The marks, restless, writhed against his skin as he ran, basic lightfoot chantment barely disturbing the ground underneath. She'd come this way, skirting the ditch and probably using that shattered piece of plywood to cross, stepping sideways *there*; he could almost see the muscle in her dancer's calves flickering as she climbed the slight hill and cut across the freeway. No traffic, it was the dead time.

He could, however, smell approaching dawn. Coffeemakers rousing, nurses and firemen finishing their night shifts, nightpixies yawning and winking out as the diurnal ones yawned and began to glimmer around eddies and swirls in the Veil, dryads and nymphs stirring in their homes of water and wood, construction workers tossing and turning as their bodies began to swim toward waking.

If he was still playing at being mortal, he'd be up already, watching the coffeemaker as it burbled, ignoring the dirty dishes piled in the sink and the persistent mildewy smell his laundry had taken on, because he didn't know how Daisy made the clothes smell sweet.

Robin had done his laundry, too, before she left. His bathroom and kitchen had both sparkled—before he'd set the chantments that would burn the whole place to the ground.

It had, in the end, been so easy.

When the sun's first fiery limb lifted over the horizon, dew steaming on every edge and the rumble of traffic in the distance becoming the mutter of an awakened monster instead of the formless grumble of a dreaming one, he checked the sky and took a deep breath, rolling the air on his tongue and concentrating. For a moment, Robin's trail blurred, so he stopped dead.

More rain on the way. His nose untangled the various threads—no Unseelie had come this way. Clouds still massed in the north, but the thunder had retreated. No rain during the night, just breathless expectancy and combat teased by a chill wind. A note of juicy green—the Gates were open, the sap was rising, the weather warming rapidly.

When his chin tipped back down, streetlamps guttering on either side of the highway as the hazy gray light strengthened, he realized where he was and where she was likely to be heading.

The last time he'd been on Highway 4 was for repaving, long tar-melting afternoons, coming home to Daisy afterward reeking of asphalt, dirt, and a haze of mortal sweat. Not much could wring the salt from a sidhe, but that had come perilously close. The last summer before her death, a golden shimmering time. They'd talked about what they would do if she got pregnant, and she had quietly thrown away her birth control

55

pills. They'd slept with the window open all that summer, the nights cool enough to bring her snuggling into his side, and he hadn't slipped out to the trashwood behind their trailer to practice with the lance's cold, shining length.

The trouble with a half-sidhe memory was that it was vivid *and* unreliable, just like the sidhe themselves.

He halted at the edge of a sea of concrete, scanning the truck stop. The diner, shabby but still obviously doing good business, was one of those low 1970s brick numbers, the big red letters on its roof probably rusted and pitted but still solid enough except for the missing E. Before dawn it would have been a welcome beacon, and the cold iron clustered around it a good way to halt or delay pursuit.

Gallow kept to the edge of the lot, finally cutting in parallel to a chainlink fence separating the diner's personal space from the diesel pumps and the long stretch of indifferently painted parking spots full of big rigs dozing in the freshness of morning. Behind the diner, two Dumpsters and a back door propped open to let out heat riding a clinking and steam-hiss cacophony of cooking. The morning rush would be well under way, a thread of burnt coffee and almost-burnt eggs, the good smell of bacon and the hot carbohydrate of pancakes on a grill.

His gaze snagged on a rusted ladder. A fading spice-tang was Robin's trail, almost washed away by cold iron and the tide-shifting of dawn.

He coiled himself, ready to leap and catch the lower rungs even though the thing looked too rusted to bear any weight, but at that moment the diner's back door banged open and a slim dark kid in a hairnet barged out, carrying two huge black trashbags. He stopped dead, and for a long, exotic moment Gallow found himself contemplating striking down a mortal, the marks painful-itching as they writhed.

The boy cocked his head. "Hey," he said. "Look, don't go looking in there, man. Hang on."

He slung the bags down, and before Gallow could speak, the boy vanished back through the door. *What the hell?*

Abruptly, Gallow realized he was unshaven, battle-filthy; his hair, though short, was wildly disarranged, and his coat much-mended along one side, as well as soaked with ditchwater and other, less salubrious fluids.

The idea that maybe the kid thought he was a homeless scrounger intent on the Dumpster's treasures actually wrung a laugh out of him, and the urge to let the lance free and strike retreated. It reminded him of leaving Summer, having to learn the ways of the mortal world again, from the faster cars to the looser manners.

Jeremiah was just about to leap, vanishing onto the roof, when the kid appeared again, this time carrying a white Styrofoam rectangle. Balanced atop it was another white paper shape, this one steaming, and he blithely edged up the narrow space between the Dumpster and the chainlink to offer both to Gallow with a small, tired smile. "Here, man." A light tenor voice, nothing in the words but gentle goodwill.

The steam was from coffee, and the smell from the rectangle was heavenly, if heaven ever passed out greasy-spoon breakfasts. Jeremiah stood, his jaw almost ajar, and the kid turned back to his garbage bags. He heaved them both into the Dumpster with practiced efficiency, tipped Gallow a wink, and stepped aside, digging in his pocket. "You better eat before it gets cold."

Gallow found his voice. "You're kind, young one." Had he even forgotten how to speak like one of them, in just a few days?

It was so damnably *easy* to slip back into the sidhe manner of speaking. And fighting, and running.

And everything else.

"Yeah, well, gotta do what you can." The kid brought out a battered pack of Marlboros, tapped one up, and lit it. His hands were chapped and water-wrinkled. A dishwasher, then, low man on the diner totem pole. "Go ahead, eat. You can sit on that box."

The box was a wooden crate, and Jeremiah lowered himself gingerly. The coffee was strong at least, and the kid had tossed a plastic fork and pats of real butter in with a stack of pancakes. There were scrambled eggs, too, and bacon.

It reminded him of Robin in his kitchen, offering a plate with a shy smile the morning after he had fought a plagued Unseelie knight.

He'd also lost the habit of mortal hunger, but he ate. It wasn't polite to refuse such a gift, offered so frankly. Had this kid been kind to a ragged little bird, too?

Companionable silence descended on the almost-alleyway. Jeremiah mopped up melted butter with the last of the pancakes, barely tasting it. The kid finished his cigarette and field-stripped it, flicking the filter through the chainlink fence. He held the Dumpster lid up so Gallow could toss the Styrofoam, and nodded, briskly. "Be careful, okay? Some of the guys around here, they like to beat up dudes for fun."

"Have they ever beaten you up?"

A broad white smile. "Nah, man, I'm too quick. Plus Natty, she owns this place, she gives 'em hell if they mess with her help. She don't like guys hanging out behind here, though. I'll get in trouble."

"I'll be gone in a few moments." Gallow hesitated. "How may I repay you, young one?"

"No worries, man, just take care."

"Wait." Gallow offered his hand. "Shake. You're an honorable man."

The smile widened, and his grip was firm. Chantment tingled under Jeremiah's palm, and a brief sparkle of gold outlined the kid as he vanished back inside, the heavy door slamming. Kind, but taking no chances. Frail mortal flesh, for all its firmness.

Not so long ago, he'd seen Robin Ragged toss a coin into a violin player's open case, and she'd thought he wanted to chide her for kindness—or that he'd assume she would do the young violinist some ill. What would she have said if she'd seen this?

He might have been kind to her, Gallow told himself, rolling his shoulders under the weight of his tattered coat. *That's a good enough reason.* He gathered himself and leapt, the ladder almost wrenching itself free of the bricks under his weight, but he was already on the roof by the time it finished groaning.

She had tarried here, among the struts and supports, but she was gone.

A few moments later, he was, too.

SILENT LUCK

11

*M*ike Ramirez left work with a spring in his step, even though the dawn shift was the worst. Bill, the walrus-sized white-clad bigot of a cook, was always in a nasty temper, Natty wasn't in the office to keep an eye on things, and the waitresses were fractious as cats during a windstorm. Bussing and washing for all of them was pretty much one serving of thankless shit after another, but he was blessed with a naturally sunny disposition and did his best.

He didn't notice the faint tracery of golden glitter on his hand, sinking into his dishwater-raw skin. He caught the 75 and made it to Saxon County Community College early, managing to stay awake through four classes, and aced two pop quizzes despite being exhausted. Coffee and sheer will kept him upright, and when he got home he handed over the day's tip-in to his stout, fiercely devoted mother and fell into bed, listening to the song of her tele-novelas through the thin wall.

He was up at 11 p.m. to catch the bus back out to Natty's diner that day, and when he walked in, Natty, her graying hair scraped back in a bun, buttonholed him: He was promoted. The cantan-kerous Bill had suffered a meltdown and quit, as usual, but this time Natty wasn't going to hire him back. "You're easier to squeeze *a day's work out of," she told Ramirez, and handed him a stack of fresh white aprons. "Get in there and get cooking."*

Happily, he'd spent long enough watching to know what to do, and even though the food was a bit slow, he didn't burn anything or turn over a wrong order all day. The good luck held through a solid week, and by the end of it he was comfortable around the grill, beginning to get faster, and whistling while he worked.

It meant better hours, better tip-in, much better pay, and benefits as well. A stroke of luck, and Mike's classes got a lot easier since he was able to get some sleep. When he finally graduated a year later, he lucked into a med school scholarship, and his mother had lost the tightness around her mouth since they'd manage to save a little. Then, just when things seemed like they were going to be hard but okay, his absent, alcoholic father finally kicked the bucket, and much to Señora Ramirez's surprise, there was a life insurance policy the cabron *had somehow kept the premiums current on, one final gesture from the otherwise useless man. She thanked God with novenas burning night and day, and Mike crossed himself whenever he thought about it.*

He barely remembered the green-eyed stranger that morning behind Natty's diner. That was the greatest—and most silent— luck of all.

HIS FILL

12

runch. Snap. To break the neck, to sink the teeth in—simple pleasures indeed. A puff of feathers, a frantic heart pounding inside a light-boned chest, and he bit the head from the pigeon with a satisfying snap of his white, white teeth.

The pixies fluttered around him, tiny dots of green-yellow, their wings buzzing and chiming. They made a game of it, flickering before night-running rats, leading them on with bursts of scent and little movements. The rats were canny, though, and grew more difficult after two or three had lost their little lives.

Once he could crawl the pixies guided him to nests where drowsy pigeons cooed softly at one another, unwaking even when his fingers deftly snatched them from warmth and safety.

Sometimes he grabbed for the pixies, but they scattered, too quick for his clutching fingers, even if they did have extra joints. Far finer than human paws, but still too slow.

It didn't matter. The danger of true death was past. He was too old to be Twisted past recovery.

Fortunately, he liked hunting. Soon the pixies fluttered around him as he unfolded, steam rising in fine traceries from pale, naked skin. He glowed in the predawn hush, nacreous as any newborn thing, and frowned slightly.

The little flittering things darted close as he whispered, coaxingly, telling them what he wanted. They spread through the Veil, winking out and winking back, their tiny brains losing the thread as soon as they left him.

He snarled, halfheartedly, picking dry feathers from between his teeth. They ached, poking through red gums, each bit of bone he ingested feeding his own skeleton. Needed more, and it was near dawn. Before the mortal sun rose, he had a certain leeway. Once its golden nail pierced the sky, his form would be set, and he was still weakened.

The iron burned his bare skin everywhere it touched as he half-fell down the fire escape, displeasure hissing between his lips. A filthy alley greeted his bruised and torn feet; he slip-stumbled along, away from the rooftops and their hidden nests.

More, he needed *more*.

At certain hours, a mortal city takes no notice of a naked man, even one pearly-glowing and sharptooth. He can weave along, flinching and hissing, through curiously deserted streets, keeping to shadows and stepping far more heavily than was his wont before freezing, his high-peaked ears twitching.

They have, those fine ears, caught a sound. A slight cough, air escaping diseased lungs.

A homeless mortal, curled in a ratty sleeping bag, dozing before cruel dawn arose. Perhaps he had congratulated himself, this man, on finding a lonely place to sleep, free of passing feet and the bright lights, or the revolving, garish blue and red of the police. *Move along, old man, can't sleep here.* Perhaps he had nipped from a bottle before stretching out, a faint alcoholic rose blooming to take the edge from the cold, sharp night. The cardboard under his sleeping bag was dry enough; above, Dalroyle Place soared, keeping its own secrets. Here at the back, the Dumpsters hid him from view, and perhaps he knew that in the morning the restaurant on the bottom floor would throw something edible into the bins.

Softly, stealthily, the naked figure crept toward the sleeping mortal. The pixies, their chiming growing agitated, hung back, some of them flushing red in anticipation.

Crunch.

Sleep-mazed and witless, the mortal still almost fought his attacker off, but the pixies descended, tiny sharp teeth nipping, their fingers yanking his hair, stabbing for his eyes with sewing-needle blades. A nuzzling at his throat, a hot gush, and the mortal man knew no more.

The naked boy settled to his feast, and the pixies crept over flesh-hill and vein-valley, biting what they could. There was an hour until dawn's rising, but they needed hunt no further.

Grinning, humming to himself, the naked boy ate his fill.

A LOVER'S KNOT
13

She should not have waited. Or she should not be here now, in this new-built suburb. The houses were large clumps of still-pristine siding in bland creamy colors, the trees spindly in tiny circles of beauty bark, each driveway wide and welcoming and precisely the same as every other. The streets had long, pretty names—*wildwood* and *marchblossom* and *azalea*. The streets were wider than average, too, their pavement black as sin and uncracked.

The only house that was different...well.

Nothing *looked* wrong. Oh, the yard was a little shaggy, but someone could have forgotten to mow over a weekend. It was the tree in the front yard, a young birch in a carefully cut hole in the turf, standing straight and tall and in exuberant leaf where every other sapling was still barely budded, that brought Robin to a halt.

They've been here.

She peered around a holly-hedge caught in scrawny adolescence, her heart pounding and her mouth dry. *No. Oh, no.*

Were they still inside? The sun had just cleared the horizon—had they come with the dawn?

Leave. Go away. If they've been here, nothing you want is inside that house.

She hesitated. It would be best to flee, lose herself in the mortal world for as long as she could.

But... she had to know.

She'd visited this place twice before, once to simply stare from the rooftop of the empty, for-sale structure across from it, and once in the middle of the night, using the lightfoot to climb like a thief and peer into windows. A mother and father, slumbering peacefully in a king-sized bed, the woman's face whole and serene, the man's arm over her and his nose buried in her hair. Robin had seen an echo of a boy's face in the mother's sleeping smile, and the father's hair was a gold she knew from stroking a child's head as he ate his bread and honey in a dusty nursery, in the very heart of Summer's realm.

Robin-mama! he would crow, and run through the orchard heedless of pitfalls, with Robin by his side. She fed him, rocked him, and the only time she herself slept dreamlessly was in her narrow bed, with Sean's weight beside her reminding her of another child, blithe laughing Daisy.

During the long, fragrant Summer dusks, she would take him to the narrow casement and teach him the names of the constellations, so different from the pale mortal stars. *Time for bed, Sean.*

Oh, please, one more, what's that one? And that?

Dead now, caught in a game much too large for him, turned to amber and shattered on a marble floor. Puck's hungry grin as the statue toppled, and underneath it all the small sound of a half-mortal heart cracking.

Her thieving night visit had also taken her to a different window. She'd peered in and seen a familiar tousled wheat-gold head, and stared long enough for the glamour to thin, sensing her attention. The changeling sleeping in Sean's bed looked well cared for, and child-plump. One of its little paws stretched out from under the covers, and she'd blinked, carefully, seeing the vestigial sixth finger under the mask of seeming.

A placeholder in the mortal realm, and how often had she thought of returning little Sean and bringing the changeling back into Summer? Or simply letting it roam free for the childcatchers to net? Sometimes a dreaming child, an especially blessed one, slipped back through the Veil. None might suspect Robin had taken a hand in affairs.

But she hadn't. A greedy little sidhe, she had kept him. *Just one more day... what harm can one more day do?*

None, until Summer had perhaps noticed how Robin cared for the little mortal.

Robin found herself clutching a holly branch, the plant reverberating as she trembled, the leaves prickling defensively as best they could. She let go, with a whispered apology, and brushed at the supple stem. A word of the Old Language, a chantment taking shape, and now any fool could see another of Summer's ilk had stood here as well. The holly stretched, whispering back to her, and Robin tilted her russet head.

How long ago?

Trees didn't count time the way mortals did, or even sidhe. Still, its memory was very fresh, of waking partly and hearing a distant song it yearned for with bole and branch. Then night, the time of darkness and soft stretching.

Yesterday. The childcatchers had been here only yesterday.

Robin brushed her hands together, though the holly had not loosed any sap. Of course they had come to take the changeling. Unwinter's attack would have done much damage; they would be retrieving every nameless placeholder they could, to bring to Summer's white hand and the wicked-sharp flint knife.

Which was worse—Unwinter's blood-freshened doorways and cold, inalterable will, or the green fields of Summer bought and anchored with nameless lives?

Idiot. This place is not safe. Leave, vanish, don't let anyone catch you here!

Silly and stupid to come.

Robin stepped out onto the bone-white sidewalk. Her heels clicked softly as she strode for the house. If any mortal was peering through a window at this hour, they would see her, but what did that matter?

What did anything matter, now?

The house had a wraparound porch. Two newspapers lay on the WELCOME mat, its fraying a comfortable sign of habitation. The door, painted a merry green, had a lovely etched-glass inset, rosevines in a lover's knot. She touched the doorknob with a single fingertip.

It was unlocked.

Why are you doing this? It could be a trap.

The front door ghosted wide. She hopped nervously over the threshold—no cold iron buried here to bar passage, of course. They lamented in Summer, sometimes, that they were forgotten. Mortals did not recognize or fear them as they once had.

The smell was awful. She peered into the living room—a television large enough to stable an elfhorse in, its face glaring blindly at a leather couch and two comfortable armchairs. The place was huge, the carpeting still fluffy, and Robin glanced into the kitchen—spick-and-span except for half a glass of water near the gleaming white sink. The countertops, some manner of plastic made to look like polished stone, glowed in the early-morning light without stone's solidity.

Dining room, empty, the table stacked with papers along one end. Downstairs bathroom, utility room leading to the garage—there was so much *space*, Stone and Throne, did they rattle in here like tiny peas in a too-big pod? Stairs, slightly creaking as she edged up them one at a time, not daring to touch the banister.

Daisy would have loved a big house like this.

The reek grew worse. Robin tried not to breathe too deeply, despite the fact that she would need her lungs full if this was a trap. Brass and a loathsome bathroom stench, reminding her of nauseating scrubbing after Daddy Snowe had "let a bomb off" in a tiny trailer toilet. *Wo00-eeee!* he'd yell. *Go fix that, Miss High-N-Mighty!*

He never made Daisy clean up. When she was born, still redheaded but unquestionably Daddy Snowe's child, he'd mellowed a little, thinking maybe Robin was his after all. Mama had sworn up and down she was, but what woman left alone with a baby and finding a protector wouldn't swear such a thing?

Three bedrooms. Had they wanted another child? Was the changeling difficult? They were usually strange but passive, sometimes called *special needs*, but once or twice they could turn into troublesome sprites indeed. No matter how disobedient they proved to be, though, the Seelie expected mortals to care for them and could grow...irate...if their "gift" was abused. In the old days, sometimes the mortals had threatened the changelings or left them on the hills to force the sidhe to bring the precious mortal children back as the placeholder withered. Risky, of course—the sidhe could take offense to that, too.

If they chose to.

Master bedroom. The door, hacked wide open, shattered bits of it still quivering from the violence of the explosion. Robin took one look into the dark cave and turned away, retching so hard her eyes filled with hot salt water. The sound echoed horribly down the stairs.

Why did they not simply take the changeling? Mortal children vanished all the time, their glowing televisions were full of reports. Any of the childcatchers could have simply come to the changeling's window and called to it, and it would have risen, with dreamy slowness, to undo any lock between it and the catchers' painful-sweet urging. Why did they have to…

She found herself stumbling down the stairs, turning away from the front door, blindly staggering through the kitchen as if she were mortal-drunk or pixie-led. *Why? Why would they—*

Oh, but she knew. Sean was dead, and the changeling taken—but Summer's wrath would not cease there. Robin had robbed the Queen of a mortal plaything before she was done with it, and had not loosed her song on Unwinter when commanded to. Of course the kin of any mortal brat Robin Ragged cherished would be punished.

There was no vengeance more thorough than Summer's when she felt herself cheated.

The back door was unlocked, too, but Robin simply blundered through it, so heedless she tumbled out onto a low, pleasant deck with an expensive gas grill crouching under a canvas sheath in one corner. Another canvas shape, dragonlike, had to be a patio table; she ran full-tilt into it with a noise like a wyrm's snapcrunching bite. Glass shattered, tubing buckled, and she regained her senses lying in a heap, the cover's tough material folded and crumpled, torn where the table had broken and sent metal jabbing through.

She'd narrowly missed spearing herself on one—now *that* would be a fine jest, to escape Unwinter and Summer both, and impale oneself on a table. The only thing better would be one of the huge umbrellas the mortals used to shield such things.

She lay there for a moment, very still, her eyes closed and throat working. Had she not, she never would have heard the slight scuffle as something darted across the patio.

Robin Ragged realized she was not alone.

Her throat relaxed, the music under her thoughts spiking into dissonance, and she turned her head, very slowly. Cradled in a twisted nest of what had no doubt been a very fine patio table, she couldn't see a damn thing.

Except the top of a pale golden head, slowly rising over the curve of damp, stretched canvas speared by glass teeth. A small, furrowed brow, and her heart caught in her throat, silencing her just as effectively as a barrow-wight's strangling fingers.

Its deepset eyes were a worn, faded blue, and its ears came to sharp points through a mat of curiously bleached hair. Under its sharp, misshapen nose a crust of snot had formed, and its wide, sloppy mouth housed picket-fence teeth. The glamour that kept it from mortal discovery was fading fast, and those teeth were sharp-white and strong.

Its lips trembled, its thin shoulders hunched, and the changeling that had held Sean's place in the mortal world let out a small piping sound.

FAIR ROBIN

14

There were no horses on the streets and their cities had turned to stone, but one thing, at least, had not changed—mortals saw what they wished to, and nothing more. Their metal chariots were wondrous enough, Crenn supposed, but the belching clouds of foulness they left behind would wrinkle even the nose of a stonetroll, and *those* were not gifted with overly refined senses.

Which could have explained this particular stonetroll, curled in a choked, noisome culvert some ten miles from the city's limits. Except for the fire-scarring on the thing's tough hide, and the fact that metal carriages whisked on a stony road above, much faster than even a steam-train. While the sound of their passage could have lulled the troll, it wasn't like one of their kind to sleep so close to sunlight.

Or with the silver gleam of a leash about its thick throat. Unwinter was hunting the Ragged as well.

The thing's trail overlaid hers, and he perhaps should not have followed so quickly, since the scent was already fading. The Ragged had not been Summer's errand girl for naught; she was sprite-fleet, vanishing like a startled naiad.

Alastair, crouched easily at the mouth of the culvert, narrowed his sharp eyes as thin trickles of nasty-smelling water slid around his boots. He'd bargained hard for his footwear from Madge the Wanderer, marveling at their thick but supple soles and how they kept his feet dry without chantment.

Crenn's nostrils twitched. Seamed, runneled flesh tingled all over his face. The scars spilled down his neck, grasping his shoulders and continuing down his chest and back. They tingled, too, and he knew the sensation too well to move.

A leash on a troll meant someone to hold it, of course. Any Unwinter hiding behind the large, gray-green, slightly snoring hulk couldn't venture out without the violet dapples of lightshield chantment on them, and Crenn needed to double back to find the Ragged's trail again...but still. Leaving an enemy alive behind you was a fool's move.

Besides, he held no love for the Unseelie.

Still, he hesitated, the sting of stagnant water and choking moss exhaling into the sunlight touching his shoulders and his brown-green hair. The moss would begin to dry soon, without Marrowdowne's shady, steady drip, drip, drip to creep between the strands.

What had she done, to fire-scar a troll and drive it this far? There was her voice, of course.

Not a scratch upon her... I will make you beautiful again.

Crenn straightened. As he did, something occurred to him. Her trail was *far* too thoroughly confused. He wasn't her only pursuer, but who else would erase her traces?

Who else would Summer send? And why ask for Crenn himself, a forgotten relic mired in a noisome swamp?

Perhaps because there was another player in this game, one the Hunter of Marrowdowne was known to have some manner of grudge against. Though grudges were as common as pixies; to have sidhe blood was almost synonymous with craving vengeance.

Crenn left the stonetroll—and whatever else it was guarding—to its sleep. It was a puzzle. First Unwinter's attack during the revels, now spring bursting free over the mortal world and Summer's errand girl to be brought back whole.

Then there was the little matter of *him*.

Gallow. Perhaps *he* was clearing the Ragged's trail, so as to have the pleasure of gutting her? It wasn't like him to kill a woman, or at least it hadn't been when Crenn had called him *brother*.

Still, you could believe a Half capable of almost anything, with the right inducement.

While Crenn might make a halfhearted effort to keep Summer appeased, the idea of thwarting the former Armormaster held *much* more appeal. Perhaps Summer had known as much.

His scars tingled afresh, thinking of doing that green-eyed Half bastard a disservice.

"Fear not, little bird," he murmured as he reached the top of the hill and peered through a screen of bushes at the metal carriages whizzing past. "Not a hair on your head shall be harmed."

First, though, he had to *find* her.

Crenn checked the sky, rolled his shoulders back, and vanished.

CHANGELING NO MORE

15

I t cowered as she worked herself free of the tangle, but it didn't vanish into the bushes alongside the deck. Where had it hidden, that childcatchers couldn't find it? Had the shock of Sean's...death...driven it into witless flight? Was that why they had vented their anger on the parents, not finding the placeholder sleeping in his bed?

It doesn't matter. She had to carefully wriggle between the glass teeth; the last thing she wanted was to leave a bloodtrail. Getting to hands and knees was tricksome, and crawling free probably destroyed whatever dignity she had left.

At least when she finally extricated herself the changeling didn't flee *her*. It crouched, a thin, bleached figure, near the grill. It was alarmingly gaunt—of course, without its mortal anchor, its substance was thinning rapidly. Its eyes, once as bright blue as Sean's, were now the color of old much-washed cotton sheets and protruded from its starveling face. It made that tiny sound again, a baby bird's pleading. A wet, filthy, red T-shirt with a picture of a dog stuck to its wasted chest; it hitched its similarly filthy jeans up with skinny, dirty fingers.

Robin slowly, so slowly, sank back on her haunches, brushing at her skirt. She pushed her hair back, and the changeling cowered, shrinking away.

"It's all right," she managed, as soft and soothing as possible. Her voice made sidhe nervous—those who knew of her, at least.

Those who didn't learned soon enough.

The changeling sank down. It had a pair of red sneakers, just as muddy and wet as the rest of its attire. It settled on its knees and reached up, touching its own tangled, pale mop.

Robin concentrated on breathing. Four in, four out. The changeling was alive, for now. There was, if she looked closely, an echo of Sean in its bird-thin grace, its fading coloring. It had lost the ability to speak—perhaps the shock. Just a faint copy, wasting away. It would dissolve into nothingness soon enough, if the childcatchers didn't come back and snatch it. No doubt Summer would use the flint knife even on this sorry specimen.

Even a changeling wasting away to nothing could still bleed.

What was I thinking? Was I even thinking at all? She dropped her hands, and the changeling did as well. Its piping stilled, and it stared at her.

The wriggling of an idea in the back of her head became more pronounced. Robin stilled, her breathing evening out. A damp morning breeze touched her bare, steaming shoulders. The deck, hard and gritty against her naked knees, stayed just as solid, but she rocked a little as the idea crept out of its hiding place and presented itself.

Don't be stupid, Robin. It's madness.

And yet.

Her hand stole out, found a glass shard tangled in the canvas. Wicked-sharp and slightly curved. The changeling stared blankly at her. It didn't judge her a threat.

Should it? It had the sense to flee from the childcatchers, or perhaps mere luck had saved it. Who could tell?

Her fingertips skated along the glass shard. It was madness. Unthinkable folly. She should simply leave the fading thing to its fate.

Then why did you come here, Robin? Why?

She picked the glass up, delicately. Thin sunshine strengthened— the clouds were clearing. It would probably be a beautiful day.

It's insane. A Half can't do what you're thinking. That much chantment will hurt you, badly.

If Summer ever found out...

A small, pained smile lit Robin's face, echoed by the changeling's ghastly grin. It copied her slight movement to pick the shard up, brushing its filthy fingertips across decking.

"Changeling," Robin said, again so softly, soothingly. "Do you want to live?"

Its mouth moved, nothing but the piping coming out.

"Do you?" she pressed.

Something struggled in its pupils, a dim spark. It stopped grinning, its forehead knitting, and for a moment it looked like a wizened old brughnie, its face a map of wrinkle-rivers.

It nodded, and its outlines blurred.

Robin set the glass shard against the back of her left forearm—not the inside, where the veins could be opened. She, after all, wanted to live as well.

If she did this, she might even be able to salvage something of her pride. Or at least make the grief and despair a little smaller.

She hissed between her teeth as she drew the glass along her flesh. It was surprisingly hard to slice, but once she'd made up her mind to do it, the sharp edge sank in, almost as if eager.

She was going to leave a bloodtrail after all.

The changeling hissed, too, and crept forward, its palms scraping the deck and its head bobbing. The hiss became that pleading little noise again.

Robin dropped the glass shard onto her skirt. The wound glowed red as sunshine steamed along the wreckage. Behind her, the kitchen door slammed, the mortal house closing itself around its secret carnage.

The changeling's mouth fastened on her arm. It suckled, experimentally, and Robin opened her mouth. The Old Language dropped like rain, chantment blurring down her arm, and when the changeling set itself more firmly, its small hands creeping up to grasp her arm, and drew again on the wound, she winced.

She held the chantment steady, even when darkness beat at the corner of her vision, and the changeling drew again. A Half wasn't supposed to do this; changelings belonged to the Queen. Their blood made corners of the sideways realms forever Summer, and her apple trees drove their roots deep to do the same. To do this was to rob the Queen, outright inexcusable theft. No sidhe of Summer would ever dream of attempting it.

Swimming weakness closed around Robin Ragged. Lungs straining, heart laboring, she held the stream of the Old Language steady. The changeling flushed, its outlines running like clay in water.

Syllables thrust up through the stream of chantment, repeated over and over. They fitted themselves together, sharp edges slicing as they fought against her hold. If she could just keep the chant long enough, they would knit themselves together, and—

A massive internal noise. Robin sagged, dimly aware of her head striking the deck as she toppled. The changeling's mouth tore away, almost taking a chunk of her arm as its teeth clicked together, and the thing threw back its head and howled as the finished chantment pierced it, reshaped it.

The oldest of magics—to create is to *name*.

Howling ceased. Groaning and shuffling, glass shattering, the creaking of metal tubing. Heavy, wet crunching sounds as the changeling-no-more writhed and spasmed, the name shaping the thing.

Birth is always painful.

Darkness, brief shutterclicks of light as her eyelids struggled to rise, then slammed down again.

When the spasming and writhing ended, a sleek wheat-gold shape lay, still as death, next to a milk-pale woman in a faded blue dress, her redgold hair oddly drained of its luster. The sun shrugged free of thin clouds, burning away haze and pouring over both of them, and for a moment the heartbeat of both creatures halted. Still, the chantment continued, its thunder fading into the distance as the act rippled through real and more-than-real.

The changeling-no-more stirred. It whined as the cramps and seizures withdrew. Its slim paws twitched, and after a little while it dragged itself to the depleted statue of a sleeping woman, curling its long body into that uncertain shelter.

DIRTY WORK
16

🌹⚔️

lose. Very close. Half the afternoon was gone, clouds massing in the north as another spring storm tiptoed its unsettled way closer and closer. Jeremiah sighed, an involuntary noise, as he scrambled up the side of an embankment and found a housing development spread before him. One of the newer ones, its pavement still tar-black, and a couple dead ends showed where they were going to build even more as soon as winter lost its grip. Bulldozing the trees that might have been here before and putting in these blocks of tofu, then planting anemic saplings—well, it was enough to make any sidhe shake their head. Even a Half.

Still, people had to have places to live. And he'd done his share of running a dozer, or a chainsaw. Each time he saw mortal buildings rising, or a mortal street running straight and true, half of him felt a nasty secret joy.

He just didn't know *which* half.

What the hell was Robin doing *here*? There was some sense to her wanderings, she was going far too directly to be simply hoping to throw off pursuit.

The sunlight dimmed, and Gallow's back prickled. The

scars writhed madly, but he denied the lance its freedom and simply turned, slow, his hands loose and easy.

Scrubwood and bushes, the freeway in the distance making a high-pitched humming. She'd come along the line of Highway 4, crossing and recrossing the river of iron cars—it was a nice trick, but he had the locket. It tugged insistently under his shirt-collar, but instead of drawing it out he focused on the stillness in the shrubbery.

And waited.

When the shape melded out of scrub and a tangle of blackberry vines, the lance poked and prodded for its freedom even more relentlessly. Gallow denied it, but his weight did shift slightly.

The man was a shade taller than Gallow but built much leaner. Brown leather cut sidhe-fashion, a jerkin and trews, and a pair of brown engineer boots, of mortal make. He still had the earring, a hoop of dull iron, and his hair was still long and brown, green tints drying out. *Looks like he's been fen-hopping. Wasn't he in Marrowdowne, last I heard?*

It didn't matter.

A gleam of eyes through the curtain of shaken-down hair, glaring. Two hilts riding his shoulders, and his capable hands were just as empty as Gallow's own.

That was also meaningless. Even without weapons, the new arrival was dangerous.

"Gallow." A baritone, rich enough to charm a bird or two from a branch and into his nets.

"Crenn." Jeremiah tilted his head.

A long silence. Clouds drifted, the sunshine intensifying, dimming again. The other man leaned forward slightly; Jeremiah did, too. So much of a battle was decided in the first few moments, before hand met hilt, far before blade met blade.

"I am," Alastair Crenn said, "not here for you."

That only leaves one other reason. Shit. "Then what for?" *If he'd get his hair out of his face, it would be easier to tell what he's thinking.* That was why he didn't, Jeremiah supposed. There were also the scars. Burning tar did things to a man.

Even a Half.

"There is a certain lady in distress." A gleam of white teeth. It couldn't be a smile; it was probably a feral grimace.

One who finds you *attractive?* That was an asshole thing to say, even if they hated each other. Still, it trembled on Gallow's tongue before he found a more diplomatic brace of words. "No doubt."

"I shall be plain."

"Please do."

"Cease following the Ragged, and I shall let you live."

What? A chill slid down Gallow's back. *Just hold on a minute.* "Summer granted her life to me, Alastair Crenn. You will not interfere." *There. That's honest, at least.* As long as Summer thought *he* wanted to kill Robin...

But Jeremiah had faced Unwinter for Robin's sake. Like an idiot, he'd telegraphed it. *My lady Robin.*

That gleaming, teeth and eyes, didn't alter. Did he wear a mask of chantment, or did he just abhor being seen so much it created a glamour all its own?

"I warn you again, *Armormaster.*" Crenn all but hissed the last word, lingering over the sibilant. "The Ragged is under my protection. And this time you have no mortals to do your dirty work."

I never did in the first place. But had he lingered too long, and Crenn paid the price? That night, the fire and screaming as the police bore down on the Hooverville shantyslum, the bubbling tar and the stink of mortal death... "I was not of Summer then, Alastair, and neither were you. I still would have spared you that, if—"

"I needed no *sparing*," the man replied, not hotly, as he once would have. No, it was a soft, deadly song of words repeated over and over in the dead watches of the night.

How did Gallow know? Because he had his own cantos to sing in that same tone. "We are not at cross purposes here—"

Crenn was already gone, down the hill in a blur, following the fading traces of Robin's passage.

Did Robin know him; had she made a bargain with him? What man would say no to the Ragged, with those eyes of hers, and that hair? Or was it just that Jeremiah was a fool? How well did Crenn know her? Did he owe her something?

Or was this a gambit of Summer's? What inducement could the Queen offer *Crenn*, of all people?

You know she's got ways. Gallow was already moving, the lightfoot blooming under his own boots. *Don't worry about that. Focus on Robin.*

You've got to get to her first.

PLAGUE

17

Pavilions stretched under a dusk-darkening sky, each tall and fair with its sides held open to permit passage. Pennons snapped in a warm breeze. In some tents, sap flowed up through stumps coaxed from warm, forgiving earth; in others, evergrape and honeywine, eldar liqueur and more potent drinks dripped into jugs and were measured out with generous hands by brown-skinned, leering satyrs. Outside the pavilions, dryads and naiads fluttered by, unwilling to approach the goatborn and not needing liquor on this marvelous night. The wind, pregnant with appleblossom and a hint of salt from the Dreaming Sea, was draught enough for them. Dwarves of the Red Clans clustered in groups, their cunning, filthy hands at work upon marvels—fireworks that would rise later, showering the crowd with light and scent and perhaps small trinkets, tiny popping chantments tossed freely to laughing nymphs or cautious brughnies, evanescent ornaments made of sighs and hair-fine glittering threads. Come dawn they would revert to cobweb and leaf, but for tonight the flash and fire was enough to delight every sidhe fortunate enough to attend.

Music roamed the crowd, bright and sprightly, Summer's

own minstrels settled in corners and nooks, perched in tree branches, plucking gitterns, lutes, pipes wailing. A vast open greensward, growing tall and fragrant and studded with star-white, starshaped *eltora* flowers, was the dance floor, and the drums of stretched skin too fine to be animal stood at the left-hand side of the temporary dais hung with dark green and the flames of jewels that echoed the stars even now beginning to glimmer above.

The drummers were motionless, their beaked and feathered masks quiescent above oiled chests and hanging arms. Some had two, some had four, and the Master of the Drums, a massive mountain of half-troll muscle with four fine upper append-ages, crouched near the huge *taiko* named Heartbeat.

They poured onto the green, the highborn fullblood. Lady and lord in velvet and silk, coruscating chantments attract-ing the gaze and quickening the pulse. Long flowing hair of every shade, high-pointed ears, the slim six-fingered or extra-jointed hands peeping from trailing sleeve. The men, fierce and beautiful at the same moment, bowed to their ladies, each pair arranged to please Summer's eye—or gratify her vanity.

"*Summer!*" The cry went up from many throats, the throng pressing against the borders of the sward, impatient for the dance. The musicians struck up a merry tune, and the full-blood highborn moved through a slow, ancient pavane, bow and curtsy, hands meeting and feet treading stately measures. The high and mighty of Summer's Court danced, each lady with an extra flutter at her left wrist. It was the fashion now, a scarf or something graceful knotted about that arm, to ape the Queen's adoption of such an ornament.

Those who had not been chosen for the dance clustered at its edges, painted lips behind piercelace bone fans, darting glitter-glances. A sharp thrill ran through them and the crowd behind—naiad, dryad, dwarf, selkie, wight and woodwight of the Seelie, those-who-could-speak. Behind them, the mortal-Tainted, from the Half to those with only a drop or two of sidhe. Behind them, more pressed of the Lesser Folk, drawn to the heat and light, the Tongueless but not nameless.

Some of the whispers held there were fewer of the mortal-Tainted this year, that some of those accorded pride of fullborn place had a mortal ancestor or two, and claimed insurance from the blackboil plague. And at the very periphery, knights in armor held guard—for the last revel had been broken.

"*Summer!*" The cry went up again, an edge to its sibilant. Did they think they could command her appearance?

The traditional dance ended, and the drummers tensed. A ripple went through the assembled, and the fullborn turned as one toward the dais.

Silence, broken only by the pennons snapping, the sough of the sweet night breeze. Normally such a dance would be held in the orchards, but a blackened scar slashed through those fleece-blossomed trees, a tang of smoke still lingered in their branches, and their bark-grown faces were shallow-drawn, not thick-graven as they had been before, though their roots were just as deep.

One moment the dais was empty. The next, before the low bench serving as a throne, there was a quiver...and *she* appeared.

Tall and fair in jade silk, her mantle deep-pine velvet, her golden hair just as deliciously lustrous as ever, the Jewel at her forehead glowing green—no hurtful spear of emerald radiance, as was usual, but a considerable light nonetheless.

"*Summer!*" they cried, as her ladies-in-waiting appeared behind her, the Veil parting lovingly, caressing them as they stepped through in her wake.

Sometimes she would toy with them, allow them to antici-pate. But not tonight. She lifted her arms, the scarf at her left wrist a deep heartsblood crimson, knotted gracefully and allowed to flutter.

"*My children!*" she cried, the ancient words of Danu herself, in the mists when the Folk were united and mortals merely a bad future-dreaming. "*Dance for me!*"

Thud. Thudthud. Heartbeat spoke, the Master of the Drums beginning his long race, and the sound reverberated through every corner of Summer, spreading out to lap at the edges of her realm.

They crowded the greensward, leaping and gamboling, the fullborn retreating to before the dais to engage in their more-mannered gyrations. The quickening Heartbeat spread through dell and clearing, forest and pasture, even the home-fast sidhe or those who paid only nominal homage to Summer hearing it through the ground, a thunder communicated through whatever foot a sidhe wore, spilling through the air itself to turn birds dizzy-drunk, even those a-nested for the night.

Heartbeat settled into a rhythm, the Master's oiled limbs weaving complicated chantment, and the first fireworks arced high over the revel, light and scent showering all underneath. Sweat sprang early, satyrs chasing nymphs who shrieked and leapt to escape, selkies whirling and splattering salt water, nai-ads sinking down to writhe on the rushed grass, a sharp expec-tancy cresting through them all.

It went on and on, whirling color and motion, fireworks flashing, the Queen motionless upon her bench, her face a stat-ue's. Tonight she was not the laughing nymph a dance some-times provoked her into seeming.

No, tonight Summer looked…worried? Certainly not, she was Queen of all she surveyed, and—

A single drop of poison in the ocean of sidhe. A lone, stumbling step, a naiad with long cinnamon hair and sharp white teeth falling, twitching as the dancers leapt away from her. Normally, the weakened or the overly mortal could drop and be trampled, their blood and bone worked into hungry earth beneath, but this was not such a thing. The crowd exploded, screams piercing even Heartbeat's thundering.

For the nymph lay, her scattered blue and silver finery smoking all about her, and twisted upon the bruised grass. The small, white, starlike flowers crisped, blackening, and died. Black flowers bloomed on the naiad's skin—she was of the Echo riverfolk, the pattern of daggered raindrops worked into her skirts said as much—and hardened, crusting as the horrified onlookers stilled.

They burst, those black cancerous boils, and the screams took on a fever-pitch. Heartbeat faltered, and the Queen rose angrily, her white hands turned to bone-slim fists, stalking through the sweating, scurrying folk.

She arrived just in time for the nymph to choke on a tide of blackened excrescence, heels drumming as the river-maiden turned to sludge herself, even sharp fishbones dissolving. The Queen's face did not change. She stared down at the bubbling, steaming mass.

When the illness struck, it took the lowborn sidhe the quickest. A highborn could stave off decline by pure will, it was rumored—but only for a while. Once the black feather brushed, it was only a question of time.

"*Plaaaaaaaaaaague!*"

Ever afterward, nobody could agree on who screamed the

single word. The sidhe fled. Howling, gibbering, they broke the pavilion supports and trampled the smallest among them. Even the Half and mortal-Tainted fled, even the Queen's ladies, mad with fear.

The blackboil plague, the scourge of the sidhe untainted by mortal blood, was loose in heretofore-inviolate Summer.

A NEW ANIMAL
18

A slow, sleepy afternoon, Daisy cuddled against her side in the sagging single bed. "What are we gonna eat, Rob?"

"I don't know." Robin lay with her arm over her eyes. In a little bit she'd get up and figure it out. There wasn't likely to be anything in the fridge. Mama was at work, and Robin was babysitter today. Daisy, usually so easy-tempered, was fractious and whining. Robin had tried everything—stories, games, even turning on the ancient black-and-white television—to no avail. A little girl was hungry, and there was nobody to feed her.

"What are we gonna eat?" Daisy whined again, and Robin pinched her, hard. "Ow! Roooob! Why'd'ja dooooooo that?"

"Shhh. Shut up." Robin tried to think, but the hole in her own belly was so big. Maybe she could chance the corner store. Stealing was bad, but Daisy was hungry and what was Robin supposed to do?

What could she take? A jar of peanut butter? Maybe too big...a stick of butter, anything?

At least when Mama let Daddy Snowe come back there would be food. But then Robin's throat might close up, making it hard to swallow when he fixed her with those paralyzing blue eyes of his and—

A short, sniveling sob from next to her, hot breath against her neck. A bright spear of hatred speared Robin—but she couldn't hate Daisy, God would surely strike her down into hell if she hated her sister.

So she stirred, a little. "I'll go to the store."

"Can I get a magazine?"

"Maybe. Let's look for quarters in the couch." Except she knew there wouldn't be any, and Robin would begin to steal. There was no way around it, and it wasn't like they would be in this park long enough for it to matter.

Sooner or later, Daddy Snowe always came back.

⁂

A deep chill woke her. *Ugh. Dreaming. Daisy. She was so small.* She pushed herself up on her hands and knees, conscious of the desire to get moving but not quite sure why. Her eyes opened, but everything was a haze. She was, for the first time in a long while, *cold.* Something hard underneath her.

A persistent nudging at her hip. Robin groaned.

That's me. I'm Robin Ragged. That's my name.

Names. So many. Mama's name, before and after Daddy Snowe. Little sister Daisy Elaine, soft and mortal and full of laughter. Daddy Snowe's names, and what he called both Mama and Robin when he was mad, and then later, among the sidhe...

Sidhe. Danger. Get up.

Waves of shivering poured through her. Her arms almost refused to straighten.

Above Half, there were truenames. Half a share of mortal blood, or more, meant no truename for you—which was a gift, since it couldn't be guessed in a riddle or used against you. It was also another pinch on a bruise, because in the Old Language, only the Named had, well, names. Everyone else was approximated.

Another nudge at her hip, an insistent nose against the silk of her skirt. Robin forced her eyes to open, to *remain* open, and stared at her dirty hands against wooden decking. Milk-pale, and the slice along the back of her left forearm smarted. Crusted over and queerly pale at its edges, it stung as she made a fist, swaying a little on her other hand.

Ouch. Why isn't it healing?

As soon as she wondered, she knew the answer. She sank back on her haunches, pushing the rest of herself upright, and found herself on an expensive deck next to a shattered table, and the prodding was the nose of a sleek, massive golden hound with wide dark eyes.

No, not so dark. More indigo, a blue so deep it mimicked summer's dusk.

Eyes, in fact, the color of Robin's own.

"Oh." A hurt little noise, as if she'd been struck.

It was as big as a *cu sith*, but not greenish as those large tail-plaited wonders. It pranced a little, its nails clicking on the wood, and nosed at her again. A candy-pink tongue flicked as it licked its sharp white teeth, but it didn't growl or bite. Its tail, fringed and fine, whipped back and forth, and Robin's child-hood distrust of dogs rose briefly, filling the back of her throat with sour heat. There was a faint reddish bloom to its fur, each hair tipped with a suggestion of crimson, and the nausea wasn't just from being so close to a canine.

Well, I've gone and done it now. She swallowed, twice, wincing. Her skirt was faded, and some of the needle-chantment was loosening. The mendings, clearly visible now, were scabs of indigo against frayed periwinkle silk.

She touched one of her curls. Faded as well, the red leached out, richer than dishwater blond but still not sidhe-vibrant.

Am I mortal now? No, the music under her thoughts still

rumbled along. The noise was faraway, though, not pressing insistently for release. Like the subway in the city, a great beast dozing.

She whispered a word in the Old Language and immediately winced. It stung her tongue dreadfully, and she tasted blood.

No chantment for a little while, then. She needed milk, but whatever was in the house behind her was almost certainly soured by deathbringing sidhe.

Besides, going back into that place, with that smell . . . no.

The hound—bigger than a Saint Bernard, the size of a pony and with enough fur to make it seem even larger—bent its head and licked at her forearm. Robin tried to snatch her arm away and almost overbalanced. The dog continued licking, mildly, and the cut eased itself together, knitting slowly as it continued.

Not a *cu sith*, then. Perhaps a dandydog, or a gebriel without a human-shaped head. It had four toes and large blunt nails, so it was more like a gytrash, but she'd never seen a gytrash this color.

A new animal, then.

It pressed its face against her shoulder, almost knocking her to the deck again, and gave a little hop of delight when she pushed at it. It was always Daisy who could coax a skeletal stray into eating from a can Robin stole from a corner store or supermarket, Daisy who lit up every time a mangy kitten wandered by. Daddy Snowe called her "pets" diseased, kicked at them with his cowboy boots.

Once, he had drowned a whole sack of mewling kittens in the rain barrel while Daisy sobbed and Robin looked on, her face frozen.

She shook the memory away, and the hound whined. It shoved its face in hers and licked her cheek, a wet, warm, *real* touch. Another whine, deep in its barrel chest.

"I know," she whispered, even though she didn't. She didn't have a single fucking clue.

Her teeth chattered, and when she wound her fingers in the hound's fur, warmth jolted down her arm, the feverish heat of a creature from the sideways realms. Her head cleared a bit, and she gazed out on the mortal backyard, blinking furiously as the sun shed a robe of cloud and poured down onto mildly shaggy grass and fence alike. An anemic sapling in the back left corner was furred with green, and when the hound folded itself down and wriggled, Robin found she could indeed hike her leg up over its back.

"Be careful," she whispered, and sagged against the creature's vital heat. "They're chasing me. You could flee, and leave me to—"

The hound growled, another low thrumming sound lifting the fine hairs all over her body. A mortal response. Her arms and legs did their best to clamp down, to keep her on its back, and it rose carefully, finding its balance.

"I wish..." There was nothing to wish for. So Robin swallowed the taste of blood and bile and whispered the name she'd knit together in the Old Language. Translation was difficult, but she wet her cracked, dry lips and tried anyway.

Thankfully, she didn't have to pronounce any chantment. The use-name was there, lying over the top of the thing's true-name in a gossamer shroud. It would be impossible to guess the real shape, the exact constellation of blood and breath below, if Robin or the hound didn't teach it.

"Pepperbuckle," she whispered. "Let's go."

Pepperbuckle threw back his shaggy head and howled, a long, trailing scarf of a cry. He bunched himself, and the world fell away underneath him.

Robin shut her eyes, clinging to warm, vital fur, and simply held on for all she was worth.

WELL DEAD BEFORE
19

The house reeked of death; he didn't bother traipsing upstairs to see what foulness lay in wait. Gallow arrived in the kitchen just as Crenn nipped through the back door, and the thought that the man might get to Robin first spurred him to even more speed. He hit the door, shivering the glass and bursting wood into shrapnel, and skidded to a halt.

Crenn whirled, going down into a crouch, his hand blurring up for the hilt on his left shoulder. Gallow's lance was already solid, lengthening, the point leafshaped now and wicked-sharp, dipping to rest at the hollow of the assassin's throat. "Don't," Jeremiah said softly. "Don't make me."

There was a patio table, smashed under a canvas cover, and the smell of chantment hung heavy in the air. A thin thread of Robin's scent, that spice and woman he hadn't realized he was missing until now.

Liar. You knew you were missing it, all along.

Crenn snarled, and the ruin of his face was clearly visible under strings of mossy hair. The boiling tar had done horrible things to flesh, and even for a Half the damage was a long time healing. His eyes glowed, bright coal-burning glimmers through the seamed and pitted flesh, and the most horrible thing was the shadows of sidhe gloss on the scars. A hideous beauty, one that Gallow might have called a lie if he didn't know the depth of the damage behind the blemishes.

He'd thought Robin's loveliness a lie once, too.

The assassin tensed. Gallow didn't, the lance humming sweetly against his palms. It had fed well last night, but there was no end to the thing's hunger.

The old Armormaster had never warned him of *that*. Would it have mattered, if he had?

"She's not here," Crenn said. It was almost obscene, how the tar poured over what the attackers had thought was a dead body had left his lips untouched. Chiseled and perfect, you could see a ghost of what he'd been before they used the cudgels on him, and the bubbling-hot liquid as well.

Jeremiah didn't let his gaze lift to scan the backyard. The locket throbbed under his T-shirt, a secret heartbeat. *Close. Very close.* Still running, too. A canny girl, his Robin.

Not yours yet, Gallow. He kept the lance steady. "You gave me a warning, Crenn. I'll give one in return: Stop chasing my lady Robin. She's not for you, *or* for Summer."

Stillness. The sun was falling, afternoon waning, and this backyard was full of chantment echoes. What had Robin done? Her song could kill, but he didn't think it likely that she'd harm a houseful of mortals.

Anyone on her trail might not be so kind, though.

"Your lady Robin?" On that scar-wrinkled face, the sneer was even uglier. "I do not think she welcomes your suit, *Gallowglass*."

What would you know of it? Just like dealing with one of the touchy mortals on a jobsite. "Just as I'm sure she won't welcome yours, if you get lucky enough to catch her."

"Oh, and now he knows the Ragged's mind as well." It would be difficult for the assassin to sound more disdainful. He straightened slowly, the lance rising in line with his throat and Gallow's weight shifting to keep it steady. *"And* mine. Why bother with dancing, Glassgallow, if you know the music so well?"

"The Ragged is *mine*. Go back to your swamp and nurse your scars." *Way to go, Jer.* Still, he needed this dealt with, and if he could provoke the man...

"Oh, they need no nursing." A wide, white, sharp smile, his shoulders loose and easy under the brown leather.

That brought up another troubling thought. Where was Puck? He had been underfoot all through the last few days, and with his hold on Robin... was he with her now?

A flash, a spat curse, the lance rasping against his palms, a propeller-movement tossing one of Crenn's blades wide. Gallow skipped back, batting the curse away with a single word, the Veil shimmering around them both, sensitized by whatever had happened before two Half started flinging violence and curses around.

Crenn was still abominably quick. Two blades and that lightfoot grace, the tar hadn't robbed him of the beauty and precision of sidhe movement. Gallow fell back, feinting, *watch that left hand, he's*...A muscle-tearing effort, blades chiming, the lance *bending*, impossibly fluid, shifting through shape and unshape to batter aside one sword, blinking aside to smack the flat of the other one and drive the assassin back. The deck groaned beneath them, glass and metal jittering under the torn canvas cover. The grill, under another cover, toppled over, and Jeremiah caught a flash of a propane tank.

Ah. Two steps to the side, the lance lengthening, Crenn pushed off the deck and landing catfoot on wet grass. His right sleeve flopped a little, high up—the lance's kiss. A thin trickle of blood slid warm down Jeremiah's temple, the initial curse having brushed him with a razor wing.

Nobody mowed, Jeremiah realized. *Whoever's upstairs was well dead before Robin arrived here. Coincidence?*

Not with the saplings in front and backyard greening like they were. "Crenn." His breath coming hard but regular. "The Ragged needs no protection from me."

A single shrug, moss greening along Crenn's forehead where salt sweat moistened the strands. One blade held *au coeur*, the other high in blackbird's-rise, the sunlight failing again behind a screen of rain-heavy cloud. He was so goddamn *fast*, and if he got inside the lance's reach Jeremiah might be forced into something other than knightly sparring.

Crenn's eyes glittered. He straightened still more, his gaze flicking across the deck and Jeremiah in a smooth, controlled arc. "And yet Summer granted you her life."

"She did." He weighed adding more. "The situation is... complex."

"It always is." Crenn's blades lowered, slowly. "Your lady Robin, hm?"

She doesn't know it yet. "Yes." He didn't relax. This was altogether too easy.

The smile widened. Crenn actually laughed, a short, bitter mouthful that might have been merry as a pixie if not for the grotesquerie his face twisted into.

He was still laughing when he vaulted the back fence, disappearing due west, and the only thing that stopped Gallow from chasing him was the sudden sharp tug on the necklace in his pocket. North and east, and fading quickly.

Priorities, Jer. How fast can she move, after all this?

"Not fast enough," he murmured, and the lance disappeared

as he bent, one ear pricked for a new arrival to muddy the situation.

Tangled in the canvas, a curve of broken glass. Rusted-red along its sharp edge, and clinging to it, three fine, curling, coppergold hairs.

Had she been forced to defend herself with this? The blood on it...

His heart, like one of Unwinter's treacherous night-mares, dropped sharply away, then returned to pound in his wrists and throat. Jeremiah sucked in a breath, glancing at the sky again.

Robin. Oh, God.

What if she'd been caught? Summer would not send only one erstwhile assassin to gather up her wayward little Half bird. Seelie had been here, the entire yard shouted it.

Jeremiah wrapped the hairs into the dried blood, hoping they'd hold. Shoved the glass in his coat's miraculously unshredded left breast pocket, and headed for the fence.

CARNIVALE
20

She tumbled, boneless, from the hound's back, with barely enough strength to keep herself from falling face-first onto blown-down chainlink fencing. Blinking, pushing her hair back, Robin staggered, and couldn't find her balance until Pepperbuckle slid along her right side, for all the world like a cat stropping a beloved human, and whined deep in his chest. Her fingers tangled in his fur again, and she limped along with him. Her shoes slipped, her calves aching savagely as the chantment in the heels fought against her mortal heaviness.

Where am I? Metal shapes rose and blurred, and she bit back a scream, thinking the dog had dragged her to the Unseelie after all.

A huge glaring white face, the size of her entire body, loomed before her with its lips rusted with old blood and its nose a crimson bulb, and terror almost robbed her of the ability to read mortal writing. Peeling paint on cheap pasteboard, and with a jolt, she realized where she was.

**SALTHOFF CARNIVALE
BEST IN THE WEST
COME INSIDE!**

"Oh," she whispered. Her heart hammered, and for a moment the place glimmered, the shape of something underneath wearing through. There was iron, though, in the tilting Ferris wheel, and also in the bigtop's skeleton full of shredded ribbons fluttering on the spring-chill, freshening breeze. Rainscent filled her nose and eyes, her hair tangling, no longer as silky. The pins shifted, and she had to clap them to her head while she struggled to walk alongside Pepperbuckle, who patiently guided them both down the central arcade.

I wonder what happened. It looks like everyone just...left. She shivered, shut her eyes. Some things could turn a place sideways—and some could wrench a place out of the stream of both mortal and sidhe, a crack between door and jamb. It was usually a disastrous occurrence, without any merriment to attract sidhe attention. *Never mind, I don't want to know.*

Pepperbuckle whined. Now they were past the arcade— there were still electrical cables, sagging on posts, buried in leaf mulch and sandy soil to trip the unwary. She hung on grimly, the creature's warmth a welcome shield. Small trailers stood on either side, the shells carnies dragged from town to town. A screen door banged, hesitated, opened under the wind's persistent fingering, banged again, the screen loose and flopping in long ribbons, as if it had been clawed.

The hound seemed to know where he was going. Robin's arm was a solid bar of pain by the time he walked her to a trailer just like all the others, turning so she could grab at a rickety railing above handmade, portable, dry-rotten steps. She climbed one, then another, clinging to the wobbling balustrade. Splinters poking her palms, she hauled herself up the third step and half-fell against the door.

When she turned, blinking against a stinging, dust-laden

wind—funny, but it seemed like the rain hadn't fallen here—Pepperbuckle was gone.

Debt repaid, I guess. I'm probably safe here for a little while. It was like thinking through mud. She tried the door; it was unlocked, and that was a good thing, because she couldn't even whisper a lock open in her current state.

Inside, more dust. It was an ancient Airstream, with a half-kitchenette and a porta-john closet of a bathroom. That didn't matter, because there was a bed, and Robin staggered across cracked, humped flooring and collapsed. The wind moaned, and the foggy idea that perhaps she wasn't in a mortal *or* sidhe space would have been frightening, but she was too tired to care.

Bang. Hiss-whine. Bang. Creak.

She woke to the entire trailer rocking on its dead, airless tires, and a wet nose in her face. Somehow the hound had squeezed through the door, its jaws clamped on a glass bottle. It nosed at her, liquid sloshing inside the glass, and she tried to push its snout away before it blew a warm, hay-scented breath over her and she realized the sloshing was something good.

She pushed herself up, wedging her back against the trailer's thin, rust-spotted wall. Had she slept? For how long? It was dark outside, but time in a between-space like this could warp in strange ways.

The bottle was milk. Full-cream, with a foil cap, and her hands shook as she managed to peel the topper off. The canine shape barely fit inside the trailer—how on *earth* had it gotten through the door?

Doesn't matter. Cu sith *can change size, a little, maybe this one can.*

She tipped the bottle to her lips, and the balm poured down her throat in long swallows. Thin trickles kissed the outside of her mouth, her chin, dotted her dress, but she didn't care. The dog whined, a high-pitched, yearning sound.

She tore the bottle away, gasping, and the world roared around her, spinning and taking on its accustomed color and depth. The Veil flexed, flexed again, unseen shapes ghosting just at the edge of her vision. A moment's worth of concentration, the music under her thoughts dipping and arrowing along at its usual volume, and she winced at the thought that she'd been afraid of losing it, even as she hated what her voice could do.

What it *had* done.

She offered the hound the bottle, but it shook its lean, graceful head, its eyes darkening a shade. It backed up, its rear ramming the kitchenette's cabinet, and the look of agonized surprise crossing its long, intelligent face wrung a tiny, betraying laugh out of her.

Pepperbuckle chuffed, a small chortling sound, as if he tried to chuckle as well. She tipped the bottle to her mouth again. Full-cream. She could taste the sun and the grass in it. Where on earth had he found such a thing?

"Good," she said, when she could breathe again for drinking. "Good boy. Good, *good* boy."

The hound wriggled again, the entire trailer rocking and groaning. He thrust his face at her again, and Robin found herself scratching behind his floppy ears, just where she'd always seen Daisy rub stray dogs. Those eyes half lidded, and now she could see the pupils were oval instead of round like a *cu sith*'s vertical slits. More like a gytrash then, those good-natured dog-sprites who guarded travelers in need—or led them into a bog and feasted on their still-writhing flesh, like kelpies, depending on their mood.

"Best boy," she whispered. A few more swallows finished the bottle, and the hound tensed. "No. No more." Robin coughed and took a closer look at her surroundings.

Nobody had been in here for quite some time. The bed she huddled on was a tiny, mildewed cot, and the walls were papered with fading photographs and once-glossy ads from old, old magazines. Flappers stared from water-spotted paper, handbills for the carnival's appearances in other cities with florid illustrations, a strongman with a waxed mustache holding up inflatable barbells, and several pictures of a solemn, dark-eyed girl on postcards stuck to the wall with creeping mold.

It was filthy, and her skin crawled, but the trembling and rippling in the fabric between the real and the more-than-real would hide her for a while. At least this particular trailer was relatively solid, and the shape shimmering underneath it didn't seem to be Summer. Perhaps part of the Low Countics, there were dry places there where the free sidhe were all dust-dancers and pixies, connaughts and *il de mus*, scatterbrained flitters and closemouth earthsalt sidhe. The interference would make tracking her difficult.

Which was good. Her legs still shook, but at least her shoes were glossy again. Her dress was the same deep blue as ever, the needle-chantments repairing themselves as her strength returned.

The hound wriggled with delight again, rocking the entire sorry heap. "Maybe we should find a more solid place to sleep, huh?"

He cocked his head and tried to sit, whacking his rear on the cabinet again. The trailer shuddered, and Robin let out another thin, half-screaming laugh. His form crackled and shimmered, and when the stretching and grinding and growling was done, he was smaller. Not by much, but just enough.

In the end, Pepperbuckle wedged himself onto the cot with her, with a long-suffering sigh, his nose planted firmly in her chest. Robin might have minded, especially the slobber, but he was warm, and she felt curiously safe, even though the dust-wind outside whispered and slithered against every surface. The milk bottle rolled on the floor, and she fell again into a thin troubled sleep, hugging a creature who smelled not of animal but of salt-sweet child, dust, and appleblossom.

BRIGHT NAIL
21

*B*efore, *there was the dreaming, the mortal world a pale baffling
shadow, and the changeling moved slowly, bumping softly into
objects made of insensate clay. Then came the silvery jolt as it was
unmoored and the scrambling away, following a blind imperative
to hide. Crouched in a storm drain, it shivered and huddled all
through the rain and big skynoise, whining softly in its throat as a
cold, fresh dawn brought the bad things, riding tall and straight
on white, white horses.*

Later, it crept about, stuffing its mouth with leaves and twigs.
So hungry. *It comprehended, vaguely, that something was not
right. Adrift and starving, until...*

The only certainty was her, *the big safe, a bright nail holding the whirling together.* She *came, and there was something...
familiar? Almost. Then there were bright rubies, and her voice,
and the dream retreating under a glare of* I, I, I.

I AM.

*So he dozed next to the bright nail, the big safe. She muttered
unhappily, tossing, and he heard more bad outside. They could not
get through the winds; his nose told him so. And what a nose! The*

world was alive again, and hers the best scent of all, but more than that, the nose told him things.

His ears flicked. Footsteps. He almost growled, but the wind rose again—this place didn't like to be found. It hated breathing and heartbeats. This place was bad too, but it couldn't hurt her.

Not while Pepperbuckle was there.

The wind rocked the trailer, trying to find a way in. Finally, its song lulled even the newborn creature to a deeper sleep, but his breathing warmth kept them both cradled. There is one thing the wind cannot eat, one thing it chokes on even as it rages, one thing even Summer and Unwinter merely play at.

That softness held the bright nail and the sleeping hound, safely.

But only for a little while.

HOW CRAVEN

22

Dusk found him increasingly frantic, holding on to calm only by sheer will and practice. Robin's scent was oddly...pale, as if bleached. The blood on the glass bothered him, too.

Then the trail simply vanished, between one breath and the next.

Jeremiah frowned. Over the fence, the trail arrowing straight for the interstate, then it dropped away. A knife-cut—one moment there, the next, gone.

Oh, Robin. He halted, a hill of scrub brush and the weeds that rose from the scars of mortal construction sloping down to a gully. Rivulets had scarred and wintercracked the hillside; behind him were blank fences holding back manicured green lawns. Here on the very fringe of the suburbs, mortal civilization stretched and retreated as fluidly as the Veil itself.

No suspicious overgreening here. The Seelie hadn't come this way. Or if they had...

The locket tugged against his chest, until he stepped past the vanishing point. Then it settled into a quivering, the feathers around a bird's heart nestled in his palm. The sky was a deep peacock's-eye blue, the sun already slipping below the horizon in a furnace of gold and indigo streaks from scudding cloud.

Someone has her.

She was canny, and fleet, but even a Half couldn't step between one place and the next, cutting a scent so cleanly. A Half could use other doors into the sideways realms, sure, and much more easily than those with only a soupçon of sidhe, but to stutter-step between mortal and not-mortal so cleanly, with such effortlessness—no.

Did she have help?

Idiot. That house was full of mortal death, Seelie all over it. Robin didn't linger there, she came out…probably fought them off, used the glass and her voice. But you need breath to sing, don't you, and it runs out.

She'd run a fine course, but someone had her now.

He was *too late.*

His knees threatened to give. Thunder spilled across the sky—another spring storm moving on, over fields shaking off winter's grip. Suppertime past and bath time coming up, as they used to say at the orphanage. Why would he remember that, of all things?

Crenn's face, ruined as it was, took him back.

Who? Not Unwinter, the Gates were open and the Unseelie barred between dusk and dawn. Later, in the full spate of the Queen's season, they would be confined to the dark of the moon as well. Summer might have sent someone to drag Robin back—the Queen had promised Gallow her life, but nothing else, and he knew well enough the power of any sidhe to twist the words as it suited them.

Just like he knew how much Summer could bend and break and still leave a victim physically whole and breathing.

Would Summer have sent Crenn as well?

Figure it out later. Right now, you've got to find a place to hide. The Unseelie are going to come out hunting; you've winnowed their numbers, and they're going to guess you're clearing Robin's trail. Unwinter himself might come out, too, since you have his goddamn horn. He touched the lump under his shirt, the cicatrice of frost on its chain much longer than the Ragged's locket. It never warmed up, and it never completely froze his flesh. It just...sat there, chill and deadly. The one weapon all sidhe feared, Seelie or not, and he had nothing to use it on. Calling the Sluagh was nothing to mess with, and you didn't give the ravening undead a name if you wanted the prey brought back alive.

How craven was he, thinking of *hiding* when Robin was... what? Who the hell had her? A free sidhe? Was there a bounty?

Of course there is, you idiot. Probably a rich one, too.

If he'd just...what could he have done? Grabbed her, forced her to stay? Bruised her again, maybe? Proven, once again, the he didn't give a damn about anything but his own selfish wants?

You let her go, you asshole, and this is what's happened. You just stood there, because it was easy. Like usual, taking the easy way out. He hadn't even left the safety of his house until night came, telling himself it was to find her and not because he knew they would come looking for him, too. The kind of lie you told yourself when you knew you were a selfish, nasty piece of sidhe—easy, hollow, and self-justifying.

The sun slipped below the rim of the earth, a subtle thrill pouring through the ground under him. Jeremiah tilted his dark head, the marks on his arms writhing madly, sting-sweet.

Unwinter had not waited for true night. He was afoot now, at the very earliest moment of dusk, and probably really pissed off.

Great. Jeremiah rubbed at his face, sighed, and turned in a full circle, deosil-sunwise, as if to shake off bad luck. If he'd been able to find the right words, maybe Robin would have stayed. Instead, she'd simply stepped over the threshold and was gone. *I am not my sister,* she'd said. As if he thought she *was.*

That's exactly what you thought she was, that's why you got involved, you sick son of a bitch.

None of this gave him a good direction to go in. He listened, intently. No thread of silver huntwhistle piercing the failing light yet. A few stipples of lightning in the distance, he counted silently until the thunder arrived, a shadow of itself.

What are my options? Weary from a day's chase and needing cover and information, well...

When he put it that way, an answer became apparent. It was probably the best one he was going to get.

It was time to visit Medvedev.

HEALED, NOT FORGOTTEN
23

❦⚔

So warm, a dozing weight against her middle, another creature's breathing a far-off ocean mouthing a warm, sandy beach. It was wonderful to rest here, between sleep and waking, her arms around that lovely warmth, her nose full of a salt-sweet sidhe smell holding tinges of sunlight and a mortal child's golden hair.

Have to get up soon. He might be hungry. Milk and honey, bread still warm from the brughnie ovens, and his little hands raised to her as she appeared.

Wait. Sean was dead.

So's Daisy. Nothing left but dreams.

Robin stirred. It wasn't the sea, it was the wind, and the waves were dust sliding along the trailer's outside. Like a falsewyrm's scales along the crusted walls of its burrow—the great drakes preferred larger caves, to keep their wings from being confined. Falsewyrms, their acid-spitting cousins, merely steamed and slithered.

The first thing she noticed was the pictures. The solemn dark-eyed girl in several of them was now tinted with fresh color, the crocheted rose at her throat blooming pink instead of sepia, its band now clearly black velvet. Faint traceries of hand-writing spidered over some of the playbills and the carnival pictures. An irritated scratching skittered under her skin as she tried to decipher some of it, so she looked away.

Pepperbuckle stretched, his legs hanging off the small bed, the paws far too large. He yawned, candy-pink tongue and triangular pearls, sharper serrations behind the blunt show-teeth. Beautiful and deadly, just like any other sidhe.

He wasn't a mollywog, cobbled together out of spare bits and given temporary life. Each part of him flowed into the next, whole and perfect. The blush of red to his fur-tips, more pronounced now, turned him almost the color of Robin's hair. His skin twitched as she petted the curve of his shoulder, and he arched into her touch. His nose, cold and wet, snuffled at her other elbow, her forearm tucked under her head. A lick from that warm, velvety tongue, and she pushed herself up on her elbow, staring at her forearm. The scar was a thin white line, already fading; she traced it with a fingernail, wincing a little as it twinged. Healed, but not forgotten.

Just like everything else.

Pepperbuckle heaved a canine sigh and had to roll back and forth to get off the bed, shaking himself once he landed with a thud much heavier than a creature his apparent size should have been able to produce. It was a good thing his spine was sidhe-flexible; he worked himself around until he was pointed at the door, then stood, ears perked and his entire attitude one of hopeful resignation.

What did a sidhe made in such a manner eat? Could he hunt for himself?

Robin sighed, ran her hands back through her hair, grimacing at the grit under her fingertips. She'd find out soon enough.

"Good boy." The bottle rolled underneath the bed as her heel tapped it, and the old instinct to dive for it so the deposit could be claimed rose briefly.

"Leave it where it is," she murmured, and Pepperbuckle tensed. "No, it's all right. Tell me, little one, is it safe to stick our noses out into the wind?"

The fine, fringed tail wagged. The hound stepped to the door, sniffed gravely, and the wagging intensified.

"You'll have to let me pass." She edged along his side, wary again. His ears flicked, she had to press her hip against him to get to the door. His heat was welcome, even if she shared it— feeling just how cold mortals were, even temporarily, left more of a chill than she wished to admit. "There."

He bolted into a hushed, windless night, and Robin peered out. The dry hiss of dust scouring the walls retreated as she hopped over the threshold, and now she could see more clearly where the hound had brought her.

Ah. The Veil curdled thick, snagged on something old and foul. The bigtop, strips of its cover fluttering scabrous even in the stillness, was where it had occurred, and Robin peered all around her, turning sunwise in a circle. Milk-fed and rested, now, she could even sense the slipping and catching in different parts of the carnival, including a throbbing brightness not far from the sad, scoured little trailer whose door banged shut behind her, the sound of a dissatisfied trap chomping after a fleet-footed morsel.

Pepperbuckle leapt, a crackling running through him as he took his larger size before throwing himself down in the fine floury dirt and rolling, all four legs waving exuberantly. Robin swallowed a laugh and felt under her hair with quick fingers. The two pins, the bone comb, the elflock, all there. The knife at her belt, the pipes secure in her hidden right pocket, a cheap blue plastic ring in her left-hand pocket. Her skirt, its needle-chantments renewed, was just as fine as ever.

And just as distinctive.

I cannot return to Summer.

Had Puck told the Queen of her betrayal? She couldn't risk it. And now, with Pepperbuckle...someone might guess. Perhaps a fullblood highborn might even sense what she had done, what a Half was never supposed to do. Robin could perhaps tread through the fringes of Summer, where none from the Court were likely to wander, but only in dire need.

If she could not return...well, there were other places to wander. Perhaps she might even come to miss the greenstone towers of Summerhome or the fragrant hills. Who knew if the hound she'd named would stay at her side? She could not depend on anything or anyone. At least at Court she'd known the risks.

She shook her head and flicked her fingers, turning widdershins once. Her hair was too distinctive, and her dress as well. She could steal mortal clothing, true, but...

Pepperbuckle leapt to his feet, shaking a small thundercloud from his fur. A spatter of moisture touched Robin's cheek; she touched it and wondered if it was raining in the mortal realms or if it was salt water. That bright, reassuring glow, at the other end of the carnival's fairway, beckoned.

The hound fell into step beside her as she set off for it. Halfway there she realized what it had to be, and why the new-named canine had brought her here. It must have seemed an attractive burrow indeed.

Especially with one corner of it fastened to a fragrant, fascinating slice of a place Robin recognized, dangerous of itself and doubly dangerous now that she had to pass unremarked. But also tempting, very tempting.

Robin glanced around. So many trailers, and Pepperbuckle could likely tell her which ones were safe. There had to be a scrap of ancient mortal cloth somewhere in this place she could use to disguise her outline.

Then, she could step into the bright glow of the Gobelin Markets and search for more permanent camouflage.

DOZY INTUITION
24

A heavy, marvelous spring rain smoked down, warm and forgiving, drenching Alastair's hair and skin. It pattered on canvas and tassels, and its song threaded through the hawker's cries. Soggy velvet and false-shining tinsel, steam-vapor from vats of bubbling dye or stew, gold-crusted pasties sending out a mouthwatering delicious vapor though the meat in them was likely to gripe you, and fruit had appeared under heavy awnings, piled in carts. Such fruit, too! Damsons ripe and juicy, the dark jewels of thumb-sized blackberries, cherries both blushing and sun-yellow, ice-cold melons piled high and proud, apples of every hue—a poetess had glimpsed such things once, and though her doggerel left a little to be desired in Crenn's opinion, she'd still managed to grasp some of the flavor of the Gobelin Markets.

The Markets were many and one, at the same time. An alley might be Morocco, bone-colored stone and desert spice, even the smoke full of sand. Another might be a winding cobblestone corner of Paris, a bookshop full of dusty tomes with a wizened wight hunching drawn-shouldered in the door, his narrow head wreathed with pipe-smoke. A bodega, reeking of exhaust and New York's dry-oil, wet-ratfur smell, stood next to a Madrid cheese shop, wax-covered wheels and thickmilk slices glowing behind dusty sugarspun glass. A noodle stand on a Taipei sidewalk jostled a Timbuktu silk-seller's stall, the Veil flexing and twisting in long almost-visible scarves. To wander the markets was to circumnavigate the globe in just a few steps, and those without sidhe blood would often fall, pale and gasping, to the paving or wooden sidewalk as they sought to enforce some rhyme and reason on what their senses were telling them. Seizures were common, and unless they had a guide to take them on the less... *active*... routes, they might find themselves meat for the gripebelly pasties.

If the purely mortal ever came here, they were desperate; you couldn't find the markets without a sidhe helper. Even those with just a touch of sidhe blood would have difficulty discovering an entrance. Some said that if you could find the edge of the markets and peer under, you'd catch a glimpse of giant chicken legs carrying the whole collage across a dreaming slice of mortal earth. Who knew?

Crenn drifted with the crowd. The long-haired, graceful ghilliedhu girls were out in force since the Gates had just been opened, craving excitement after winter's long sleep. Other dryads, too, including the whitethorn women with their generous hips and spike-mailed hands. One of them might have been his own dam, if her tree still stood, but he was Half and easily forgotten even if he had been calved on a night of storm and groaning.

Still, sometimes he watched them, wondering. Such questions were pointless, but could only be used against you if they were spoken.

Dwarves cried at the corners, their metalwork bright and inviting, their filthy fingers lingering over filigree and wrapped hilts. Poisonsellers and lightfingers chanted in shadowy corners, mostly outcast drow and trow, their dark-adapted eyes luminous. The perfume of sidhe from either Court and the Free Counties as well crept into the blood and breath, a subtle exhilaration. The Enforcers, their black leather masks and long black coats functional instead of decorative, were not often seen—but they were about.

The goblins valued peace, because it was more profitable than the alternatives.

If you wandered long enough, the market began to make a mad manner of sense. Crenn carefully halted every so often to let the current pass him by, his target at precisely the right distance—far enough away it couldn't sense him and hide *or* quiver with eagerness thinking him a danger or a client, close enough that the patchwork around it didn't change *too* much, kept less fluid by his attention. No two paths through the market were the same, ever, so to thread its needle-shops you had to work on a dozy intuition, almost dream-logic but not quite, chantment dripping from every surface like water-weeds. A ram-headed bloodybone jack slid past, his horns tipped with ocher and the glint in his eye bespeaking business; once a satyr pranced his way a clip-clop, keeping to the wall opposite and watching for any dryad. They vanished as soon as the beast appeared and came back when he was out of sight, tossing their hair and waving their long fingers. Pixies sparkled, clustering rips and rents in the eddying chantment, colors breathing through them in spectrum waves.

Patience, Crenn. Patience.

Few of them took any notice of the rain except a few burning-hobs covered in layers of burlap, their footprints steaming, adding to the white veils. No wyrmkin, and no aetherists at all. No cloud-hoolins, or canine spirits.

That was strange. What was even stranger was the lack of Unseelie. In the markets, most violence was set aside.

His patience, as usual, was finally rewarded.

A tall shadow wrapped in a dark cloak hurried along, his boots noiseless and his manner bespeaking familiarity with the markets. He stepped firmly but not heavily, the light-foot used as a warrior would, the broad shoulders familiar-strange.

Predictable. Still, he couldn't underestimate the cursed man. Gallow slipped away oily-quick from trouble, and had even in those days when neither he nor Crenn knew of the sideways realms—only that they both bore a mark, perhaps of the Devil himself. The orphanage hadn't been able to hold them both, not once Gallow figured out how to whisper locks into opening. Alastair learned by watching, but it simply hadn't occurred to him that the locks were not immutable. It had taken the other boy to spark their rebellion.

He had followed Jer's lead, then and afterward.

That was when the trains were the chariots of foulmouth princes reeking of harsh cheap tobacco and too-few baths, when a man had to get drunk on possibility if he couldn't pay for moonshine, or he could get rich running barrels of corn liquor across the ridges, dodging lightning and the blue serge bulls. When the deputies with their shiny badges could catch you, shooting, stamping and kicking until you fled consciousness, then douse you with bubbling pitch and foul tar and set you afire...and all your buddies, the men who called you *friend*, ran away. Except one who came back and could only work a halfhearted healing because he knew no chantment other than opening locks or sweet-talking a mortal woman or two.

Like schoolteacher Sarah, in her faded blue dress. You never forgot your first, even if she was mortal. Even if she was nothing more than a pipe dream.

So we're thinking about Sarah now? Cut it out.

Crenn's true prey had vanished. Gallow had some means of locating her, and he was going to some trouble to do so.

My lady Robin.

There had been talk, in Summer, of Gallow leaving his post of privilege. A long while ago, a whisper had surfaced that he'd done so for a mortal doxy. Rumor wore many shades, most of lie but some of half-truth, and Robin Ragged was a Half. It had something to do with the breaching of Summer's borders, and Summer herself taking time to send *him* after the girl—stipulating that not a feather of the Ragged's plumage was to be plucked.

Certainly Summer had sworn, so there were two possibilities: The Queen had a further use for the Ragged...or vengeance. And while Summer had uses for all who came into her snow-white, grasping hands, only the latter would move a queen to spend such attention on a small, nagging detail when her wider realm was in danger of rotting on the vine.

The cloaked stranger passed through the age-blackened door, too tall to do so without bending. A slice of dimpled, golden light widened, filled with his shadow, and narrowed to oblivion again.

Crenn took another few steps, staying within range as the door drifted. The sign above it was two doves, one singing, the other broken-necked, both being swallowed by a fanciful, greedy-mawed snake, and a more fitting sigil for the sidhe who squatted toadlike in that hole and dispensed high-priced solace to the desperate could hardly be devised.

It seemed the Gallowglass was owed a favor by none less than the linchpin of the Markets himself, old Medvedev the goblin prince. Crenn's smile, toothy and ruinous, vanished as his head came up and he sniffed, rolling the air over his tongue on the exhale to gather the new tang.

Interesting.

Somewhere else in the Markets' pile, a new ferment had been added.

The Unseelie had arrived.

A-HORSE AND A-HOUND

25

Oh, go away." A round, white, bald-shaven pate barely rose, reflecting mellow light from the forest of pierced-tin lanterns hanging from a low, smoke-blackened ceiling. The mountain of flesh held a head that had sunk forward, round chin resting on a billow of chest covered with expensive acid-green silk, its sheen of constant greasy sweat collecting in creases. The fishbelly cast of a creature that never saw daylight might have turned the stomach, if the sheer bulk of the goblin didn't. Size meant status among them, and wealth. "Whoever you are, you reek." Slightly nasal, the words were breathed in an asthmatic wheeze.

Really, the wonder was that such a fat-swathed creature could speak at all, that he didn't expire from his own weight. When was the last time the great doge had bestirred himself?

Who knew?

"It's a lack of bathwater." The door swung closed behind Jeremiah, nipping at his heels as if it sensed his weariness. He pushed his hood back, wrinkling his nose slightly—the cloak, while waxed and reasonably effective at keeping him dry, was still full of the musty earthsmell from its former owner. It would take more than a few yards of cloth to throw pursuers off his trail, but the rain might help.

For anything else, though, he'd need more.

"There's much of it falling, tonight." Tiny black eyes, almost lost in great slabs of cheek, traveled over Gallow from top to toe and twinkled a little, perhaps even merrily. "Wellnow. By woodland and by brook, what's come along to cook?"

So you know I'm hunted. "A fish too spine-boned for most, oh my gracious host." Any amusement Gallow might feel at exchange of greetings drained away. Normally there were pixies crawling over every acre of Medvedev Dadalo the Builder's satin- and brocade-robed bulk as he lolled on his cushions. The contraption behind him, its silver belly bubbling and its pipes emitting steam-jets of various colors and fragrances, was hushed, and one of his secondary sets of hands, wasted and thin, only toyed with the silver mouthpiece. No movement behind the screens of dark, heavy, carved wood, either, lesser seam-headed and ungainly goblins scurrying to carry and fetch, currying favor and bringing rumor or tribute.

The markets were a goblin affair, the Vene Venesa Clan's doges—and those who found it profitable to seek alliance with them—jealously guarding their fiefdoms and renting out stall and building space, stitching the disparate pieces into a whole, performing whatever strange, ancient chantment was necessary to keep such a cobbled-together heap going. Technically, the doges were all "equal"—but Med was first among them. The linchpin of the Markets, they called him—or, less complimentarily, the Head Gobbler, which could have been anything from a comment on his sexual proclivities to a warning about his preferred snack.

"The sweetest meat," Medvedev wheezed, "may rest inside the sharpest shell. Greetings, Armormaster. To what do I owe this honor?"

As if you can't guess. "Perhaps I am lonely for your excellent company, O worker of wonders."

The shuddering, heaving, cracking sound that rumbled on and on was Medvedev's laugh. Faint pinpricks of foxfire glow twinkled around him—pixies struggling to coalesce, perhaps sensing some mischief they were not a part of. The Veil behaved strangely in the Markets; sometimes it was whispered that Summer and Unwinter both did not precisely *fear* the doges, but held them in some caution. The market-folk held themselves nominally among the free sidhe, but even Puck Goodfellow, the closest thing to a leader the free folk had, was not often seen in the noisome alleys and patchwork stalls, crowded shops and throbbing taverns.

Could it have been Puck who spirited Robin away? Cheating the Fatherless of something he had his claws in was no small proposition.

Finally, Med's chuckles ceased. He blinked, heaving his bulk from side to side a little, the entire room groaning and swaying as he did so. The lanterns danced crazily, the chantment-steadied candleflames inside sputtering and belching black smoke. Gallow had seen Med laugh before, but it was...disconcerting, each time. "I wondered how long it would be before your shadow darkened my doorstep."

"Did you now." Exhaustion hung on Jeremiah. Even highborn fullbloods needed rest. How much wearier would Half flesh and blood become before he committed some stupidity?

If he hadn't already.

"Oh, yes. I have heard rumors, and I thought to myself, *Now, what would make most sense for Gallow to do?*" Another burbling laugh. "Then I thought, *Certainly he would avoid me. That would be wisest.*"

"It might." Gallow let the cloak slip from his shoulders. The material made a soft whispering sound before landing with a sodden thump on the parquet flooring, and it was almost worth the sudden chill to see Medvedev's nose wrinkle. It wasn't quite an insult, but then, neither was Med's roundabout threat to sell him to the highest bidder. "I have not long been known for wisdom, sagacious one. Unlike yourself."

"For blood, and for a certain rough charity, but aye, not wisdom. I shall ask outright, what brings you here?"

Rough charity? "Can you not guess?"

"Unwinter seeks thee, and Summer is weakened by recent frolics. A marvelous moment. Much profit to be had, if one makes the right decisions." His primary hands spread, seven extra-jointed fingers on each, their orange-tinted nails long-curving and scraped clean daily by lesser goblins. Medvedev scratched at part of the mass of satin, a slice of quivering pale skin briefly visible. The orange veins crawling through it matched his nails, and writhed just under the surface.

Those weren't the same as Jeremiah's markings. Iron would burn through that flesh and sicken the fat beneath, and just thinking about it made his arms tingle-burn. Medvedev had elected to meet him alone, balancing out the risk of Jeremiah's suspicion.

Everything even, tit for tat, just like a sidhe.

His shoulders relaxed a trifle. Medvedev lifted the hookah-pipe and took a long, bubbling draft. Another good sign.

"Unwinter's coin may not be to a purse's liking." Gallow let his hands hang loose and easy.

"Oh, it rarely is." The left of Med's primary set of hands flickered, digging deep in folds of clothed fat. "Ah, here it is. This is what you left with me, lo those many seasons ago." A flicker, and it whizzed through the air. Jeremiah's hand flashed out and he caught it, feeling the tingle of the simple chantment to ease the weight of the round black carrying-boll. Just as heavy as he remembered, its wizened surface running with foxfire gleams as it recognized him. "Should you tire of playing catch-and-hide with the twins, there is always room for another Enforcer in my markets."

Jeremiah placed his hand at his heart, bowing slightly as his fist compressed the ball and he stowed it, safely enough, in his pocket. As soon as he found a quiet corner, it would be time to open it up and change. "You honor me, oh greatest of doges. I presume the salary would be adequate." *Not that I ever want to go back to enforcing. Leaves a bad taste in the mouth.*

The doge did not have a chance to reply, for the door behind Gallow was wrenched open, a burst of rainy air and the peppermusk of danger breathing through. Jeremiah found himself spinning aside, the lance resolving between his palms and the leafshaped tip swelling with red light as iron crackled into being.

It was Crenn, soaked to the bone and wearing a wide, white, fey smile, disconcerting on his ruined face. "Unseelie! They are riding the Markets, a-horse and a-hound!"

Med's piggy little eyes narrowed still further, and Crenn struck the lancetip away from its pause near his throat, a contemptuous little slap.

"Are you moontouched, or—" Whatever else Gallow would say was lost in a breathless rolling static unsound, the hairs all over his body trying to stand straight up in response.

Dimly, from outside, the silver huntwhistles stitched together the roil of falling rain.

"In my market?" The room quaked afresh, Medvedev's bulk rising. He rocked from side to side, velvet and satin tearing, and pixies blossomed into being around him, their chiming little cries adding to the creak-groaning din. "A-horse and a-hound? *In my market?*"

Chitterings, bangings, squeals. Shadows moving behind the carved screens. A lamp fell, its sides crumpling as one of the goblin's fists flashed out, and Jeremiah ducked the sudden missile. He stepped aside, the lance vanishing as he grabbed Crenn's jerkin, leather slipping under callused fingers. The door hadn't managed to close itself yet, and it wanted to, but Gallow drove a shoulder against it, and they both tumbled out into slashing rain, rolling in a puddle; Gallow gained his feet more through luck than skill.

The long line of cobbled-together architecture holding the nerve-center of the Markets flexed, an undulating snake uncoiling itself for the first time in a century or so. Distant screams echoed with the huntwhistles, their silver net thrilling through the ultrasonic, scraping sidhe skin and freezing the heart of each pelting raindrop. "You *idiot!*" Gallow yelled as Crenn rose, water and ice sluicing from every edge and surface. "Did you have to?"

"How do you think they knew you were here?" Crenn yelled back. "The moment you started bargaining for that stupid cloak, the goblins started scurrying!"

"They scurry all night, and half the day, too!" His arms ached, *ached* with the desire to let the lance free and end this stupid bastard once and for all. "Now I'll never..." *Shut up, Jeremiah. Just shut up.*

"Cry me upriver later." Crenn's hands flicked up, the twin swords shirring free. Their blades ran with water, and the moss was back in his hair, threading the draggled mop with verdant green. "For now, Armormaster, we are to run. And fight."

"Why should I follow *you?*"

"Because," Crenn replied, reasonably enough, "I won't have Unwinter robbing me of the pleasure of killing you myself. Now *run.*"

A MEMORY ATTACHED
26

The best thing she found was a long black velvet cape-coat in what must have been a fortune-teller's tent, dusty and moth-eaten but large enough to blur her outline. With the hood up and a thin black dust-stiffened scarf, embroidered with itchy tarnished spangles, wrapped around the lower half of her face, she could be safely anonymous—obviously sidhe, but perhaps a nymph of any drier sort, since a naiad would drip-damp through the alleyways.

It didn't matter, because as soon as she approached the slice of the Markets holding the edge of this place moored to both sideways realms and mortal, she heard a pattering of raindrops.

She took her time, examining the border from the shadows in the lee of a deserted cotton-candy stand. Wherever the rain touched, puffs of dust splattered up, ghost-outlines of open mouths before an uneasy breeze whisked them away. When the border shifted they dried quickly, leaving strange ringed ripples in the dirt. A long time ago, maybe mortals would see those dapples in a forgotten corner of the world and know the Folk had been about.

No more, though.

The sleeves were long, so she could cover her hands once she stepped over—gloves would be necessary, and a kerchief for her hair, and perhaps a pretty bauble to anchor a glamour to, since her locket was gone. *That* would be the most expensive article, since all the rest could be stolen if need be, and she would have to trade something significant for anything shiny and sidhe-wrought. The ring in her pocket would do, perhaps. It was bright and tawdry and had a memory attached.

Could she attach a glamour to a bright piece of mortal plastic? Not a very good one, and the hour or so required to do so suddenly didn't feel like one she had the luxury of spending. A nameless tension bloomed under her ribs, her heart beating fast and thin in her ears.

Pepperbuckle squeezed against her side, his warm, solid shoulder against her hip. She found her hand lying on his ruff, caressing absently as he leaned into the touch. What did this beast eat? Could she afford to feed him?

"Are you hungry?" she whispered. "What on earth do you eat, little one?" *Little one*, as if he wasn't a beast large enough to be ridden.

His tail wagged once, but his ear-perked attention didn't waver. He regarded the Markets with cocked head and tense hindquarters.

Robin took a deep breath, glided out of the comforting shadows. The hound moved with her, pacing regally, but slowed as they drew near the shifting, dancing border. He whined, and perhaps she simply imagined it, but there were words buried in that low, worried sound.

"I know," she soothed. "You don't have to come with me." *It's probably best if you don't.*

That earned her a single reproachful look, his head barely turning. Then he focused on the border, slowing still more.

Robin halted just at the very edge of the curtain of dapples, one of her heels striking a pebble loose in the dirt and sliding sideways a fraction before steadying. Her head tilted, and for a moment she and Pepperbuckle stood in exactly the same attitude of *listening*, her pale hand lost in the slowly rising hair between his shoulderblades. A shudder rippled through her, crown-to-toes, and its twin worked down through Pepperbuckle. His nails lengthened slightly, digging into bleached-bone dust.

What is that?

Commotion strained through the shifting border, faraway shouting. The Markets were a cacophony at the best of times, but this sounded . . . wrong.

If she hadn't hesitated, the Markets might not have moved, fluidly sliding past. The alleyway that held some small bit of them tethered to this lonely place was off to her left, tucked on the other side of a long row of joined-together, mobile tin shacks that used to dispense greasy mortal food. Echoes of past crowds shuffled around Robin, the ghosts of hungry mortals and footsore children gawping, given a simulacrum of heat and motion by the disturbance. Something was *definitely* afoot, and she was just about to turn and seek another exit when a familiar shadow darted in front of her, running with his head up and a second shadow pacing him.

Black hair cut aggressively short, the broad shoulders and deceptively light footsteps, a flash of green eyes. He was in the same dun coat, a heavy thing with leather elbow-patches, raspy corduroy her fingers still remembered threading needle-chantment through. It was sadly tattered now, and he looked like he'd been rolled through a flood and a few muddy creeks as well. A hurtful pang went through her—what was he *doing*? Of course, Unwinter would be after him, too. She had thought him far cannier than *this*, to be caught running at night through the Gobelin.

I am not my sister. She could never be blithe, laughing, fully mortal Daisy.

And yet.

Her skin twitched all over. An invisible string tugged sharply, some item of hers, maybe with a simple location-chantment on it, carried by the running man. Through the borderline interference came the silvery, ultrasonic thrills even mortals would be able to sense.

All the breath left her. Pepperbuckle growled, and her hand slipped free of his ruff. She could not ask the changeling-hound, whatever affection he bore her, to run toward death.

Robin filled her lungs again and lunged forward, her heels clattering as she bounded onto the cobblestones, after Jeremiah Gallow.

THE GOBELIN

27

"Idiot!"

It was amazing Crenn had the breath to keep hurling his opinion of Jeremiah's intelligence hither and yon. Gallow landed *hard*, breath driven from him by the impact, and whirled. The lance burst into being, blossoming between his palms, and he set its butt against the ground as the rider behind them blew the huntwhistle again, a cold thrill yanking on every nerve Gallow possessed.

"Moron!" Crenn yelled, and the swordblades blurred, solid arcs of silver, driving back the two drow who sought to pull him down. One fell clutching at the spurting stump of a severed arm, the other gutsplit and throat-cut at almost the same moment, and Crenn darted forward as the Unseelie knight on his nightmare destrier, its foam-splattering mouth champing, hit the lance. *"Halfwit!"*

More precisely, the destrier hit, shock grating through Jeremiah and away, his boots scraping the cobbled floor of this part of the markets. The lance groaned, its hungry blade finding a quivering clot, the point around which the elfmount coalesced. The shape of the battle changed inside Gallow's head, so he yanked the lance aside, *hard*, tearing the small, hidden ball-heart free of its moorings. The destrier exploded into smoke, and it wasn't just the furious pace of combat—the Markets themselves were writhing. Goblins howled, wooden and metal shutters slamming closed, ghilliedhu girls ran shrieking, long hair flying and white flesh flashing.

He'd asked Robin if she was ghilliedhu, once.

"You goddamn brainless pig!"

If Crenn was yelling, he obviously didn't consider the situation overly dire. Or Jeremiah had managed to irritate the man past bearing. Either was equally likely.

The shops and stalls were closing themselves, the more fortunate barring their doors and windows against the appearance of Unseelie, the poorer stall-folk buttoning themselves up, the stalls retreating like frightened anemones, vanishing into cracks, alley-mouths snapping shut.

Thrashing almost-real tentacles cracked cobblestones before their spent force released itself in puffs of vapor, Crenn facing another clot of drow, low, slinking shapes with coin-bright eyes flooding behind the knight, who rose from the ruin of his mount with slow, terrible grace. The rain showed no sign of slackening, and as much as Gallow would have liked to shed his wet, clinging coat, he knew he needed the faint armor it provided—and if he managed by some miracle to shake pursuit, he would be glad of its cover. Half didn't feel the weather much, but this damp could get a man down.

"Scumsucking cretin!" Crenn continued, at top volume.

A high-crowned helm, a mailed fist covered in exquisite dwarven metalwork clasping a heavy hilt. Broadsword instead of curved new-moon blade, and the lance hummed as sick heat poured up Gallow's arms, beating back his exhaustion. The marks stung with sweet pain, the destrier's hold on the physical disrupted and the resultant energy sucked into the blade's ever-hungry heart.

"*Gallow*," the knight breathed, and behind him the lamp-eyes brightened, low, slinking forms sliding out of shadow and confusion. The hounds, with their needle-teeth and their tough hides. So many of them, and—

"Robin," he whispered, and *moved*.

Crunching. Squealing, a vicious burst of toothed sound, a golden blur. It distracted him, broadsword grinding against lancehaft, the armored weight telling against a lighter foe, and the ground beneath him heaved. A rolling, creaking, snapping thunder, growing steadily closer, was a goblin doge's fury. Something had descended on the hounds, a blur of coppergold, and—

His side unseamed itself, a lick of fire, and Gallow cried out. The lance shrieked, the haft bending as it sought to recover, but he was falling. It wasn't the ground, it was his side, a hot spear of agony in his vitals, his head bounced against cobblestone and there was *another* sound.

A deep, beautiful wall of pure golden music, loud enough to shake a man's bones to jelly, hit the knight from the side. The Unseelie, knocked off his feet, vanished in the flood of light, and there was only one thing that could make such a noise and such a marvelous glow. He'd seen it before.

Or maybe it was death, and heaven opening up for whatever part of him was mortal.

It went on and on, then stopped as suddenly as it had started. Light, clicking footsteps—a woman in heels, running. So familiar, everything in him rising to meet that sound, but the blade in his side twisted again and he bit back a scream. The lance had vanished, he was weak as a kitten, spilled here on the ground with the rain pounding along the length of his body and a furnace lit in his belly.

Oh, shit. The clarity of the thought took him by surprise.

Guess she didn't get all the poison out after all.

A FACE TO MATCH
28

🌹⚔️

Asidhe in sodden black velvet fell to her knees next to Gallow. Had the bastard managed to get himself killed by an Unseelie after all? It beggared belief. One moment the idiot had been fine while Crenn dealt with the massed drow, the next he was on the ground and a gigantic golden noise blasted by, picking up and shaking everything in front of it, flinging the knight—a highborn fullblood, but too big and ponderous to give Gallow any trouble, or so Crenn had thought—*through* the knot of drow, flash-frying an Unseelie hound or two in the process.

"Jeremiah? *Gallow?* Open your eyes, you idiot!" A woman's voice. Husky contralto.

Crenn's blades whirled, shedding water and brackish, red-tinted drow-blood. A sidhe dog the size of a pony—perhaps a gebriel, but without a human head—crouched before the remaining Unwinter dogs, its redgold fur standing up in a stripe along its back. It was a handsome beast, and the snap of its teeth said it meant business. The Unseelie dogs obviously thought so as well, and vanished back through the Veil, one or two making a halfhearted dart toward the new arrival before backing away, shredding into nothingness.

The eyes were always the last to go.

The big beast cocked his head and stopped growling once they were gone. He shook himself—*definitely* a he—and turned, looking at the woman in black.

Who had her hands at Gallow's shoulders, ineffectually trying to heave him up. A thread of her scent washed through the rain: dust, the good healthy oil-heat-haze of a dog, and a familiar thread of spice and fruit, as if she were a nymph.

Well, now.

"Oh, you...ugh. Oh, no." She sounded frantic. Glanced up, and a slice of her pale face became visible. She pushed the hood back, just a little, water fringing off its edges, and spied him. There was a scarf over her mouth, but it was steam-smoking, something had punched a hole clear through it. "You! Are you here to kill him?"

How can I answer that? Crenn opened his mouth, shut it.

She pushed the scarf's ruins down, irritably. Blue eyes. Deep summerblue, thickly fringed with dark lashes. A sweet mouth, pulled tight as if with fear or pain, high pretty cheekbones. A water-darkened curl stuck to her damp cheek, and something inside Alastair Crenn turned over, *hard*.

"Are you?" she persisted, and almost overbalanced, trying to haul a Half male several pounds heavier than her upright. "You fought with him. Are you granting him aid?"

What can I... "Oh, *fuck*." He didn't have to work very hard to sound disgusted. The blades sheathed themselves, habitual movements, and Crenn shook his head, his hair sodden and curtaining his ugliness most effectively. The moss was coming back, too. Reminding him, as if he needed it. "Of all the... fine. *Fine*."

Between the two of them, they got Gallow upright. The man hung like wet laundry, and hissed in short, sharp breaths.

"We need an exit," she said, peering past him into the rain. The hound, its fur slicking down, loped toward her, its every line expressing self-satisfaction. "Oh, good boy. *Good* boy, Pepperbuckle. Best boy."

Pepperbuckle? Not a bad name. "I am Alastair."

"Fair greetings, sir." She began trying to haul Gallow after the dog, who looked over his shoulder expectantly. "I'm Rob."

I know who you are. By all rights, he should dump the Armormaster here and take her. It was the perfect opportunity. He could return her to Summer, go back to his swamp, and . . .

I will make you beautiful again.

As beautiful as this Half girl? It didn't seem possible.

Her fingers slipped in Gallow's belt; Crenn took a firmer hold. Got the man's arm over his shoulders, and things became much easier. "Do you know him, then?"

"No," she replied, shortly. "Not well, anyway. But he saved my life." She tugged him forward, her slight strength not helping very much.

Gallow groaned, and some sense came back into his half-closed, glittering eyes. The pounding of the rain eased a little. "Augh. *Damn* it."

"He speaks." Crenn snorted, heaved him over a puddle. Behind them, the thunder of the Markets expelling intruders intensified. The doges would remember a dent put in their profits from this night's madness. "Are you blooded, Gallowglass?"

"No." Jeremiah coughed and started weakly trying to help. Which made things *much* easier, and the girl slipped away from under his arm and walked after the hound, skipping back nervously every few steps as if she wished to hurry them along. "What...are you...doing here?"

"I could ask you the same." Sharply, and her footsteps clicked. Did she have hooves? No rumor had ever spoken of her as a beastmaster. Where had she found the sidhe dog? "You're a fool, Gallow."

"That's what...he says." Another cough, and Gallow spat a gobbet of something that steamed as it hit. "Ugh. Not fun. Not fun at all."

"Oh, good boy!" she cried, and Crenn's boots slipped. "There's a door here. The Markets are angry, it's getting closer, but I hear no more of *them*."

"Best to be safe." Crenn's voice sounded unnatural, even to himself. Guttural, harsh after hers. "You are the *luckiest* bastard, Glass-gallow."

The Armormaster steadied, and the exit—an alley much darker than its surroundings, with pinpricks of red and white light smearing as the mortal realm outside it struggled to hold on to the slippery sideways more-than-real—swallowed them. The tiptapping of her footsteps suddenly made sense.

Heels. She's wearing heels. Black ones, shining sidhe-glossed, turning her walk into a graceful sway.

They dropped into the mortal realm with a thud, the rain cutting off cleanly, and Jeremiah shook himself free of Crenn's grasp. The girl turned, her hood slipping and falling free, her damp hair a glory of tangled golden curls with a red tint, even in this dim cold light. A wet shushing sound came from the lights at the end of the alley—*cars*, he told himself. *Cars.*

She studied him warily, the dog at her hip now regarding him with the same bright interest, its coat a rougher copy of her coloring. One pale hand knotted in the beast's fur, as if to steady herself, and her summerdusk eyes narrowed. "I know of you." The contralto made the words a song, and a pleasant shiver went down Crenn's back, along with rainwater. "The Hunter of Marrowdowne himself."

"Yes," he heard himself say. "And you're the Ragged. A beautiful song, and a face to match."

Now what was he going to do?

FREELY GIVEN
29

Pepperbuckle, warm and vital, leaned against her. She didn't even know what slice of mortal earth they'd stumbled onto, but it didn't smell familiar. Gallow slumped wearily, his hand pressed to his side, and the bolt of wine-red fear that went through her almost knocked her a-stagger into the hound. "Does it hurt much?" A timid, soft tone, just like Mama tending an invalid.

He shrugged, the tatters of his coat flapping a little. "It's easing. See?" More gently than she'd ever heard him speak. He peeled his hand away with a slight grimace. "That was a timely arrival."

"No less than your own, not so long ago." *Are we at quits? Tell me we are. Tell me to go away.*

"I thought you taken." He peered at the dog. "Where's that from?"

"*He* is from elsewhere." The quarter-lie slipped easily from her tongue, and he did not press her.

Instead, he straightened and cast a wary eye at the other man. "Well. You've found the lady you sought, Crenn."

"So I have." Easily enough. "And so have you."

He was leaner than Gallow, and his hair was moss-grown, sodden as her own stolen coat. He kept it shaken over his face—rumor had him as either beautiful or supernally ugly, but few braved his parts of the fens to find out. There had been a time when good hard coin could have tempted him out of the swamps to track a sidhe or beast, no matter how fleet or canny; there were other, darker whispers about what he charged to end a single life. The sidhe did not use the word *assassin* lightly, but he was named thus every once in a while.

She did not loosen her grip on Pepperbuckle, but she did back away a few cautious steps, and the hound moved with her, perhaps thinking it a game.

A Half who hunted beasts in the fens at the edges of Summer's lands could easily kill a new-made hound, *cu sith*, gytrash, or... otherwise.

Gallow moved forward, half staggering, as if he intended to put himself between Crenn and Robin's own self. Which would make it difficult for her to use the song, if she had to. *Damn* the man. It wasn't the first time—she could have drawn Unwinter neatly away, had he not openly *challenged* the lord of the Unseelie.

So Crenn of Marrowdowne had been hunting her. There was only one explanation. "What does she want of me?"

"Who?" Crenn cocked his shaggy head. It was too dark to see much, and that might have been a blessing.

The velvet, stiff with dust and full of spring rain, chilled against her skin. "Do not play the fool," Robin returned, hard and fast. "What other reason would you have to come seeking *me*, Crenn-creek?"

The silence that followed was broken only by the sound of traffic, tires shushing on cold pavement, and a distant murmur of a mortal crowd. The hunter's shoulders dropped slightly, but he did not move hand to bladehilt. Instead, he hooked his thumbs in his broad leather belt and regarded her, his eyes mere glimmers through ropes of matted, mossy hair.

"Ah. That answers *that*." Jeremiah straightened. "Why *did* Summer send you after my lady Robin, Alastair?"

My lady Robin. It was the second time he'd said it, and Robin told herself it was respectful, nothing more. They had fought together, and an Armormaster would place a value on that sort of thing. It meant nothing else. The warmth in her chest was Pepperbuckle's nearness, and that was all.

"The lady Robin Ragged is under my protection." Crenn didn't move. "It seems likely she may need it, since the Queen granted her life to the Gallow-glass as a boon, during the Gate revel. He must have brought her a rich gift to claim such a prize."

Oh, he did indeed. Glass ampoules. I wonder if she has had cause to open one, yet? It did not surprise her. Perhaps Crenn thought such news would make her distrust Gallow more than she already did and view the hunter of Marrowdowne more kindly?

If you distrust Gallow so much, Robin, why did you run to save him? If she did not, why had she left him in his trailer?

Why bother asking, when she knew the answer? *Daisy.* And the other ghost standing between them, a dead mortal child broken into slivers on a marble floor.

"I brought *her* what I did in order to buy the Ragged's life." Gallow turned away from the man, as if he feared no attack from that quarter. "Not that it concerns you, Half. Robin? Are you well?"

She meant to push him out of the way, if the hunter made a sudden movement. But Crenn stayed stock-still, and Jeremiah Gallow stepped close to her. His hands met her shoulders, and

Pepperbuckle's inquiring growl shook her. Or was it something else, some internal earthquake communicating itself from him? Her hand did not relax, knotted in rough, rising fur.

"Are you all right?" Gallow peered at her face in the dimness, his light irises catching a stray reflection of headlamp shine, or simply glowing as a sidhe's could when fired by high emotion—or good sport. "I thought you taken, by Seelie or worse."

Not that there could be much worse. She shook her head. "I'm... well enough. You—the wound. It pains you?"

He shrugged, his wet coat flopping. His thumbs moved slightly against wet velvet. "It's not bad now; we're in the mortal. We shouldn't linger. The Hunt won't take kindly to being balked, and may find our trail."

Not likely, with the Markets closed up. Still, there was profit to be made, so the goblins wouldn't keep it sealed for very long. Perhaps only until dawn, which was more than enough time to scatter again. Now that she knew a hunter was after her, well...

And yet, he said *protection.* So Summer wished her whole? Such news was not as comforting as one might think.

"I can find my own way, thank you." But she didn't move. Why? "You asked my life of the Queen? Truly?"

"She granted it with good grace. Robin—"

After you took her the ampoules. Has she opened one? "Then I'd best be merrily away, in case you intend to offer her another gift at my expense. She will no doubt welcome thee warmly, Armormaster."

"Robin—"

"Leave her be, Gallow. The lady wants no part of your suit." The hunter laughed. It was a rich, mellow voice he had, deep and fine, but too bitter to be even remotely soothing.

"You stay out of this, *Al.*"

They know each other, in some fashion. Interesting. In the end, though, it didn't matter.

She found the strength to push his warm hands from her shoulders. "You may stay and argue, sirs, but I'd best be gone." *Where are we? A mortal city, and—*

Pepperbuckle's head made another quick movement. His low, thrumming growl rattled the Dumpsters along one side of the alley, and she was suddenly conscious of her own weariness. Would every night for the rest of her perhaps-short life be this tiresome?

"Robin." Very quietly, Jeremiah Gallow spoke. "You'll not stir a step without me. I mean to see you safely through this."

Do you mean what you say? No matter what he *meant*, if the Queen had sent Crenn and also thought Gallow sought to kill her himself, setting them both at each other might buy Robin precious time to escape what either of them had planned for her. "And what safety can you promise me, *Armormaster*? A man is led by the string in his trousers, and I know who holds the end of yours."

"I don't think you do. Come." He yanked on his torn sleeves, settling them as best he could. "This is not the place to wait for dawn."

A thin thrill of silver, far in the distance, underscored the words. Robin shuddered and set off for the mouth of the alley. Pepperbuckle paced beside her, but his great head drooped. He was probably hungry, and she hadn't the faintest idea of what to feed him. "I know," she whispered to him, and perhaps to Gallow as well. *I know many things, but none of what I'd like to.*

"Lady Ragged." The hunter, trotting after her but observing a careful distance. "Your *cu sith*, does he like fowl?"

I don't know. "He may, sir."

"Then I shall find him some. He drove off Unwinter's dogs and did me a service. It's the least I can do."

Why, how kind of you. As if she didn't know better than to trust a man's good humor, especially a sidhe's. "I ask the price for this favor."

"Freely given, little bird. You interest me."

Well, that was a relief, and absolved her of any commitment to repay. "I am not easily snared."

"Christ." Gallow caught up with her, moving stiffly, his hand sealed to his side again. "You've become a sweet-talker, Crenn. Don't listen to him."

I have little choice. She smoothed Pepperbuckle's ruff, peering out of the alley's cave-mouth. She sniffed, deeply. No familiarity, and very little sidhe-tang in the air.

Well, it will have to be good enough. She tested the wind, found it chill but favorable, and set off in search of a hole to spend what remained of the night in.

And—useless to deny it—to see if Gallow would follow.

SEEK ANY CURE
30

It was Crenn who found the abandoned warehouse, Crenn who brought Robin's sidhe-dog sleepy, city-fat pigeons from the rafters—which the dog swallowed whole, at first, then settled into cracking and slurping at the bones of after three—and Crenn who built a fire, striking a spark from flint and a knifeblade, nursing the glitter with shreds of sere winter-weeds before tossing larger chunks of wooden pallets on the tiny, hungry blaze. Fire-chantment would draw other sidhe, if there were any about, but this mortal magic stood lesser chance of doing so. The iron in the warehouse walls was a better protection.

The smoke drifted up, thinning to almost-lost before finding a gaping hole in the roof at the south end of the cavernous space and escaping into the night. As long as they kept the fire small, it would likely go unnoticed.

Robin sat curled against the dog's side. The thing was the size of a pony, and it looked nothing like a *cu sith* or a gebriel, or any other hound Jeremiah had seen among the sidhe. Its coat almost-matched her hair, and its eyes were just a shade or two lighter than hers. Where had she found it?

Did it matter?

Gallow peeled the shirt away from his side, examining the wound in the firelight. Crenn, crouching easily, equidistant from both him and Robin, hissed a little through his teeth as he recognized what had made the slice on Gallow's side.

This particular scar was livid, unlike the pale others criss-crossing Jeremiah's belly. He'd lost some of the blurring of mortal life and was just as lean-muscular as he had been before Daisy. The body remembered.

You just couldn't hide from what you were, ever.

He squeezed his fingers along the scar. Clear drops welled from the lower end, and he pressed a filthy, oil-soaked rag from the warehouse floor against them. The fabric smoked as the poison ate at it.

"What did you do this time, Jer?" Crenn tossed another pallet-bit on the fire, taking care to keep his hair shaken down. You could only see the gleams of his eyes and a few odd flashes of copper flesh, nothing to build a coherent picture on. Maybe he didn't want to show Robin his ruined face.

Jeremiah bared his teeth, occupied in catching the last bits of the poison.

It was Robin who answered, softly. "He challenged the Lord of the Hunt himself." The dog's crunch-slurp and low, happy growl underscored her words.

"Why on earth did you do that?" Crenn leaned forward a little, as if he couldn't believe his ears and needed confirmation. "Even for you, Gallow-my-glass, it's a stupid move."

Jeremiah flung the rag away, into a dark corner. It hissed, a soft, caustic sound, and he immediately felt better. It would be short-lived. What could he say? "Seemed like a good idea at the time."

Crenn's laugh, short and disdainful, fell dead instead of echoing in the cavernous space. Another piece of pallet cracked in his capable hands. "I had heard you besotted with a maid, old man. Is that what this is?"

"No," Robin said, immediately.

Just as Jeremiah said, "Yes."

Another short silence, this one full of sharp edges under the crackling of the fire. Crenn glanced at Robin, back at Jeremiah. Shrugged, easily. "Does your hound require more, fair Robin?"

"I think he's all right." She stroked the dog's shoulder. It made another low, happy noise. "You are very kind, sir."

"Who could not be, to you?"

Oh, for God's sake. Irritation bit at Jeremiah's nerves. "You were never a womanizer before, Alastair."

"I am not now, either." A glitter of teeth, another sharp crack of wood. "I'll leave that to you. Remember Chicago?"

They'd drunk their way through every speakeasy in that town, and there had been that pair of dancers—Mona and someone else, both with long legs and marcel waves. He couldn't remember their faces, but he did remember the fight where he got knifed, and Crenn turning on the low-level mobster with that wide, white, unsettling grin under his fedora...

"I'd rather not." Gallow exhaled, hard, shaking off memory. The firelight painted Robin's black coat with gold, turned her hair into a lower, sullen flame. She was right there, drooping next to the dog, whole and breathing. She looked... tired, in the way only a sidhe girl could. No bloodshot eyes, no dark circles, but a certain wan transparency. Sodden and in motheaten velvet—where had she found it?—she looked...

There weren't words.

Oh, for fuck's sake, Jeremiah.

She studied Crenn, a faint line between her dark eyebrows. "You two are... friends?"

"We used to be." He stretched his hands out to the fire. Smears of wet dirt across the back, grime under his fingernails—looking from that to Robin's pale, flawless cheek did something strange to his chest. A nameless aching.

"Ah." She asked no more. Swayed slightly, and the dog glanced back at her. It clearly considered Robin its mistress. The blood-clotted glass shard was safe in Gallow's coat pocket, and that was a good thing. Who knew what someone else would do with it?

Did she think he meant to carry her head back to Summer? Still? "Robin?"

"Hm?" Her eyelids were falling. She could fall asleep at a moment's notice, just like any battle-weary soldier.

"What I did, I did to free you from Summer. And Unwinter—" His side twinged, sharply. The longer he spent in the sideways realms, the more the poison would swell itself inside the healed-over wound.

Unwinter's prey never truly escaped.

"Why did you do that?" She shivered, pulling the damp velvet closer. Wise, not risking a chantment to dry it, even if they were relatively safe here. "I had not time to ask, before."

"Do what?" *Don't ask me this with Crenn listening. It's not the time.*

"You let him strike you." She sagged still further, curling to pillow her head on the tawny-red shoulder.

"There was no *letting*." Still, though, he hadn't been thinking.

"He meant to kill me, before I could sing."

He would have, too. Jeremiah hadn't really *decided*. Everything in him had simply rebelled at the thought of Unwinter's blade cleaving the life from Robin Ragged's slim, so-vulnerable frame. "I know. Sleep, Robin. I'll wake thee, should trouble approach."

She closed her eyes. The hound cracked another bone, slurping, and sighed.

Crenn said nothing for a long while. He cracked no more wood, and the tilt of his head could mean he was studying the beast or the woman. The fire settled into its temporary home, more comfortable than any other creature except perhaps the dog, who eventually put his head down in the ruins of an albino pigeon and began to snore.

Finally, the hunter settled cross-legged, the swordhilts short, stubby wings behind his shoulders. "You're marked by Unwinter."

Stating the obvious, Crenn. "I have a plan."

"Don't you always. Is she yours, then?" A slight movement, thrusting his scarred chin at Robin.

She looked so peaceful. Glowing, serene, almost childlike, reminding him of Daisy's tranquil face on the pillow next to his own, lit with the innocence of mortal rest. But Daisy had been the mortal shadow, and Robin the flame. It could burn the poison right out of him, that heat. "What do you care? And what does Summer really want, Crenn? I didn't figure you for an errand-boy." Two questions for one, an insult to boot, and he would likely not get a single answer. Unless they were speaking as they once had. As friends, as mortal men, the rough camaraderie of roofers or haulers, construction mockery or the half-insulting beer-banter that passed for affection among them.

How much mortal was left in Alastair? Or in himself, for that matter?

"I care little what Summer wants." The hunter tossed another piece of dry wood onto the fire, and sparks whirled up. "I care little for your courtship, either."

"Then why are you still here?" *And not back in your swamp, nursing your grudges?*

"Perhaps she interests me." Crenn shrugged. "Or perhaps I'm simply waiting to rob you of something *you* care for, Gallow. Which would you prefer?"

Don't make me kill you. "There's your mistake, Al. There's nothing left I care for." The words sounded hollow even as he spoke them. "My wife was Robin's half sister, and she is long dead."

"Ah. Shall I ask permission to court your kinswoman, oh Gallowglass?"

"She needs no trouble from you, Alastair Crenn. Your quarrel is with me."

"Is it?" Another short laugh. He had many of them, it seemed, each one bleaker than the last. "Get some rest."

"And trust you?"

"You're marked; all I have to do is wait. There's only one thing that can cure you."

"Yes." His throat was dry. "But before I seek any cure, there is business to finish." *Figure out how to trade the Horn to Unwinter, and get a good bargain for it. Then, to get Robin somewhere Summer can't—*

"Indeed. I'll take the first watch."

That felt familiar. Even fresh out of the orphanage, they had understood the need for watchfulness. Jeremiah took one last long look at Robin, sleeping peacefully. He stretched out on his side on the cold cracked concrete, pillowing his head on his left arm, and stared at the fire. He'd need all the rest he could get.

Especially if Robin took it into her head to slip over the borders into the sideways realms again.

Crenn fed the fire in handfuls and spoke no more. Gallow finally fell into a thin, troubled rest, his side aching and the taste of lies in his mouth.

BAD JUJU
31

They called old Pete Craddock crazy. He coulda told them what was, really. Crazy was the goddamn capitalists. Crazy was the nine-to-fivers in their offices. Crazy was the gummint that sent a boy to the jungles to murder Commies and then, when he came back, spat on him and called him a babykiller.

It was a damp night, even though the rain had stopped, and he pushed his cart down the sidewalk as dawn came up. Unbroken bottles piled high in the cart, and Pete's bootsole was flapping a little. His head hurt from the cheap rye, but he had enough empties to turn in. You got up early, just like you did on the farm or in the service, and you got your work done. Those what stayed in bed lost out, or were throat-cut by the little crawling gooks in black pajamas.

Rail-thin almost-elderly mortal man in a blue knit cap and boots held together with worn-down duct tape, shuffling down the pavement, bobbing his head as his long brown coat flopped. Winter had been damn hard, but down here you could set yourself up in one of the empty warehouses, if you knew how to get in. If you looked for the forgotten spaces.

A flicker of motion ahead. Pete's head jerked up, his bloodshot muddy-hazel eyes narrowing.

Sometimes they came after him. If it wasn't the pajamas it was the longhairs, and if it wasn't them it was the pig cops who didn't give a damn if you were a ghost, if you'd died for your country in a goddamn rice paddy and couldn't get a woman or a place to stay now because everything slipped right through a ghost's hands.

The world was full of assholes. They'd set Jimmy McClintock on fire, poor Jim lost in a glue-sniffing stupor. Those drugs would get to you, bad juju. Liquor was much better. It warmed a man up, set him straight.

In fact, Pete often thought, liquor was even better than a woman. It didn't nag you to death.

The flicker came again. His bootsole flopped as he slowed, staring.

The old Emberly warehouse was locked up tight. The fence around it was topped with razor wire and pretty damn solid. At first Pete thought the delirious tremens had him, because there was a man balanced on the top of the chainlink, stepping between the sharp coils. Dressed all in brown leather, with a shock of nasty matted hair that looked almost green in the predawn glow. He coiled himself, the top bar of the chainlink fence flexing slightly, the wire rattling, and leapt, landing on concrete soft as a whisper.

The man rolled his shoulders back, and Pete realized he had stopped dead, his jaw hanging. The tattered garbage bags covering his prizes flapped, a soft rustle as the usual dawn exhale filled the city.

It was enough to make him think about Bad Mandy who lived under the overpass, smelling of sour lavender and whispering about the things that lived in the cracks and corners. "Aliens, dontcha know. Some of them can fly. They hide, and only come out when you're not looking."

Bad Mandy, with her blackened teeth and her hissing, jabbing two fingers at you. "Don't you look at me!" she'd yowl. "Don't you dare!"

The man in brown darted into the alley across the street between two falling-down brick heaps. He made no noise at all, but the fence was still quivering. Pete's mouth was dry, as if he was back in the jungle with the shadows under every leaf, the steam and the stink and the shit and the blood.

Trembling, Pete pushed his cart forward, wincing as the wheels grated. So loud in the hush, how hadn't he noticed it before? What if the man came back, or suspected Pete had seen him?

He sped up. His bootsole flapped harder and harder. Rancid sweat burned all over his body. By the time he hit Caroline Street he was running flat-out, the cart juddering madly, bottles jouncing free of the garbage bags, shattering like bombs.

He was two blocks away from the collection center, and only one from the police station, when the massive heart attack seized his chest and dug its claws in without mercy. He screamed, a short cry because he had no breath left, and toppled to the cold pavement. The cart continued down the sidewalk, rolling with slow majesty before tipping, spilling glass and dirty clothes, a sleeping bag, and various other items into the road—a snail's shell, brutally upended. Its wheels came to a stop, finally, and there was silence for a little while longer.

ASK AND BEGONE

32

A fair, fine morning in Summer, but nary a sprite or nymph was to be seen. Crystals of dew sprinkling the lush grass, the finely carved leaves, and the glowing flowers went unharvested. No dancing in the dells, and Summerhome did not throb with merriment. The pennons hung listless, the green and white walls smoke-tarnished, the shell-white paths glowing as bleached bone under a harsh-glaring sun. No balmy breeze, no music floating in the air, and the orchard's blossoms had closed tight. No open frills on the gnarled black branches, just white buds, shy and hard as a kraken girl's nipple.

The crystalline steps were repaired but dull. The visitor's glove-soled feet brushed them, and he blinked out of sight before the massive door. He appeared on the other side of it, stepping out of nowhere as casually as a mortal on a Sunday stroll.

Who was it, to tread so bravely, when Summer's door had not opened that morning? The Queen of Seelie was not accepting visitors. Perhaps he had an invitation?

He passed lightly over the shifting map of Summer's domain in the eternally twilit rotunda, glancing down only once to see the damage wrought by Unwinter's raid. So much had been restored, but the edges of the map paled alarmingly. Half of the fens were gone, the Dreaming Sea reaching hungrily inland, the borders with the Low Counties ran and blurred much faster than they should, and the deep scars, as if a gauntleted fist had raked across the map, were still discernible.

The doors to the Great Hall were closed as well, but he simply skipped through the Veil and came to a halt just inside them, observing the empty, cavernous space. The hangings were now the deep, clotted red of dried blood, hanging utterly still. The couch on the dais was no longer choked with pillows.

Perhaps she found them too soft.

On the couch, she sat, straight and slim. The red scarf knotted around her wrist dripped down the front of her dress of black spiderweb and sigh, its many misty, shifting draperies blurring her outline. Her hair was just as long and golden as ever, its waves hardening as she raised her head and saw who stood before her.

"You," she said tonelessly.

He swept her a fine bow, hand wide as if holding a feathered cap free, one toe pointed just so. "Me. Hail Summer, light of Seelie, Jewel of Danu."

Her aristocratic nostrils might have flared a millimeter. That was all. She watched him straighten, and if she noticed any change in him, she did not inquire. No, she sat white and still, her slim fists clenched. The Jewel on her forehead gave a single brilliant flash, settled back to a low punky glow. No minstrels behind the carven screens above, no handmaidens waiting upon her, no knights in attendance.

He turned in a complete circle, widdershins, looking about him with much interest. Finally, his irises flaring with yellow-green light around the black tarns of hourglass pupils, he faced her again and mimed shock and surprise, his mobile mouth stretching wide, his features contorting.

Whatever she thought of this display remained a mystery. When she did speak, the words dropped listless from her carmine lips. She moved them as little as possible. "What do you want?"

"Many things, oh Summer. But is this any way for old friends to greet each other? Your hospitality grows a little thin of late, I should say."

"What. Do you. Want." A tremble passed through the throneroom, and the visitor affected not to notice.

"You had better manners when you were a serving-girl, my dear."

Another tremor slid through the room, this one more definite. Summer's blue, blue eyes narrowed a fraction.

That was all.

Finally, he sighed, an almost-comical expression of resignation playing over his youthful face. "I shall match rudeness with its own kind, then." He stepped forward, easily, and again, until he stood in the exact center of the hall. "And I will ask very simply, so you may understand me."

"Ask and begone." Summer did not move.

"With good grace." Puck, called Goodfellow by some, the closest thing to a leader the free sidhe had, bared his sharp teeth in his V-shaped grin. All things considered, he was looking very well, though his leathers were new, and a pair of sharp eyes might have noticed a certain absence of items at his belt. "I have searched as you bade me and found nothing but hints of your knights striking death into mortals. This will not do. Where is my girl, oh Seelie's Dawn? Where, oh where, is *my Robin Ragged*?"

INVITED GUESTS

33

🥀⚔

allow." She prodded his shoulder, felt at his clammy forehead. "Hist, *Gallow.*"

He groaned, woke with a start. She clapped her hand over
his mouth to capture any startled cry.

"Listen," she whispered. "Crenn is gone; he left just a few
moments ago. Wake. We must move."

Gallow blinked. This close, she could see the fine lines at the
corners of his eyes—he had been much older than her when
he first stepped into the sideways realms. His skin was too
cold, and sweat-slick besides. As long as he stayed in the mortal
realm, he wouldn't sicken further; one step into the sideways
and the poison would begin to swell in the wound again. He
nodded, his black hair rasping against his sleeve, and she eased
her fingers away.

"He's gone?" he whispered.

She let her hand fall and matched his quiet tone. "As soon
as dawn rose. I do not like the thought of where he might hie
himself to. We must away."

"Okay." He nodded, levered himself up with a grunt. Stood,
rubbing the sleep from his green eyes with one hand, and the

set of his shoulders would have told her he was in pain, even if he had not winced a little, digging in his pocket with the other hand. "Half a minute."

"He'll return, probably with reinforcements." She restrained the urge to hop from foot to foot. "If Summer wants me, it's best not to stay where her messenger left us."

"Where's your dog?"

Does it matter? "Looking for a safer place to hide. It's dawn; come along or I shall leave you."

"I wouldn't recommend that." He rolled something in his palm, then cracked it, like a nut in a brughnie's capable, horn-hard hands. A red glimmer, creaking leather, and she averted her eyes as he stripped off the rags of his dun coat and shirt. Muscle flickered under pale skin, and he struggled into a gossamer doublet pulled from a carrying-boll. She recognized it now—goblin work, and fine, capable of carrying almost any weight. "A few seconds now might save us trouble later."

"I have difficulty believing anything will *save* us trouble now." She found herself stepping forward, tugging at the under-doublet laces to settle them aright, as if he were a child or a lover.

The leather was supple, varnished-red armor, with a jingle of whisper-light and iron-hard chain worked into the hide. Dwarven work, very fine, but not of a cut Summer's knights would willingly wear. It was, perhaps, just the thing for a lanceman who needed a balance between agility and a fair measure of protection. Was that what he'd gone into the Markets for?

"What else have you in there?" *Why am I whispering?*

"Want to dig and take a look?" A lopsided grin, and he bent to his boots.

She found herself smiling as well and smoothed her face as well as she could. She turned in a circle, first deosil then widdershins, wishing Crenn wasn't so *quiet*. If he came back now—

A few more moments, and she turned back to find Jeremiah Gallow running a hand back over his short hair. He offered her the boll, his palm cupped a-cradle and his dirty fingers shaking slightly. "Here."

She took it, marveling at its lightness, running her fingers over the patterned surface. "A beautiful piece of work."

"Should be. I paid enough for it. My Summer armor's back at the bus station."

Why tell me? She shrugged as he picked up his tattered coat again, digging in its pockets. She looked away, unwilling to witness any other secrets he might be carrying. "You planned to leave, then?"

"What? Summer? Oh. I wasn't always...well." He dropped the coat, kicked at it with one booted foot. Now they weren't mortal shoes, but hobleaf-boots, light and supple to the wearer, heavy as stone to the insect crushed beneath them, and worth a pretty penny. "I was not always Summer, Robin. Let's go."

"Wait." She offered him the boll again. "You must need this."

"No." Gallow looked down at her, and there was the mark of fever on his cheeks, a slight hectic flush. His green eyes glittered dangerously. "You may find a use for it, or for anything in it. It's yours."

"I have nothing to offer in return."

"I didn't ask you for anything in return. Come on."

As if you know where we're going. "Not that way. Here." She slipped the boll into her own pocket. If he was in a giving mood, well enough. If it was a trap, she could rid herself of it later, couldn't she?

A door on the south side was chained shut, but the padlock

holding the chain was more than happy to click open under a sidhe's gentle coaxing. The hinges were rusty, too, but she pushed it open, wincing at the scraping, and peered out. Thin sunshine fell over a weedy gravel driveway, shadows sharp as knives, and a flash of tawny-russet was Pepperbuckle, slinking along the fence at the end of the gravel.

The touch surprised her. Gallow's hand closed loosely about her wrist. "Do you really think I'd kill you for Summer?"

She pulled away, or tried to. "Come along."

Sunshine, a balm against her skin. It felt good, even wan as early-morning spring light could be, and she pulled Gallow along. He turned loose of her wrist only to slip his fingers through hers—his gauntlets had retracted, a marvelous bit of workmanship. Warm skin, calluses scraping, and she wondered why it felt…well, natural, to hold his hand.

"Tell me." He didn't squeeze, but his hand caged hers securely.

"I don't know." There it was, in plainest truth. Pepperbuckle's pads didn't disarrange the gravel at all; he nosed at her excitedly and pranced, clearly proud of himself. "You might give me some lee to run, for Daisy's sake."

His fingers tightened. There was a weak spot in the fencing here, she spread her free hand against it and pushed. Chantment sparked on her fingers, and a curtain of chainlink drew aside. She hopped through; Gallow had to bend, much taller than her. Pepperbuckle nipped along at Gallow's heels, and when they were done the chantment loosened and the fence snapped back into place. She exhaled, shaking a slight stiffness from her fingers.

"I would not betray thee, Robin." A little formally. He'd fallen back into sidhe-speech now, with its arcane etiquette and architecture. "What I did, I did to protect you."

"So you say." *You stole from me.* Was she supposed to believe he felt so much for her dead sister he would risk his own skin for just a fading echo of her in Robin's own face?

"Summer didn't send Crenn to kill you, at least. Just to bring you back."

"No doubt what she has planned for me is worse than a simple stabbing." She tested the wind and glanced at Pepperbuckle, who took off trotting along the fence, tail high, the very picture of a hound with a mission. He glanced back, and she hurried to keep up. Gallow moved well enough in her wake, but even in the hobleaf-boots his steps were heavier than their wont. "Especially if…"

"Especially if she knows you invited guests to her revel."

Robin halted. Her breath caught, and her back prickled with gooseflesh.

He *knew.* How?

Stop. He's only guessing.

He was at her back now, so close she could feel the fever-heat of him. "What hold does Puck have on you?" His breath brushed her ear, another chill running down her spine. "I'll protect you, Robin."

A lucky guess, nothing more. "Protect me?" Her throat was dry, and the music under her thoughts took on a slow, sonorous quality. Was she going to have to unleash it on *him*? "You're poisoned, Gallow. All I have to do is wait." *Just as Crenn said.*

"That's why you woke me up instead of just slipping out with your dog?"

The world threatened to tilt out from underneath her.

Pepperbuckle trotted back, ears perked and his ruff rising, and she saw something hopeful in the distance, glowing white. Atop it, one of the more hated symbols perched, its stubby arms thrust stiffly out. Her heart tore a little further. Funny, how she'd thought she had already suffered enough.

There was always more to be drawn from that well.

"Please," Gallow breathed in her ear, and she shut her eyes, as if she could pretend he meant any of the words that would follow. "*Please*, Robin."

The mothering darkness behind her lids, a false friend, offered no comfort. "Let go of me."

He did.

She took two steps, rubbing at her left wrist as if he'd injured it. Her skin ran with electricity at his nearness, at the chill left by moving away from his warmth. She opened her eyes as Pepperbuckle halted, ears pinpricked and tail stiff, its fringe moving slightly as morning breeze touched it. Exhaust, cold iron, the filth of mortal living. Summer was more fragrant, but much more dangerous. A pretty sweet, wrapped in gold to hide the poison.

Was Unwinter better? Did she care enough to find out?

"There's a church," she said, hollowly. "You'll be safe enough there."

"And you?"

She shook her head, her hair bouncing, and set off down the sidewalk again. The street curved down a hillside, shambling warehouses rising on either side, early light tinting even the tired facades with gold.

Her velvet coat was no longer so dusty. Pepperbuckle's heat had dried it quite nicely last night, and she could perhaps needle-chantment some of its threadbare patches. Some of the rips would mend of their own accord as the heat and chantment-aura of a part-sidhe worked out through her skin and into the cloth.

"Robin." Gallow, behind her. "I was frantic, searching for

you. I cleared your trail of all the Unseelie I could find. I have something Unwinter himself wants, and I mean to trade it to him for your protection."

Oh, Daisy would be proud of you. "Very kind of you."

"Aren't you going to ask me why?"

"You must have loved Daisy very much." She sped up, her heels clicking, a familiar sound. "We must hurry. The assassin of Marrowdowne will no doubt track us easily."

Thankfully, finally, he spoke no more, just stepped heavily behind her. His breath came hard and fast, but she didn't slow.

BELIEVE NO MAN
34

*D*amn the woman. The stitch in his side gripped even harder, and sweat stung all over him. Still, he kept going, grimly determined to keep her in sight. The dog gave him many a dubious look, but at least there were no mortals about to witness a huge russet hound, the woman with the fiery hair in tattered black velvet, and the man in her wake wearing armor he didn't have the strength to glamour.

He kept his gaze fixed on the back of her head. What was she thinking? Daisy hadn't been this...difficult. But then, Daisy hadn't been to Court, and hadn't survived among the sidhe. Simple, uncomplicated, sunny, that was his dead wife.

Except she'd never breathed a word about her sister. How much had she suspected? Or was Robin just a family secret? A Half's talents could make things difficult, among mortals. Had Robin been sent away, a shameful blot on the past?

Puck had found her, and brought her to Summer. Now Jeremiah was thinking there was more to the story. Far, far more, but some turn of it escaped him.

If he could manage to earn her trust, she might tell him enough to make the whole story visible. The more he knew, the better he could play both ends to keep her safe. Or as safe as possible even after the poison eventually claimed him.

The sun mounted higher. A buzz and blur of traffic began, drawing nearer, a snake-rattle of warning.

She finally noticed he was lagging. His feet didn't want to work quite right. Was this what mortals felt, what they called *sick*? It was different from being wounded.

Much different.

Her fingers, warm against his forehead. The armor was too heavy; now he was thinking he shouldn't have put it on. The sidewalk glittered with chips of quartz, even the cracks and seams full of rich dirt and tiny green sprouts. His toes caught, he stumbled, and Robin was speaking to him.

"You're fevered. How long were you in the Markets, Gallow?"

Long enough to find you. His tongue fit oddly in his mouth, so he didn't say it. Greasy sweat all over him—going without rest, without anything but mortal food, then fighting a running battle through the Gobelins with the poison breeding silently in his side. Movement—she was under his arm, now, and he leaned on her drunkenly. A hot weight on his other side was the dog, pressing close, and Robin whispering. Glamour-chantment, prickling all over him to disguise their bizarre appearances, digging at the scar in his side with tiny diamond claws.

"Why didn't you tell me it was this bad? Oh, *damn* it." She stumbled, too, righted both of them, and a long reeling time later there was a rattling. She propped him against a stone wall, and he lost himself in the veins, cracks, moss, small spots of lichen. "No, Pepperbuckle, stay back. Back. It will hurt you." More rattling, a whisper of lock-opening chantment, and the raw edge of fear in her voice was wrong.

180

"Come now," she coaxed, and he blindly followed. Smears of daylight, he tripped over an edge and fell. Instinct tucked his shoulder, tried to make him roll; the world turned over and a short, stunned cry echoed all around him.

The haze cleared. His side ached furiously. He curled around it, the armor flowing with him. It was much more comfortable than mortal clothes, but still, he'd rather be home in bed, with Daisy bringing him something fine and cold to drink and—

Daisy's dead. Watch where you are now, Gallow.

"*No*, Pepperbuckle!" Robin, a low, hoarse frantic voice. "It will hurt you, you're sidhe, oh, by the Stone...oh."

He tilted his head, gravel digging into his hair and the scalp beneath. The world was cockeyed because he lay spilled on his unwounded side, and he watched as a sideways dog whose coat matched Robin's glorious mane stepped daintily over an invisible border, framed by high iron gates. It looked vaguely familiar.

The dog shook out its paws, as if walking on glass, and avoided the iron to either side. It stepped, high and dainty, its tail beginning to droop, then wagging just a little. Jeremiah's head rolled along the ground, and he looked up.

Seen from this angle, the steeple with its Celtic cross was straight out of a horror movie or a surrealist's nightmare. The steps leading to the church door hung askew, like a cartoon staircase.

Daisy had loved cartoons. He'd never told her he could remember when they didn't exist, a time before the glowing television screens in even the poorest of houses. So many things he didn't tell her.

"Stone and Throne," Robin whispered. Clicking and shifting as she stepped over the gravel, as mincingly as the hound. Come to think of it, the dog almost moved like she did—a quick hop, a distrustful glance, a slight shake of its proud head. "Here, Gallow. Can you stand?"

He found his arms and legs would obey him, but only just. "Church." He managed to sound only breathless. "Nice."

"I didn't think…" Maddeningly, she stopped there. Continued guiding him up the steps. The dog stayed at the foot, its low whine rattling through Gallow's bones. "Yes, stay there. Just a moment."

The door reared above them. How strange, it looked just like the entry to the Great Hall in Summerhome. "Good dog," he said. "Can't come up the steps, though. Right?"

"Hush." She propped him against the right-hand door, bent to the left one. Whispered at its keyhole, and he watched as her curls bounced and settled, how the black velvet cloaked her, the flawless-pale slice of one cheek. "Here. Go in, lock the door. Find a place to hide."

"You think the lock will deter another Half?" *Stay with me.* The words stuck in his throat.

"I'll lead him away. *You* simply stay there, and I'll return."

"What if you don't?"

The left-hand hinges creaked as she pushed at the door. "Nobody has caught me yet, and it's daylight. If Crenn comes, we shall see."

"He's tricky. Don't believe him."

A faint smile, warming her eyes just a touch. "Oh, Gallow. I believe no man."

It stung, but only briefly. "Can I know what your plan is?"

"No. Concentrate on surviving until dusk."

"Fine." *I'm a coward. Hiding in a church while a woman guards me.* "If I wasn't poisoned—"

"You'd find some other way to be annoying, Gallow. Go,

rest. Under the altar's best, even another Half can't drag you from there."

"Come in with me." He couldn't help himself.

She glanced over her shoulder. The dog made a low grinding sound. A full-sidhe beast stepping onto holy ground would be uncomfortable, to put it mildly. If the dog was Seelie, it could stand the discomfort for a few moments; free sidhe, not so long.

Unwinter, of course, couldn't stand it at all.

"Robin." He leaned on the door, so she couldn't pull it shut. "I want to tell you something."

"Save it for tonight, Gallow." But she leaned forward, and her lips met his stubbled cheek. The touch burned through him, a soft vital fire, much different from the sick fever-heat of poison. "Now go, and hide."

SOME WAY THROUGH

35

Pepperbuckle slouched, his shoulders moving with sleek grace, and leapt. A *crunch*, pigeons scattered, but one hung from his jaws, flapping furiously until he shook his head with a snap. He settled down, hunkering behind the waist-high half-wall bordering this particular flat roof.

"Good boy," Robin said, though the mess he made of the birds turned her stomach. He could no doubt catch rats, too—and perhaps even housecats, if the mood took him. She'd worried for nothing. Instinct prompted survival, even in the heart of such a new-made beast, so she followed her own share of intuition and moved at a lazy pace, alert for any whisper of sidhe or pursuit.

Sunlight poured over this city, rich golden springshine. The rain had retreated, and under the reek of exhaust and warming pavements came a thread of cut grass, the mineral tang of warming earth. Well past noon, with Pepperbuckle clearly very capable of feeding himself, and her hands trembling just a little when she thought of what she intended to do. She moved just enough, from one quarter of the town to the next to make her difficult to track, but not enough to tire her overmuch. She even stole a pint of heavy cream and drank it settled on the roof of a library, watching a storm threaten to the northwest before it evaporated under the assault of sunshine.

The Markets had thrown them far away indeed. She was certain she was still in America, though, and the sun hung at its accustomed Midwest angle in the sky, but this was not a city Summer had entrances in. Unwinter could be reached from everywhere, but stepping over into Summer from here would require first finding some slice of the free sidhe's lands under the surface of the mortal.

She stayed well away from the parks and the vacant lots, the strange-tilted alleys or the triple or quintuple crossroads. Away from the mobile homes and the shabby edges of urban renewal, because the in-between places were where sidhe most often came through. In the sleepy time of afternoon, when traffic lulled and cats napped, she stole again—a quart of whipping cream from a large supermarket with a crammed parking lot—and began finding her way back to the church.

Pepperbuckle whined as she slipped through the gates again. "No," she whispered, pulling them closed behind her. "You can't, little one. Go, hunt, hide."

He tried to snake his nose through, and pulled back with a smothered yelp as the iron brushed his whiskers. Sidhe enough for that, even if he could stand consecrated ground for a short while. Her own mortal blood probably provided some insurance. Would it wear off?

She didn't have time to find out.

"I'm sorry," she whispered, reaching through the bars and rubbing behind his ear, the way he liked. He stared at her reproachfully. "No. Go hide. Survive. If I see morning, I'll find thee."

He whined and yipped as she walked up the gravel path again, stopping to sniff deeply every few steps, testing the air. The hound didn't fall quiet until she bent to whisper to the lock on the main doors, again. Her chest ached, and her eyes were full of suspicious dampness.

The further away the changeling-dog was from the danger Robin brought with her, the better.

Her skin crawled a little as she stepped over the threshold, into dark, calm, incense-scented quiet. She slipped through the entryway, her heels hushed against hardwood, and into the main space, the walls soaring away and the windows on the west side glowing with late-afternoon light. "Gallow?" she whispered, and the word feather-brushed the dim quiet.

"Here," came the reply, and she hurried toward it, past the neat rows of age-polished pews. A ghost of snuffed candles, a faint astringency of cheap blessed wine, the cloying of dying flowers stacked on the altar. Hanging above its white-robed bulk was a gruesome sight—a wooden man nailed to rough splintered beams, his face a mask of suffering. She averted her gaze—the highborn talked about the Pale God and his followers, scorn and trepidation mingling in the words. Robin could have told them that the Protestants didn't really believe in anything but money, and the Catholics were too busy being guilty, like Daddy Snowe always said, but why bother? The finer points of mortal religion were lost on Robin as well as the highborn sidhe, and neither felt the lack much.

Still, it was...disconcerting, to see torture displayed so openly in what was supposed to be a holy place. Even Summer would not kill a changeling so unglamourously.

Unwinter might, but he did not pretend to be sacred.

Jeremiah was on the steps to the altar, sprawled like a knight in an illustration, his hair disarranged and the armor a blot of crimson. Just like Sevrilo in the Four Corners song, taking refuge against Braghn Moran's fury—the very same dark-haired Braghn Moran who was now one of Summer's favored knights. Had he survived Unwinter's raid?

Did Ilara Feathersalt, the golden-haired fullblood Robin had spied leaving Summerhome one misty morning, care if he had?

"I brought you cream." She could no longer hear Pepperbuckle. Robin wiped at her eyes, as if the incense-smell bothered her. "Do these places often stand empty?"

"Depends on the day of the week." Eyes glittering, cheeks bright with fever, he was handsome as only a sidhe could be. Had Daisy ever seen him like this, with his pretense at being just another gray, sullen mortal man turned to ashes by the fever-glare? "The priest came in a little while ago. Didn't see me."

"Good." She perched on her knees next to him, helped him sit up. "Is it very bad?"

"I'm just weak right now." He watched her while she opened the carton and shook his head when she offered it. "You first."

Was he being chivalrous? She offered it again, folding his callused, too-warm fingers around the waxed cardboard. "I already did. Drink."

"So what's this plan of yours?" He tipped the cardboard carton to his mouth, taking long swallows, and she debated the wisdom of telling him. When he broke away from the carton, gasping, he gave her a sharp glance. "Let me guess. You wish to summon Unwinter."

How did you . . . She shook her head. "I hate being predictable."

"It makes sense. It'll also help me. I can trade this for the poison taken off, and probably protection for you." His free hand patted at his chest.

"Trade what?" She restrained the urge to wipe at his mouth. He wasn't a child.

"You didn't see that bit?" He took another long draft of cream, exhaled slightly. "God, that's better. Almost forgot what cream does. I, ah, I stole Unwinter's Horn."

She'd seen it dangling from its chain as she sought to draw the poison from his wound with new bread. "I know, I saw it. But *why?*" Why would anyone do such a thing?

"Seemed like a good idea." The fever-flush abated, and his gaze lost that dangerous glitter. "You think he'll trade an antidote and the protection of one little sidhe girl for that?"

"It's more likely he'll hang you on a gibbet and *take* it. And skin me slowly to boot, to put me on my own gibbet next to yours."

"At least we'll be together." Sweat stood out on his forehead, great clear drops, but he was no longer gasping, and his gaze took back its accustomed sharpness.

It was easy to see why Daisy had liked him, now. "Why did you go to the markets?"

"To get my armor. And to see if Medvedev would offer you shelter."

"You know him that well?"

"He owes me."

"For what?" *Too many questions.* But if they kept him from speaking on other matters, it was a good thing. At least he wasn't requiring similar answers from her—or at least, not to the same degree.

"I was not always of Summer, Robin." He finished the quart in a few more long swallows and exhaled a long, satisfied breath. "Thank you."

She took the carton back, avoiding his fingers now. Silence between them, as the windows on the west side dimmed. The obstruction in her throat was dangerous; she concentrated on breathing. Four in, four out. The song was her protection, and the discipline of breath helped steady her as well.

He watched her while she set the empty container aside and smoothed her velvet sleeves over her hands. Some few of the holes and shiny patches were amenable to needle-chantment, and in a little while the robe would be no more tattered than any other piece of sidhe finery.

She never would have dared to wear velvet at Court. "I hear Unwinter is a cheerless place," she said, finally.

"If it is, your presence will no doubt brighten it."

Where had the old Gallow, the Half who apparently hated anything sidhe, gone? This man seemed a little softer. "Should I trust you?"

"Do you think you could?"

"I'm not... my sister, Gallow. I never will be."

"I don't want you to be."

Very well, then. She pushed herself upright, the carton dangling in her right hand. "There's another door. I'll make certain it's clear."

"Robin." He reached up, and she surprised herself, her left hand catching his. "Try to trust me. It will help us both survive."

"Will it?" She squeezed gingerly, surprising herself again. "We shall find some way through, then. I will do all I can for you, Jeremiah Gallow." *Whether it's for Daisy's sake, or for... other reasons.*

"And I will do anything for you, Robin Ragged." He sagged back onto the steps, his fingers slackening and his eyes closing, and Robin closed her mouth with a snap. It was, perhaps, merely the fever talking. No sidhe would give such an open-ended promise, especially not to a Half known for running Summer's errands.

The windows darkened still more, and she shook herself. There was no time for indecision.

Not when she planned to face Unwinter himself.

BE WELCOME HERE
36

Dusk came with a cold wind, and he tried not to lean too hard on Robin's slenderness. She was stronger than she looked, but it irked him nonetheless. Out a side door and down a flight of moss-cornered steps, Robin freezing as footsteps echoed. It was the priest, a corpulent blackbird with a reddened nose, swaying heavily down an indifferently paved path between laurel bushes. He heaved along, humming as his black shoes squeaked, and Robin looked up at Jeremiah. Her lips parted, just a little—was she thinking of unloosing that wall of noise on the mortal?

He shook his head. *Don't.*

The footsteps passed them, a slow, majestic treading. "Lord," the man said, "have mercy. Have mercy on all of us." A thick drawl, maybe Texan, slowed the words and gave them a rhythm.

What would be the reaction, Gallow wondered, if one of them said *amen*? Causing a heart attack in one of the Pale God's followers might be something the Unseelie would count as sport.

"Especially all those in need of sanctuary." The priest paused on the other side of the laurels. "May they be welcome here, O Lord, and should they need supper or a friendly ear, why, let them know the parsonage is just a few steps down this path, here. Thank you, Lord. Amen."

The crunching continued, and the priest's head did not turn. He rocked past, patting at his well-cushioned belly, and disappeared between more rustling laurels.

Robin's blue, blue gaze met his again, and her lips were still slightly apart. She looked almost stunned, and if the scar on his side hadn't chosen that moment to twitch again, sending a bolt of pain through his middle, he might have tucked his chin and bent down, and found out if her mouth was as soft as it looked. Maybe she would make the slight humming noise Daisy did when he kissed her, a satisfied little purr, or . . .

Jesus, Jeremiah.

Did she read it on his face? No way to tell, because she immediately glanced away, a worried frown aimed at the priest's retreating back. "Can't even chantment," she whispered, and urged him forward.

"Why would you?" he whispered back.

"To ease his pains. He's old." She steadied him, his armor silent now, the marks on his arms and chest strangely quiescent.

The graveyard was well maintained. Had the priest been walking among his less-active parishioners? How had the man known?

He'd been careful, dammit. Or as careful as he could be hiding under pews and sniffing the dust of so many shuffling, sanctified feet. Headstones leaned into umbrous dusk, this way and that, dewed with mineral-smelling sprinkler water. His boots didn't slip in the muddy wetness, neither did her heels sink in.

At least the lightfoot hadn't deserted him. Yet.

He felt the edge of the consecration approaching, the ground sloping down to an empty lot. The scar heated up, a phantom blade digging in. "Where's your dog?" The breathlessness was returning, too.

"I told him to hide, and hunt. He's safer away from me."

Of course you did. "Jesus, Robin. How did you survive Court?"

"Better than *you*, apparently." She halted, which meant he was forced to. "Stay here. Do you hear me? Do *not* do what you did last time. I could have escaped Unwinter handily enough, but for your little display."

"Could you? Puck helped, you know."

Her shoulders tensed. "Did he?"

"Yes." His arm tightened as she tried to pull away. "What hold does he have on you, Robin?"

"None." She pulled away, and he had to let her. He swayed. *Christ. I'll have enough trouble keeping upright.* "None, now. Gallow?"

"For God's sake, Robin. It's Jer, to you."

"Is that what Daisy called you?"

"Daisy's *dead*." It didn't hurt to say it this time.

She half-turned, looking over her velvet-draped shoulder at him. Black didn't blend at night; it was *too* dark. A long pause, her tongue darting out to nervously wet her lips. "I wish I'd drawn all the poison out."

"You did all you could." He searched for something else to say, something to ease her mind or keep her from this last desperate gamble.

Another shake of her russet head, and she turned away, drawing the hood up as if to hide her hair. She walked, straight and slim and graceful as a ghilliedhu girl, toward the shifting border between graveyard and empty lot. The stone wall had

195

been partly pulled down, maybe by age or maybe by coincidence, and a chainlink patch stretched from one edge of the hole to the other, to keep out kids and the curious, not to mention desecrators masquerading as thrillseekers. It was like looking through a different hole, maybe, into the days when the Folk ruled every place the churches didn't rise, their green fields dangerous at night for every mortal outside the circle of firelight and iron.

A pale flash was her right hand, her fingers closing around chainlink. The sun dipped fully below the rim of the earth, a subtle thrill running along every inch of Jeremiah's sweating body, and the scar flamed again, almost driving him to his knees.

"Unwinter," she said clearly. "Lord of the Hunt, lord of the Unhallowed, Lord of Unseelie, I name thee. I am Robin Ragged, and I invoke thy presence. Lord Harne of Unwinter, a handmaiden calls."

Silence. Even the faraway urban blur of traffic faded. A faint soundless wind began, and in the distance, the first high ultrasonic thrill of a huntwhistle rose.

GOD'S HOUSE
37

*F*ather *Ernest McKenzie had once been a boxer, and he could,
he supposed, still slug a sinner if need be. He'd thought about it
when he realized there was someone else in the church this morning. Who knows what had alerted him—a faint scuffling noise,
the warmth of another breathing body, or perhaps he was going
crazy. But when you spent so many hours in a building, you got a
sense of its fullness, and its emptiness, too.*

*He had almost called the police, too, but then ... well, it was
God's house, wasn't it? If someone would steal from God, there
was likely to be a damn good reason, and one old, asthmatic priest
was not hero material.*

*What the intruder didn't know was that there was a second
entrance, and even a man as large as the good Father assigned
to this slowly dying parish could creep silently into the choirloft. It was there he heard their voices in the afternoon—a man
and a woman. Most of what they said was nonsense, of course,
but the tones—soft, caring, a pretty contralto voice and a man's
baritone—oh, the tones reminded him of so much. Like Amelia,
who could have had him instead of God, if she'd accepted his ring.
But she hadn't, and the polio took her, and a few years later he was*

ordained. Surely the Blessed Virgin would forgive a poor sinner who prayed to Her but saw a dead woman's face in Her place?

"I would do anything for you," the man said, quiet as if he were in the confessional, and it sounded true. You could tell, after a while, what truth sounded like—or you thought you could, in those close confines.

The rest of it was…odd. He didn't dare peek through the screens, knowing the choirloft had a few squeaky boards in its floor. He stood in the door and strained his ears; it sounded like they were on the run. Criminals, perhaps…but that was God's business, wasn't it? Or the Devil's. Either way, not Father McKenzie's.

He retreated softly as they did, taking the back passages until he could slip out through the locked southern door, and he skirted the entire front of the church to give them time. His heart beat, fast and thin, as he tried not to hurry down the gravel path at the side. The prayers became audible as he approached the side door in the laurels, but he didn't look. Let him imagine them, both young, the man and the woman relying on each other in an uncertain world. How had they slipped through locked doors? Who knew? He would call a locksmith tomorrow morning.

Or maybe not. It was God's house, not his. Surely the Lord would keep the locks or not, as it suited him.

The good Father did, however, lock the parsonage doors and made sure every window was locked as well. That done, he retreated to his bedroom window, and with the lights off he could see two shadows in the graveyard, leaning on each other. The smaller shadow left the taller one and walked to the chainlink fence. Halted. There were no graves along that strip—maybe the smaller shape had bolt cutters, and the cost of repairing the fence would no doubt make little difference to God, but Father McKen-

zie was just a sinner, and he had just started to berate himself for not calling the police, because even if it was God's house McKenzie was the steward and a good steward was responsible...

The fear began. It crawled down Ernest McKenzie's back, a cold prickling sweat, his useless balls drawing up under his skivvies and his hands beginning to shake. Was it delayed reaction, or—

A foxfire glimmer in the wastefield beyond the fence. That land nominally belonged to Our Lady of Perpetual Heart, but even the faithful were choosing cemeteries over the hallowed earth now. The Father gripped the windowsill, watching the shimmer coalesce. It was a cold glow, and he remembered the stories they had scared one another with in summer camp. Corpseglow and will o'wisps, ghost tumbleweeds and pale riders, childhood fears crowding rank and thick through the cracking carapace of adulthood.

"Hail Mary," his dry lips whispered, "full of grace. Look over this sinner, please. Look over this sinner."

A shadow in the glow, a wrongness, *and he went to his knees in front of the window, his heart thunder-straining. He rested his sweating forehead against the sill, and even if it was God's house, even if he had offered sanctuary and a hot meal, he knew he would not be opening his doors this night. He squeezed his eyes shut, but he could still see the corpseglow. Was it his sins coming for him? Had they been demons, thumbing their nose at God, hiding in his very church?*

"Hail Mary, full of grace... pray for this sinner, now and at the hour of..."

The glow burned behind his eyelids. Ernest McKenzie thought of Amelia, her buckteeth and fair blond face, her faded gingham dress and the torrid, hot-biscuit odor of her sweat, and he wept. His heart kept hammering, filling his ears and throat and wrists, and he spilled over onto the floor, his head hitting hardwood with a faraway thunk.

There was one mercy, probably from whomever he prayed to. The heart attack was swift, and he felt no pain, sliding quickly from his large mortal shell.

His last, semiconscious thought was of the space between Amelia's neck and her shoulder, a tender hollow he had always wanted to kiss...

LITTLE DOVE

38

A single point of greenish foxfire, at the height of a tall rider. The darkness closed around it, and her breath puffed out in a white cloud. Sere winter grass, just barely greening underneath its cold-blasted coat, flattened and flash-froze as the clawed hooves of a creature from the black-sanded shores touching Unwinter's ash-choked country spread against a cushion of screaming, frigid air.

The light shivered over a high-crowned helm, over the spikes of armored shoulders, down the tattered, thick velvet of a heartsblood cloak, the red so deep it was almost black. Under the helm, two vicious, bloodred sparks; the sable armor flowed with him as Unwinter tightened his gauntleted fists, each one bearing an extra finger, each finger bearing extra joints. Dwarf-made and beautiful, the blackened metal ran with chill brilliance as the un-horse, a night-mare birthed from the Dreaming Sea and grown large on choice meats and struggling prey, caracoled with beautiful, awful grace.

The hounds came next, the mucus-yellow lamps of their eyes firing first, their bodies piling through the rift in the Veil Unwinter had torn. Should she feel special, because he'd appeared as soon as the words left her mouth? For once, a full-blood highborn had done the bidding of a Half.

Don't get cocky. Her mouth was dry. She kept breathing, four in, four out, watching those cold gleams above the helm's visor. The reins, neatly dressed, hung with that same heartsblood velvet; the destrier's caparison was pretty enough, she supposed, if you hadn't ever seen the knights of Summer go riding on a moonlit evening, over the rolling hills on a snow-white path.

All the same, there was a certain grace in the refusal to sugar the deadliness, to put a candy shell upon his cruelty.

The metal under her fingers burned. Enough cold iron to keep the hounds back, and the consecration, though weakening here at the edge of the graveyard, was still solid enough to hold an Unseelie at bay.

Even this one.

Unwinter's head lifted slightly. A faint noise behind Robin—she suppressed a sigh of irritation. Would the man never *listen*?

"*Little dove.*" A deep voice, its edges sharp-cold enough to numb while they sliced. Like a clear-running Arctic stream, jagged rocks along the bottom. "*You are foolhardy, to invoke me thus.*"

I hope not. "Milord. I am grateful for your company."

"*Little liar.*" A slight note of amusement, perhaps. "*I abide by your father's terms.*"

For a lunatic moment she thought he meant Daddy Snowe. Then she remembered Puck, standing on the concrete at the edge of Amberline Park, and her own betrayal of Summer.

Could you call it betrayal, though? There had been Sean, the changeling child begged as a boon, and stolen from *her* as well, encased in amber and shattered on the marble floor. Sean was dead, and it was Summer's fault—except, deep down, Robin knew it was her own, as well. *Just one more day, just let me keep him one more day.*

Well, she had, one day too long. Now there was the bitter price to pay, over and over, for the rest of the life she was scrambling so hard to retain.

"I have something that will interest you, milord." Very careful, her hand knotted in the fence though the metal threatened to ice itself to her skin. "You are a fair and generous lord, I have heard, and I would ask—"

"You want the Half hiding behind you not to burn, little dove. It is not so hard to guess." A low, grinding chuckle. *"What will you give me in exchange, Ragged?"*

"She'll give you this, Harne of Unwinter," Jeremiah Gallow said from behind her. He was much closer now. "Your Horn, in exchange for your protection of the Ragged. In every possible way, with all standard and extraordinary provisions, for eternity."

A long silence. Ragged's fingers tingled. Tucked in the pipes, a secret cargo, lay another thing she could trade. Was Gallow silly or feverish enough to think it would be that easy?

"And what of yourself, Gallow-my-glass? You challenged me to a duel. Dare you decline now?"

"Oh no." Gallow actually laughed, a short, bitter sound. He sounded, in fact, almost exactly like Crenn the assassin. "I shall fight you, and welcome. Will you give your word, Unwinter?"

The bloody glimmers in the helm's depths narrowed slightly. *"The Ragged is welcome in my dominions. Those who hold fealty to me shall extend her welcome, and protect such a precious bauble."*

"Why have your hounds been hunting her?"

"Where else shall I find my challenger, but by dogging his lady's footsteps? Come now." The sparks under his rimed helm

intensified. The hounds wove about his destrier's feet as the nightmare-beast pawed. A chunk of frozen sod lifted. *"I long to test your mettle again, Armormaster. Did you find her embraces palled, and sought one closer your station?"*

The way he said *her* made the word a curse, and there was no question of whom he meant. Just as, when Summer said *him* when she spoke of her erstwhile lord, there was none.

"No more than you did, sirrah." Gallow's hand closed around Robin's shoulder, fever-warm, slightly sweating. She almost gasped—it was *madness* to speak this way to Unwinter. Her knees were suspiciously rubbery.

Silence greeted this sally. The destrier pawed again, and the hounds darted forward, a living, liquid wave. The chain-link snapped, crackling as sidhe flesh touched threads tainted with cold iron, and Gallow's hand became a vise, dragging her away.

"Hasty, hasty," Gallow said as the hounds squealed, cringing back and smoking.

"You cannot stay there forever." Unwinter, equally fey.

"STOP!" Robin yelled, and the song trembled under the surface of the word. The chainlink rattled again, flushing with gold for a brief moment, and the squealing intensified. She shook Gallow's hand from her shoulder, and clutched her fists in the long, draggled velvet. Who was the fortune-teller who had worn this coat before her?

I hope she had better luck, whoever she was. She cleared her throat, inhaled—and Unwinter's destrier stepped mincingly aside. Perhaps the song had hurt him, last time. "I would trade too, Unwinter."

"Careful, little dove." Unwinter pulled the reins tight, and the destrier's neck arched painfully. *"You amuse me, but my patience grows thin."*

"What would you give me, Unwinter, for the cure to the plague? And for knowledge I hold of its cursed source?"

For now she knew, beyond a doubt, precisely who had loosed the blackboil upon the sidhe. Had Summer tried one of the ampoules yet?

"Robin?" Jeremiah's whisper, hot and fierce, in her ear.

Unwinter considered her. Her knees were definitely trembling now. To throw away such an advantage, to let one such as this know what she carried...

Who was mad, now? They were all moontouched.

A low groaning sound rose. The chain rattled, invisible hands pulling at it. It wasn't her knees.

"Give me the thing about his neck, little dove, and I shall honor you—"

Whatever the lord of the Hunt wished to honor her with remained unspoken. The ground tilted, and Robin screamed, a short curlew cry flaring with desperate gold. Jeremiah's own yell, rougher and less sonorous, rose, too. The stone walls holding the graveyard in quivered, jelly-shaken, and the chainlink rattled venomously. Solid earth fell away underfoot, cracks widening in the graveyard's surface, a crazyquilt of crevices. Headstones tilted, Robin's shoes scrabbled for purchase as she leapt, the chantments Morische the Cobbler had wedded to them snapping and crackling as they fought gravity itself. Earth crumbling, the stink of ground hallowed by dead and blessing rising—the nightmare of every sidhe, mortal clay suddenly animate again, and hungry for revenge against its tormenters.

More noise, over the groaning of riven earth. Battle-cries, the clashing of sword, shield, and lance. Elfhorses and Unseelie steeds trumpeting, familiar barking and howling, snapping and growling. *Summer knights? Attacking here? How did they—*

Robin fell into blackness, and fell deeper. Every solidity vanished, and she barely felt the small, horn-hard hands catching her, slowing her descent. Rock groaned, cradling her, and she tumbled, breathless, through space and the Veil itself, unable even to find a four-count of air to loose the song, her only weapon.

Her second-to-last thought was of Gallow. Had he fallen, too?

And her last, frankly more worrisome:

Why on earth are the dwarves interfering?

FINDERGAST'S MERCY
39

eing this far underground made him... nervous. Their halls were beautiful, certainly. Hilzhunger's territory was obsidian-walled, wet black stone running with its own fey light when the Veil shifted. It was an open question, whether the dwarves were truly *below* or just preferred close confines and their corners of the sideways realms obliged. If the sidhe had philosophers among them, they might have debated the matter endlessly. As it was, none cared enough to truly find out, and perhaps such a mystery was best left unexamined.

Crenn rolled his shoulders back, loosening the tension, and watched Findergast bobble around the cot. Sprawled on it, Jeremiah Gallow gasped for breath, his harsh coughing echoing from the hard, glassy walls. His hair slicked to his skull, his armor's chestpiece pushed up to show a slice of belly, his eyes closed and the fever burning in him, he looked almost mortal.

Almost.

Findergast had the misfortune of being beardless, but his skill as a chirurgeon more than made up for it. Dwarves could not bear to craft an ugly object, it was said, and this one's dirty, hardened hands couldn't bear to set a bone improperly, or allow a sickened creature to die—if it could be prevented, and more important, if he were paid well enough. The gleaming torc of soft mellow gold at his neck, worked with triskelions and hammerglyphs, marked him as one of Hilzhunger's clan. The Red were nominally allied with Summer; the Black dwarves bowed to none but often found Unwinter more congenial to trade with.

Summer's habit of sending her Armormaster to fetch trinkets the dwarves did not wish overmuch to part with was perhaps responsible for some of their reticence.

"Just *look* at this," Findergast muttered. "Where does he get such marvelous poison, I'd like to know? Even that blasted boy's isn't as virulent."

Can you treat him? Crenn didn't say it out loud. Why Summer would want him kept alive was not Alastair's business, and in any case, could he be said to care?

"*Robiiiiin,*" the man moaned, striking out with fists, feet, and weird uncoordinated grace. Findergast wove around the strikes, which were slow enough to permit such a dance.

So he did care for something. Crenn's smile would have been wolfish if not for the persistent unease crawling between his shoulderblades. The girl's voice was nothing to trifle with, even when she wasn't singing. Not only that, but Summer...well. She had been waiting for him, as if she expected he would slip through the Veil and bring her news first, instead of the girl herself.

Bring her to me. And make certain the dwarves care for Gallow. Summer had even deigned to caress Crenn's shoulder, and the dual shiver of loathing and curdled desire made his moss-matted hair sway. She'd laughed, the bright bell-note of a sidhe girl, but her eyes were so black, and the Jewel had flashed once, warningly.

Whatever Summer had planned for Robin Ragged was not likely to be pleasant. Another thing Crenn shouldn't care about; it wasn't his business.

The dwarves had performed as promised, and Summer's payment for the first half of their services was already being melted in their furnaces. The other half would be handed over when the poison burning through Gallow was ameliorated. Summer couldn't be foolish enough to expect even the greatest of dwarven healers to check Unwinter's venom. At least, not completely.

Just like she couldn't have sent Braghn Moran to treat with Hilzhunger; the dwarves would not let a full sidhe through their gates. Wise of them, with the plague about.

"Good, he's some fight left in him. Strong, very strong. Let me see, let me see." Findergast strode to the table along one side of the low room, full of alembics, bubbling chantment-pots, vile substances in mortar and in jar, candles burning with straight, wax-white flames. The gas-blue flames under some of the bubbling glass bulbs were tiny flamesprites, crunching on tiny sipping mouthfuls of kharcoal while they performed for their host. The light ran wetly over flowing designs carved in the obsidian walls, and Crenn suppressed another shudder.

How did they *breathe* down here?

Scraping, cursing, muttering, the healer worked. Foul-smelling pastes steamed against the wound on Gallow's side, blackening and crisping as they interacted with the clear, welling poison oozing from its seamed surface. Gallow stilled, his muttering ceased. Crenn let out a soft breath.

Finally, the healer glared at him. "You're still here?"

"I have a commission." *One I don't much care for.* Still, there was the promise.

I will make you beautiful again.

What good would it do him? He longed to be back in his swamp, listening to the trees and water seethe with life about him, the pale haunches or scaled hips of naiads fleeing when he approached unless he was silent as death itself. There was good hunting in Marrowdowne, amid the hanging curtains of moss, between the huge black trunks and on the sodden humps of what passed for land.

Except that was not *home*. There was no such word, for a Half. Both worlds open, neither accepting.

Child's play to track the two fugitives, even when he left the prey in its burrow while he ran to inform Summer, just like a falcon dizzied by the Queen's candy-breath. All the time, it burned inside him—Robin steadying Gallow as he walked, refusing to leave him, Robin standing at the chainlink with her chin held high, not a quaver to be found in her beautiful contralto as she invoked Unwinter.

What was it about Gallow that could snare such a girl? And if Crenn could suss out what such a snare was made of, could he, perhaps...

Findergast wrinkled his long, elegant nose. He oiled his long black curls, and the gold beads in them winked as the glow in the walls rippled. "I can stave it. Not completely. How long does *she* want him to last?" No question who the *she* was. He looked, Crenn decided, as if he wanted to spit, but could not bear to foul the slippery, elegantly patterned floor.

"As long as possible."

"Very well. Begone, so I may work." He waved a beringed, filthy hand—they cultivated dirt in certain ways, preferring honest earth to lying perfume. *The nose lies, except in metal,* their proverb ran.

Crenn nodded. He turned on his heel, and Gallow stirred again.

"Al! Where are you? Al! Al!" Frantic, the cry breaking.

Was he reliving that night, the hot wind and the leather-soled mortal men, most of them with temporary "deputy" badges, breaking the shantyslum camp, catching everyone unawares? It was the children Crenn had thought of, and their teacher. Even in Hoovervilles there were attempts at civilization, and Sarah was gentle with even the youngest of them, a schoolteacher of a mortal girl sidhe-beautiful in her blossoming.

That night, though...

Running toward the school-tent, through the screams and the shouting, before the thunder had felled him—a mortal bullet, cold lead, had passed through his belly, touching his spine and throwing him to the ground. Gutshot was a death sentence, and they thought they *had* killed him, kicking and beating his prone body before pouring the pitch and tar over him, lighting it just as an afterthought *or* a warning to the rest of shantyville.

Move on, that warning said. Some of the others had been tarred and feathered, most of them not surviving the shock.

Only mortal, after all.

It took more than a bullet to kill a Half, but tar and flaming pitch was enough to burn one. Waking to find Gallow looming over him, his face a mask and the scarring turning Crenn to a river of melt when before... and Sarah, turning away, flinching before she sobbed into Gallow's shoulder.

Oh, so we're thinking of Sarah again? He shook the idea away, his hair whipping. A mortal girl, nothing more. Long withered and dead. The betrayal hadn't hurt, he told himself. It didn't matter that Gallow had probably been with Sarah that night, despite knowing how Alastair... felt.

He couldn't even remember her face, now. Instead, what he saw was Robin Ragged, on her knees beside the fallen Gallow, and her determination, her strength. Loyalty was rare among the sidhe. How did Gallow *do* it? A woman who fought off a stonetroll, a woman whose voice rang with gold and whose touch... except Crenn would never feel those fingers, would he?

Doesn't matter, Crenn told himself. *Do your job, then you can put this behind you.*

Such a canny, loyal sidhe girl didn't deserve a faithless bastard like Jeremiah Gallow. Crenn was doing her a favor.

Bringing her to Summer is a favor, Alastair? A mark of affection?

He told that little voice inside his head to take itself elsewhere. Perhaps Summer only wanted information from the Ragged, and... well, instead of the promised price, Crenn might well beg a boon of Summer herself. He would not be so silly as to simply ask Summer for Robin's *life*. When one stooped to prey, one did so for the whole beast, not merely its eyes or its liver.

Is that what you want?

Crenn's stride lengthened, and he began to hurry.

It was time to collect the Ragged.

WONDROUS TURN
40

꙳⚔

Robin woke confused, lunging up from a narrow pallet to find herself under the blank-faced guard of two crossbow-wielding dwarves in unfamiliar regalia. They prodded her through deserted halls to an iron-bound door, and she suspected their fingers ached to squeeze the triggers.

It was Hilzhunger, a Red chieftain, who greeted her with belching, unctuous niceties. He perched on his masterchair, a pile of fluid, twisted obsidian like a breaking wave, his grimy fingers scratching under the gold chains festooning his neck. Tall for his ilk, and portly even by the standards of dwarves, he was also, by their standards, prodigiously filthy. The gold at his fingers, ears, neck, and wrist gleamed even through the blackness, chantment-clean. No dross would ever taint dwarf-made shinies. They preferred to worship silver, as Danu's reflection, but gold was wealth measured and displayed.

Robin forced her hands to relax. "Your hospitality is generous, sir, and your intervention was most...timely," she murmured. Realmakers were held in some esteem among both the Black and the Red clans, but she'd never bargained with Hilzhunger before. His clan specialized in glasswork and finely made practical items, not the pretty, dangerous baubles Summer coveted. Either he had been richly paid to interfere...or he *expected* to be.

She'd never heard of dwarves breaking the sanctity of consecrated ground before. Although, really, they didn't have to—all they had to do was work *underneath*, and what they wanted would fall through their roofs.

Where had all the bodies gone?

I don't want to know.

"You're a braw maiden, to be speaking to Unwinter so." The chieftain continued scratching under his golden collar. A fine crimson satin waistcoat, red leather trews, and blood-colored boots—he had dressed for the occasion, and Robin's grimy velvet was a sorry statement indeed. A few moments of chantment would clean it, but she had not been allowed that luxury.

No, the squat, frowning guards at the door, their crossbows aimed at her, had precluded such niceties in these unfamiliar halls, choking-close as every dwarf palace seemed to a sidhe used to Summer's light and air. Or even the mortal world's wide, cold sky.

"Thank you." She half-turned, allowed her gaze to drift over the guards. Leather and chain, supple dwarven work armoring them, and no doubt should she make a sudden movement or loud noise, a bolt would sing from their cunning little weapons. "I am...uncertain of your welcome, sir."

"I know of your voice, cuckoo-girl." Was that sweat on his forehead? Little jewels in the crimson light, the walls thrumming uneasily. "A good turn doesn't mean you'll give me another."

"You've been paid for the first turn, or you wouldn't have danced it. I wonder where my lord Armormaster landed."

The chieftain showed his teeth, white pickets through a bush of black beard. "Why do you care?"

This was getting worse and worse. Still, she had to try. "Good turns can be repaid."

"Indeed they can." Hilzhunger kept glancing across the central firepit, its low umber glow the result of the flamesprites curled up, sleeping, on a banked bed of blackrock and kharcoal. The dwarves largely slept when their burning sprites did, and there were rumors that they had a particular chantment to make said sprites large enough to enjoy a couching with. *How else*, a Summer wit would say with a smile, *do you suppose their numbers increase?*

It was the main door to his hall the dwarf kept glancing at. Alternatives raced through Robin's brain, each one discarded as it arose. She swayed slightly, as if exhausted. "I dislike the thought of straining so gracious a hospitality as you offer, sir, and had best be on my way."

"No strain at all, cuckoo-girl." His grin stretched even wider, and Robin began to have a very, very bad feeling about this indeed.

It wasn't the main door, however. It was a smaller side door, a single narrow leaf, sliding aside to reveal another crimson-laced passageway beyond. The figure slipping through, moss-haired and broad-shouldered, almost looked like Gallow for a moment, and her traitorous heart leapt before she realized who it truly was.

Crenn paced silently into the hall. Robin tensed. "Crenn."

He didn't pause; a slice of his chin was visible for a moment, coppery skin flashing too quickly for her to guess at its true dimensions. "Please, it's Alastair, for you. I am relieved to find you unharmed. Your hound, is he well?"

I hope he is. "I do not know." Still, that he would inquire warmed her, a little. Had he vanished to bring more pigeons to Pepperbuckle? Who could tell? He didn't seem insulted that she and Gallow had flown.

Was he an ally?

Robin, you are too old to believe in a tale like that.

Crenn's head shook slightly, his expression hidden by his hair. "That saddens me. He is a fine creature."

"That's all very well." Hilzhunger shifted in his chair. The firepit crackled, its chantment-laden rim shivering uneasily. "I'd rather this be over with, though, if you don't mind."

"I would like nothing more than to be on my merry way from your domain, sir." She took a single step toward the firepit, a calculated risk. The crossbows did not sing. "Alastair... have you seen Gallow? Is he well?"

"As well as can be expected." He kept moving toward her, his face hidden. Moss in his hair had darkened, drying. The crimson light was kind to him, perhaps, but she still could not see his expression, and that made her even more uneasy. "Tended by a healer, last I saw."

That means little, but thank you. "No doubt a certain lady engineered this wondrous turn of events." *What does he want? What does Summer want, other than vengeance upon me? But she swore my life to Gallow. What can Crenn do to me?*

She discovered she did not want to find out. He kept approaching, one gliding step at a time, and Robin darted a glance at Hilzhunger, whose lips parted slightly, avid interest all over his beard-choked face. The precious-metal beads woven into his hair twinkled merrily at her.

"Halt," Robin said, very calmly. "Or I shall sing."

Crenn shrugged, took another step. "The clans are not bound

to Summer's promise, little bird, and I would hate to see you bleed."

Four in, four out. "You won't see it." The tension all through her now. "Don't make me do this, Crenn."

For the first time, he shook his hair back, his face rising from behind the matted, mossy strands.

Dark eyes, little difference between pupil and iris, kharcoal lashes. His mouth would have been beautiful if he hadn't been grimacing, and one-third of his face was... well, just as attractive. High cheekbones, knife-sharp, a proud nose, and those coal-dark eyes.

The remainder was a river of scarring, seamed and puckered meltflesh. His right eye drooped a little, but at least he hadn't lost it. The scarring almost swallowed his perfect mouth, and spread down his neck.

Someone had *done* that to him. Robin gasped, and he blurred forward with the eerie darting speed of a sidhe assassin. Down in a tangle of arms and legs, her throat relaxed and the song gathering itself to strike, snakelike, before his fingers, cruelly bruising, found her mouth. A gobbet of something foul forced between her lips, she choked, and numbness spread through tongue and jaw. She thrashed, biting, clawing, kicking, and it took him several moments to subdue her, holding her chin in a vise of callused fingers, sealing her lips closed. She couldn't *breathe*; she choked afresh and struck out all the more desperately, elbowing him in his fine eye, her fingernails under skin, peeling furrows away. Hot blood, she was still kicking when he levered himself off her, bent down, and pulled her to her feet.

She spat the herb-gobbet out, but her throat had gone numb. It reeked of crushed strawberries and mint, and her nightmare had become real.

Shusweed. She struck at him again, but he evaded her fists easily, catching her wrist and pinning her arm behind her back. She opened her mouth, but nothing came out. A gag of the crushed root, very much like mallow, could rob a sidhe of her voice—and leave her helpless.

Crenn nodded at Hilzhunger. "I should like safe passage to the agreed exit, chieftain. Your emissary there will receive the other half of the payment."

The dwarf waved a languid hand, and Robin stared helplessly at him. Crenn dragged her along, his hands cruel now, and she tried to scream, to let the song through. It beat inside her, ineffectual fury thundering in deep spiked minor chords, but it was locked securely in her chest and could not find release.

A LITTLE BIRD TO RESCUE
41

Jeremiah's legs felt odd, disconnected from the rest of him. Forcing his eyes to open took a great deal of concentrated effort, and once they opened, all he could see was red.

Well. This is a new thing. He blinked several times, a shiver pouring down his body as acrid sweat broke out. Salted with mortal metal, but with a smoke-ice edge, the shuddering should have brought him to his feet, the lance springing into being between his palms.

He managed a twitch. Strength returned slowly, his vision cleared, and he stared at a ceiling that was unquestionably dwarven work, glossy blackstone carved with their angular writing, stylized beasts running from tiny hunters. The bloody light slid over them, tricks of vision or chantment spurring them to seeming-movement. A stag, its throat cut, kept running. The hunters fell upon one another with axes and bows, their tiny sharp-carved mouths open wide in soundless screams.

Weird. Like professional wrestling, only in stone.

A scraping sound. His body obeyed him now, and he propped himself up on his elbows. The cot underneath him, though too small, was sturdily built. The other smell—of earth and metal and simmering sidhe sweat—told him, if not the particulars, then at least the general of where he was.

Dwarves. Great. Maybe they owed Robin a favor or two? She'd disappeared through a dwarven-made door not so long ago.

Robin. Where is she? The earth had opened up. One moment Unwinter, the next, falling. The dwarves had intervened. Why?

The sliding scrape became the patter of glove-shod feet, and a familiar shape danced into view. A slim sidhe boy, his irises burning yellowgreen and his pupils hourglass-shaped bowed, his leather jerkin bright as a new penny and not yet supple with use. The points of his ears poked up through a mat of frayed brown silk, and his wide cheery smile gleamed pink instead of white. The light was kind to him, making his cheeks as smooth as a mortal baby's ass, and his grin was full of good cheer that stopped just short before plunging over the brink of homicidal.

"Welladay!" Puck Goodfellow cried, and Jeremiah finished pushing himself upright. "Look who has awakened, and is colt-staggering."

Trundling along in the Fatherless's wake was a sour-faced, beardless dwarf who cut the free sidhe a wide berth on his way to a table loaded with burners, alembics, and piles of odds and ends. Jeremiah swung his legs off the cot.

It was always better to face Goodfellow on one's feet. Or as close to it as one could manage.

"Puck. A pleasure to see you." A lie, but not an insult.

A slight movement behind Puck was the beardless dwarf, who snorted, striding across to the table. He began clinking and rummaging with great officiousness. "Save your love songs. The sooner I'm shed of you both, the better."

"Charming, isn't he?" Puck hopped sideways, a dancing step. "A great healer among the clans. Nothing but the best for you, Gallow."

"I'm honored." *There's bound to be a price for this.*

"Can't stave it off forever." The beardless dwarf stalked to the edge of the cot. He held a bubbling, foul-smelling flagon. "You drink this, and I've got four more doses for you. More I cannot give."

Four doses? "You have my thanks," Jeremiah said cautiously.

"No need. We were paid for your life."

"Oh?" *By whom?*

"Drink." The dwarf shoved the flagon into his hands. "I suggest quickly, too, before it cools, since it's even worse then."

It smelled of manure and tasted like skunked beer and cinders. Jeremiah gagged, sputtered, and managed to get down every dreg. Puck whistled innocently, examining the walls.

The healer took the cup back and handed him a pouch. It clinked, and inside were four crystalline vials holding blue-tinted sludge. "One daily. They'll lose efficacy nearer the end, but better than nothing."

More than I thought I'd get. "I suppose I shouldn't swim for half an hour after taking one."

The healer stared at him, clearly unamused. "I know who you are, *Gallowglass.* Unwinter's poison interests me, or I'd have left you to rot. I had kin among Finnion's clan."

The marks twitched, writhing under Jeremiah's skin. His first education in the hunger of the lance; they had not expected him to survive, and dumped him in a dark room to molder. But he had, and when he woke...well. No love lost between him and any of the stone-shapers. "Then you'll have weregilt soon."

"A colossal waste either way," the healer said with a sniff, and strode for the door. "Best get moving. Some of Hilzhunger's aren't as patient as I."

So it's Hilzhunger who has me. Great. Okay. Where the hell am I going? He glanced at Puck Goodfellow, who looked vastly amused by this entire exchange. Jeremiah coughed, the draught threatening to come back up. The cough turned into a word, the only possible reason the Fatherless could be standing here so far below the free earth. "Robin."

Puck's grin did not alter one whit, but he paused. "Yes, Gallow-my-glass. We have a little bird to rescue."

"What is thy interest in the Ragged, Goodfellow?"

Puck still did not move. His eyes flamed yellowgreen, and the strength flooding back into Jeremiah's body was welcome.

But not enough.

"Oh, the Ragged delights me." Puck turned, skipping. "Such a fine voice."

And you used her to invite Unwinter into Summer. What hold did Puck have on her?

None, now, she'd said. It didn't matter. All that mattered was finding her.

"I might ask you the same," Goodfellow continued, as he strode for the door left ajar by the healer. Glove-shod, and in new leathers. There was something off about him, too. "What do you intend with my little Ragged, Armormaster?"

Your little Ragged? "My lady Ragged has many enemies."

Puck laughed, capering, and pushed the door wider. "Indeed she does, sirrah. Indeed. A hunter has snared her, and who knows what Summer intends? We must hasten."

"Crenn." *Of course. He was off alerting the dwarves, or Summer herself. He's grown canny. Did he predict Robin?*

How could he, when I can't?

"What reward could *she* offer him, do you imagine?" Puck's laugh, merry and raw, bounced off the stone. "He bears you a grudge, I've heard."

"So many do." It was work to keep up with Puck, and Jeremiah began to suspect that were he to fall behind, the Fatherless might not stop. The antidote—or as close to an antidote as a dwarven healer could manage—burned in his limbs. False strength, maybe, but he'd take it.

The scar on his side twitched, but Jeremiah broke into a run, following the brown-haired boy.

WHEN YOU ARE MAD

42

reen hills of Summer lay in the distance under a blue dusk, the stars just beginning to twinkle in indigo. The white paths gleamed, and the orchard was a cloud of fleece, cupped around Summerhome's familiar, beautiful towers. Pennants snapped in the freshening breeze, bringing the spice and velvet of appleblossom scent to every corner of Seelie. Even this one, where worn stone steps rose between juicy green thorn-vines, their tangles starred with small yellow roses bearing only five petals apiece. Pixies glimmered and fluttered among the vines, clouds of pinprick light as they chimed excitedly. Some pointed at Robin, their mouths tiny *O*'s of surprise, showing sharp ivory fangs.

Robin dug her heels in, but Crenn was much stronger. He didn't hurt her, but he did prod her in the ribs a little ungently. Her throat, still numb, tingled a little, and she gagged afresh on the strawberry-mint of shusweed.

The stairs went up, and up, and up. One of the roses snapped shut, a pixie's wings beating frantically inside it, the tiny thing's glow fading while the tight-cupped petals *squeezed*. A formless murmur filled the air, and Robin blinked away furious, scalding tears. *You bastard. You utter bastard.*

She had sometimes contemplated what it would be like, to be robbed of the song's power. To be just as helpless as a mortal girl under her stepfather's belt.

The thought spurred fresh panic, and she almost dove to the side, into the thorns. Better than what probably awaited her at the top of these stairs, no doubt. Or maybe he was just going to toss her from the cliff—for the murmur, growing louder now, was the mouthing of the Dreamless Sea upon the sugar-white Seelie shore. The chalk cliffs rose high, kissed with low cloud on some mornings. If not for the chantment in Robin's heels, the hunter might have had to carry her.

Now *there* was a thought. But if she went limp and made him drag her, he would.

He yanked her back from the edge of the step. "Shhh, pretty girl." Hot breath in her ear. "It will be done soon."

Oh, it certainly will. Hate you. I wish Gallow were here to kill you.

Except Gallow had probably perished of poison by now, even if Hilzhunger's clan had a healer skilled enough to stave off some of the effects. They had no love for him, and it would suit them to hand his corpse over to Unwinter and perhaps claim a rich reward.

She kicked at Crenn; he avoided the strike, and she spat a mouthful of shusweed juice at him. It flung wide, spattering the vines, and they writhed with dissatisfaction.

"*Stop* it." Crenn grabbed her arms, shook her so her head bobbled. She tried to knee him; he spun her, his arm a bar across her throat. "*Listen* to me, pretty. She cannot kill you, Gallow saw to that. Endure."

Fine thing for you to say. She longed to open her mouth and let the song free. She could produce nothing more than a formless croak.

Helpless. Again.

"You'll have help," he whispered, those lips pressing against her ear. His breath was sidhe-warm, sweet with drugging certainty. "I paid them for Gallow's life and to spare; now *you'll* have help, too."

He is already dead, and you are a liar twice and thrice over.

"*Listen.* I'll only say this once." His arm tightened. She had rarely been so close to a man before. Hard muscle, the woodsmoke of a sidhe's fury, an indefinable tang of lemon and *male*, along with a fresh green edge that was probably swampwater and moss. "He comes too late, or not at all, does the Gallowglass. I speak from experience. He's not worth you, pretty girl." A pause, she tried to kick him again, clawing at his arm with broken fingernails. He exhaled sharply, and she wondered if he was going to do what men always did when a woman was helpless. "You have more friends than you know," he finished. "Remember that, and endure."

He half-carried her up the next few steps, then twisted her arm behind her back, his fingers gripping just short of bruising.

Oh, fine friends indeed. None of them will aid me. That was the most important lesson she'd ever learned, in the sideways realms or the mortal.

When it counted, you were always alone.

She kept pitching from side to side, seeking escape. He was so damnably *strong*, and he hadn't lost hold of her once.

The last step came as a surprise. She pivoted, seeking to throw him back down the long chain of stone edges, but he gave one of his bitter little laughs and pushed, neatly throwing her off-balance instead. Dusk had deepened while they climbed, and a salt wind tugged at Robin's curls, fingered her velvet coat, and stung her eyes.

He means to throw me from the cliff. Her entire body turned cold. But there was no cliff. The vines tangled over a rough stone wall barring the Dreaming Sea from view, and she looked up.

And up, and up. A tower rose from this thorn-grown courtyard. White, but it didn't glimmer like Summerhome. Instead, it was matte, except at the very top where a hurtful glitter gave one piercing flash. No doubt that high spire caught the last gleam of Seelie's sun.

Or something else.

Robin's mouth turned dry.

There, at the foot of the steps leading to the tower's single narrow, graceful entrance, stood Summer.

Just as lovely as ever, her long golden hair in rippling waves, her mantle deepest pine, its long sleeves brushing the ground. The Jewel at her forehead was dull, a foxfire glow instead of a beacon, and her face was one of the sharper ones, cheekbones like blades and her scarlet mouth lush-cruel. A crimson scarf was knotted about her right wrist, floating and flowing as the wind tugged at it, and over her head pixies flittered in complicated patterns, drawn by the faint glow ribboning upward just as fireflies would be, down in the shadowed dells.

The first feeling was shock. *She's changed.*

But how? She was ageless, eternal, so all the songs said. The change was difficult to pin down, too. Robin had no time to think, observe, and suss it out, because Summer spoke.

"Robin," the Queen of Seelie murmured. "Robin, Robin, Robin."

Shudders seized Robin Ragged, racked through her, and Crenn grabbed her arm to keep her upright. Summer's eyes, black from lid to lid, held few sparkles now. They danced where the very center of the pupils should be, and if you drew close, breathing in her drugging breath, you could watch those lights forever—and not feel a single thing as the flint blade pierced your chest.

The changelings rarely struggled. When one did, Summer gazed upon it exactly like this, and it stilled soon enough. Even those closed in wicker towers and set alight with elf-fire did not scream, for she stared into each one's face for a long moment before they were led, small and docile, to the oven. Little gingerbread dolls, ready to be consumed for her glory, to keep Seelie just sideways enough and safely away from the deeper folds of the Veil.

At least Pepperbuckle is out of her reach. Robin sagged in Crenn's grip.

"My little Ragged. How you wound me." The Queen sighed. "I longed to see your face, but you were gone."

You bitch. You killed Sean.

Except she could not lay that death fully on Summer's threshold. It had been Robin who thought *just one more day, just one more day,* keeping him because she could not bear... and now, Sean was dead, his parents were dead. Everyone was dead.

Except Robin. And this sidhe bitch who ruled everything she looked upon.

"I brought her." After the soft music of Summer's tones, Crenn's words were harsh. Robin lunged, almost broke free of his hold—but he dragged her back. "Without a scratch, though that took some doing. Unwinter wants her, too."

"He may not have her." The Queen smiled, her pearly teeth peeping past those carmine lips. "Not until I am finished, and I am not yet."

Crenn nodded. "You promised her life to Gallow, I'm told."

"Rumor again, huntsman?" Her smile widened. "Her life I did pledge, at the spring revel, no less. I do not intend to deprive her of one moment of it."

"Then what do you aim to do?"

Now her gaze turned to Crenn. "Nothing that concerns you."

"I haven't been paid yet." He shook Robin, but halfheartedly. She sagged, her fury turned to ashes now. What was the point?

What was the point of *anything*?

At least she'd avenged Sean, and Daisy. And Pepperbuckle was safe.

At least that.

"You think me false? Come." Summer indicated the tower's narrow, arched mouth. "Just a few more steps, and you'll have delivered. Then you'll be beautiful again, Alastair Crenn. You've done what no other knight of Summer could do."

He made no reply. Just stood there, holding her arm.

She tried to yank away. Velvet tore. She shoved him, and his hand fell free.

"Nothing to say, Robin? No song to sing?" The Queen shook her head. "I expected more. Ah, I see. Shusweed." Summer sighed. "Well, Crenn. Bring her hither."

Robin hopped away from him, her heels clicking. She lifted her chin, glaring at him, *willing* him to . . . what?

Gallow would not do this. She swiped at her mussed hair, settled her torn coat. *He is dead now, and there is no hope. But I won't scream and struggle. She'll like that too much.*

Robin Ragged lifted her chin, stalked for the tower.

The Queen smiled, a benevolent, pacific expression. Robin drew abreast of her, glanced back at Crenn. Hoped he could read the disdain on her features. *You bastard. You're ugly* within, *and that's where it counts. No amount of glamour will ever make you half as fine as Jeremiah Gallow, even if he's a cursed male.*

When she turned back, Summer still smiled. "Tell me," she murmured, "what do you see when you look into a mirror, you little Half slut?"

Robin's mouth was dry, and the shusweed numbness still sank its claws into her throat. Still, she had a gobbet of dry phlegm.

She hawked, just as the boys in the trailer parks did, and spat directly at Summer. *I wish I were plagued. Then maybe you'd take it, and sicken and die, you whorebag.*

For the first time, the Queen of Seelie actually looked *shocked.* Her eyes swelled, her mouth dropped open, and Robin might have enjoyed that if she hadn't already been moving. She flung herself up the three low stairs and plunged through the entryway.

Whatever Summer had in store, at least it was Robin's own choice to face it, now.

WHAT I HAVE WROUGHT
43

The redheaded girl spat at the Queen of Seelie, launched herself…and vanished into the high-arched, narrow black mouth of the tower. Its dull sides brightened slightly, and Crenn stared.

Why did she do that?

The tower shuddered, and the aperture slammed itself shut. Smooth and seamless-white, it rose, and the glitter at its top turned blood-red.

Summer's face twisted. Even enraged, she was beautiful, but Crenn took a step back. That paleness, slim and enticing, was clotted cream, and his gorge rose for a brief pointless moment. No man could look at Summer and stay unmoved, true. Maybe it was just that he'd spent so long without any female attention at all—his entire body tightened, the swelling where a man felt everything first before the brain kicked in eating at his belly.

Summer laughed, her face smoothing into a young girl's, altering seamlessly. A warm wind rose, mouthing the tower's rough bisque.

"Silly girl." The Seelie Queen glided away from the steps. Her step was light as a leaf, and the appleblossom reek on the wind intensified as she drifted closer. "And you, huntsman. Questioning me."

She's here alone. Without guards. He was armed, too. The thought vanished in a red flash, but she probably heard it anyway.

"Still, I promised you." Ever closer, a playful breeze, but his sensitive hunter's nose caught a whiff of something foul. *What is that? And why is she glamouring so hard?*

She was very close now. Close enough to dizzy a man. The blossom-scent filled his nose, made his eyes water.

"You did well," she whispered. Her breath touched his hair— when had he closed his eyes? The tower was still glowing behind his eyelids. What was in there?

The Ragged, sleeping, her face pale and peaceful. Her fierce loyalty. *He saved my life,* she'd said, her expression softening ever so little. Facing down Unwinter himself, and spitting in Summer's face to boot. A woman like that could make a man immortal, or so close he couldn't tell the difference.

A woman like that was worth...

It was deathly silent except for the Dreaming Sea's endless song. Sweat greased him, and he was suddenly aware that his breeches were too tight, he smelled of the salt of mortal sweat and Marrowdowne fens as well as exhaust and cold iron. There was a rotting reek wafting from Summer's robe, and he stepped back before he could help it, his bootheel catching a stray thorn-vine and grinding, sharply. Crushed, it oozed heavy, sticky sap, and the vines shifted against one another with creaking, cracking groans.

Summer stood very still. "Afraid of a woman? And I was told you were *brave.*"

"I did what you asked." What was that smell? He'd never

come across its like in Seelie before, not even in the deepest, greenest bits of Marrowdowne where the bones of giant beasts submerged in the peat bogs and the spongy masses could drag even a kelpie or a lightfoot pondrunner down in moments.

They were ancient, the choke-thick hummocks of moss-hung Marrowdowne, and *hungry*.

"I did not *ask*, Alastair Crenn." A glacial cold in Summer's tone, now. One soft white hand reached out, touched his shoulder, then bit, cruelly. Her nails were claws now, sliding through his shirt and jerkin, pricking at skin underneath. "I am *Summer*."

Crenn screamed. Fire roared through him, as if the pitch had been set alight again. He fell, tangling in the thornvines, which hissed and blackened as Summer crooned in the Old Language. Chantment ran spiked rowels under his skin, and he thrashed among the hissing, cringing vines. Thorns striped him, only pinpricking their warnings; Summer laughed, a tiger's low, coughing growl, and they were blasted away from his struggling form, curling and shriveling.

She took her time, grinding the pain in. When she finally released him, her laughter was just as chill, and just as merry as ever. She surveyed his supine form with gleaming black eyes.

"Come to Court soon, Crenn; for I shall wish to see what I will have wrought."

He lay, panting and wrung-wet with sweat, and listened to her soft footsteps recede. She was singing, in a lovely lilting nymph's voice. It was part of Belgasson's Lay, when his lover Andariel was shut in a blackstone tower at the edge of Unwinter, and died of longing before he could return from the last of the Sundering Wars to free her.

"Oh beauty's pain, and pain is pain, and nothing else will do;

For all the world's a trap, my love, without the thought of you…"
A jingle, a jangle, and Summer was gone, taking the hideous scent under her appleblossom perfume with her.

God. He twitched, weak as a kitten. The vines cringed, tasting her displeasure.

It took two tries for Crenn to get to hands and knees. The scars burned, but when he scrubbed at his face with dirty hands, he felt only smooth skin. His shoulders were no longer ridged with thickened tissue, and he felt under his shirt. No trace of the horrific burning remained, and the pain was already receding.

He retched, dry, coughing heaves turning him inside out. Crawled across blackened stone, his skin moving fluidly, sweetly, the hitching of scarring gone. His nose was no longer a ruin and his cheeks were soft again, though he could feel a stubble-rasp he'd forgotten.

The burns had not grown hair.

Three steps before the tower. They were cold; he snatched his hands back, pushed himself upright. His knees threatened to give. He felt the chillscorch through his boots as he stepped thrice up, nervously.

The tower swayed, gently. Deathly silent, except for the billowing of the Dreaming Sea.

He spread his hands against the stone. It throbbed a little, uneasily, as if the entire edifice was a harpstring plucked by the salt wind.

The door's vanished. God. Jesus Christ, God forgive me. What have I done?

HOME TO VISIT

44

S tairs. She climbed, and climbed, occasionally passing slits in the tower's wall, just wide enough to peer out and take a sip of fresh air. All in all, it was dank, and cobwebbed, and slightly musty, but not so bad.

A Half in Summer wouldn't starve. She might grow attenuated, true, and solitary confinement could waste one away. It was, Robin thought, hacking and spitting again, nice to have nobody to worry about. No need to guard her expression, or keep her thoughts hidden. She'd never lived alone—first there was Mama, and then Daddy Snowe and Daisy, and then Court. Summerhome was always bustling, and the rhythm of Court life didn't permit much solitude.

This might not be so bad. Unless the whole thing was stairs. She was heartily tired of stairs. What else was there to do but go up?

Once the shusweed wore off, she could use her voice. There was little the song couldn't destroy. Summer had to have known that and accounted for as much, so Robin would have to be careful. She would have to—

The end came as a surprise. The last stair gave onto a small antechamber, and there was a wooden door, just slightly open. Rich golden light outlined it, made a wedge on the dusty floor. Possibly electric—but it couldn't be; this was *Summer*.

Whatever's in there is likely to be nasty.

It startled her into a harsh wheeze that might have been a laugh if she hadn't been numbed by shusweed. Nothing mattered in the slightest anymore. Everything Robin made the mistake of caring for withered. She was poison, and at least here in the tower she couldn't harm anyone else.

Summer had probably done her a favor.

Another wheeze. Robin wiped at her cheeks, surprised to find she was not weeping. Even the anger was gone, cold ashes.

She approached the door, cautiously, step by step. Her calves burned, though her shoes were just as light as ever. *If I never see another stair again, it'll be too soon.* She peered around it, squinting against the brightness.

A small round room, prosaic and wood-floored. There was a fire burning in a granite hearth, and the light was multiplied by the shining walls. Small chips of glass, perhaps? The dancing flames illuminated those sparkling tiles, and Robin stepped forward, dimly aware the door was swinging open on its own. Everything behind her receded, and when she glanced back, the stairs and the platform were gone. Instead, a solid sheet of mirror watched her, water-clear, showing a Robin repeated into infinity.

Bedraggled in torn black velvet, her hair tangle-tumbled and her cheeks chapped, her mouth half ajar as if she were moontouched or halfwit, her pupils pinpricks and...

Oh God. God. No.

Behind her, a misty shape. It solidified, and Robin stared. *It's not possible. Not possible. Just glamour. It's not real.*

It was a redheaded woman older than Robin's apparent age,

her features a softer, blurred copy of Robin's own. She wore sensible shoes, a neatly hemmed blue dress, and she was covered with bright mortal blood. Tiny stars of safety glass winked in her hair, longer than Robin's and with less curl. Some of her teeth had been knocked out.

Of course, Daisy had died in a car accident. Puck had pixie-led her car, and . . .

"Robin," the Daisy-phantom said, lisping a little as her tongue brushed against where teeth should be with soft sliding noises. *"It's so good to see you."*

More gossamer shapes began to solidify. Robin backed up, frantic, her hands stretched behind her, searching for the surface of the mirror, to put her back against it. The gleaming tiles had grown together seamlessly; there was no corner to retreat to.

Nothing, just cool air, no matter how quickly she moved. Her own horrified expression, repeated over and over, and there was Mama wasted away by the cancer, leaning on an IV pole, her stentorious machine-assisted breathing a death-knight's bellows. A young golden-blond boy, his skin studded and scarred with amber slivers, reaching toward her with fingers that dropped heavy, resinous, tinkling shards. *"Robin-mama!"* he piped. *"You've come back!"*

She could only make harsh cawing sounds. The shusweed was wearing off, but too slowly.

A darker shadow loomed behind her. She whirled, and the short mortal man with slicked-back gingery hair smiled, a looped leather belt cracking as he jerked his fists apart. *"Now look at this,"* he said, and it was Daddy Snowe's sneering, booming voice, so deep for such a little man. He wore his workboots, and they clopped on the faded linoleum as he stalked toward her. *"Look who's come home to visit."*

239

Robin blundered away. The screams stopped in her throat, her heart racing; she tripped and fell headlong. It was the floor of the trailer in Seneida again, staring at the gleaming lino under the dinette table as Daddy Snowe's boots thudded behind her. She'd washed every inch of the floor, but he always found a streak, and when he did—

"*Home at last,*" they chorused, and little tinkling bits of amber and glass fell as Daisy and Sean crowded close. "*You're back, Robin. Back where you belong.*"

Daddy Snowe's belt cracked again, leather snapping against itself.

HUNGER FORGOTTEN

45

※

There was the fire-ground, where he could not walk for long, and she told him to leave her. Hunt and hide, she said, and her word was law . . . but still, he lingered. It was not right. He smelled danger, and treachery, and could not express it. The sun sank, and he slunk about the edges of the fire-ground.

Then they came, dangerous ones he had fought off before, reeking of spice-ice and cinders, with their hounds very like him but so cold, so cold. The ground shook, and Pepperbuckle curled into a holly-bush against the stone wall, trembling, his flanks dark with sweat. Her last despairing cry tore through him, and an invisible cord stretched almost to the snapping point.

When the moon rose he burst from the holly, its leaves combing his fine coat, and pierced a fine gossamer Veil. Instinct turned him topsy-turvy; he spilled into a balmy evening full of dangerous, delightful scents. Nose to the ground, the hound ran, coursing along Summer's green hills, following a maddening, faint, flaring trail—for his mistress-mother was elsewhere, in a realm he could not enter, though he could step through the gossamer into others lying just a few degrees off, fanned atop one another, rubbing through and echoing, shifting in dreamy succession. The darker ones, with their cinders and bone-white flashes, the crimson touches, he stayed well away from—but if she had gone there, he would follow.

A long time passed as he ran, hoping to catch a scent, following that tenuous cord. Through sunshine and dusk, time shifting as the sideways realms did, stepping through mortal shadows to avoid larger beasts that might slow him, resting often under bushes or tucked in safe, dozy hollows...

Suddenly, the cord-chord was plucked. It resounded all through him, and Pepperbuckle halted, head upflung, lips skinning back from sharp ivory teeth, damp nose lifted and flaring, his fine tail—dragging for quite some time now—perking, then twitching, then wagging furiously.

He turned, needle-north, and the wind that reached him smelled of salt and stone, and a faint breath of her.

The hound danced for joy, his padded feet kicking up fragrant dry leaves. He set off, any shadow of weariness or hunger forgotten. In the distance a spur of stone rose from the cliffs, glowing dull-white except for the top, where a diamond of bloody light bloomed.

Pepperbuckle ran.

SCORN

46

Stepping over the border into a Summer afternoon was a hideous jolt, and the scar along his side burned. Jeremiah had to halt to breathe, but Puck did not leave him behind. Instead, the boy-sidhe crouched, his ear-tips perked through the frayed silken mat of brown hair, his leathers creaking just a little too much. This shaded dell, tucked some distance away from one of the bone-white paths, was ringed by fragrant, secretive-whispering cedars.

Puck drove his slim brown fingers into the loam, muttering a word or two of chantment. He whistled, and pixies appeared, their tiny flittering glows bleached by daylight. Jeremiah's breath came back, the dwarven draught burning like a coal in his stomach. He leaned against one of the cedars, glad a dryad wasn't peering out of the bark. The entire sisterhood of this ring were probably out a-marketing—cedar-nymphs were naturally gregarious, fragrant beings.

The pixies chimed around Puck, excited little voices babbling in a mix of languages. They picked words up everywhere and forgot them just as quickly, interlacing them with chantment-tongue. The Fatherless simply listened, head cocked, clutching the soft, forgiving loam.

Finally, he straightened. "Come, Glass-gallow." He brushed his hands together, as if ridding them of stain, and the pixies scattered, winking out or hiding under cedar boughs. "We have an appointment to keep."

"With Robin?" Something was different, but fogged by poison and exhaustion he couldn't quite put his finger on it. What he wouldn't give to be at home in his trailer, curled up in bed, hopefully with a sleeping warmth beside him—Robin in his arms, and her quiet breathing mixing with his.

That would be nice, wouldn't it? Pay attention, Jeremiah.

"Why do you inquire so, Glass-my-gallow?"

Because we're in Summer, and it looks like you're receiving word from little pixie spies. He shrugged, but whatever he would have said was lost under the merry clopping of bell-chiming hooves.

Jeremiah peered out through the cedars. Beside him, Goodfellow crowded, smelling of leather, crushed sap—and old dried blood. Had he been wounded recently?

Something's off with him. Have to think about it.

Summer knights, four of them, gathered around a palanquin roped between two bridge-trolls, one of the few Unseelie clans that could stand direct sunlight. Still, the trolls looked miserable, and their silvery chain-collars steamed.

The palanquin itself, of black wood and silver chasings, bore fluttering pennons on high, flexible rods. A stylized fist, silver-embroidered on black silk, grasped fruitlessly at the breeze.

Gallow let out a soft breath. "An envoy." From Unwinter, no less.

"Seeking parlay, no doubt. He keeps thinking she will listen to reason." Puck's giggle was just as high and carefree as

Summer's ever was. "I could tell him differently, but would he credit it?"

"Summer has the Ragged," Jeremiah guessed. His head was clearing, but not nearly quickly enough.

"She does indeed." A snarl drifted across Puck's face. It wasn't like the Fatherless to take such an interest in a *female*, let alone a female sidhe. He'd extended himself mightily for Robin, and forced her into breaking Summer's borders to boot.

It changed the game somewhat, to think he would have to balance the Fatherless against Unwinter and Summer both. The very idea made Gallow even more tired. Four vials, not even a week's worth of leeway before he'd be right back where he started, hallucinating all his failures and dying of fever. "Then let's go."

"Rushing blindly in, Armormaster?"

"If you've a better idea, Goodfellow, I will bide to hear it."

"No, indeed. Let us begone, then."

Summerhome throbbed with gaiety. Nymphs trip-skipped through the halls, brughnies scurrying behind them to gather up dropped ribbons and pearl-drops of crystallized salt or dew-pearl. No fullblood highborn ladies, though—at this hour, they would be retired to soft shaded bowers, dressing for the evening's merriment. More brughnies monkeyed on the walls, shaking the dust out of tapestries, coaxing fresh green woodbine into twining under the sconces. The kitchens would be a steaming inferno by now, no doubt Summer would feast the envoy royally.

Still, it wasn't the same. There was an edge to the laughter, and the knights on guard duty did not so much as smile at the sidhe girls and their fluttering draperies. No cloud-dog gebriels cavorted over Summerhome's towers, and the torch-lighting hobs did not jest or sing. Music did roil and runnel through the halls, but it was not the joyous drumbeat that could force a mortal heart to match its pace. Instead, skirling pipes throbbed on the edge of dissonance, seeking to sound happy, perhaps, but without any true joy. The knights on duty did not smile at *all*, in fact, their mouths cruel lines under full helm and armor.

None glanced at Jeremiah *or* Puck, which was even odder. They were not challenged, which led to a very unpleasant conclusion: Puck, at least, was expected.

I have four vials. Four days of grace. Not enough.

Instead of striking for the great hall, where any revel would be held, Puck turned to the far edge of the rotunda, and the Red Door opened like a flower.

The chamber beyond, reserved for weightier affairs than dances and fetes, was robed with Summer's green, from fir to sage, holly to sedge. Brambles grew up the walls, tangling over the sconces; fireflies and small floating bits of chantment-glittering thistledown filled the hall with soft light. Unwinter's parlay—a tall, severe-faced highborn fullblood in black, with the clenched-fist sigil patterned over his cloak and his ebony armor flowing with him—had just dropped to one knee before Summer and was rising.

She stood, in a heavy green mantle, straight and proud. Thornvines crawled up the robe's back, forming a high frame above her golden head and a torc around her white, white throat. Bright veins of pale gold moved fluidly along the vine-cables, winking into gemlike brilliance at the points. Dwarven work, metal married to wood, and her hair was looped and coaxed through the vines, the whole fantastical architecture twinkling with pixieglow and fireflies drunk on the chantment she exuded.

Summer knights ranged along either side of the chamber, and on the second step of the dais, just where the Armormaster would stand, Broghan Trollsbane met Gallow's gaze. Black of eye and hair, his veins a faint blue map under flour-pale skin, he wore the glass badge on his breast, and Jeremiah could have laughed. Broghan, as Armormaster? He was dangerous, certainly, but only if you were clumsy.

Which I am now. Arrogant to think he was anything near his prime.

Still, the lance could be cold iron. That gave him an edge against any fullborn.

The Queen of Seelie's smile widened. A cloying of spice and burnt-leaf smoke rode heavy between the pillars marching down the chamber, each one twined with brambles. Harvest-incense, far too soon in the season for it, but who would tell *her* that?

The Jewel at her forehead flashed once, settled back into a low dull-green glow. "Fatherless." Summer's tone, dulcet honey, pulled on every nerve-string. The knights ranged along the pillars tensed, Broghan the Black almost swayed, and the envoy, his long, aquiline face with its gloss of sidhe beauty turning into a mask of disdain as his elegant, gloved, six-fingered hand twitched for a gem-chased swordhilt. The violet tree-ring dapples of lightshielding chantment on every inch of visible skin turned a darker shade, perhaps because the Unwinter knight recognized him.

"*Gallow,*" he said, the consonants sharp as knives. "He is ours."

Summer's laugh, low velvet, stroked along the floor, curled around each man. "Cease your yapping, Unwinter hound."

"I have brought him." Puck folded his arms. "I went to no little trouble to do so, oh Seelie's jewel."

"What is *trouble*, to one such as you? You shall find your maiden in a white tower, enjoying the finest of hospitality." Summer clasped her own white, six-fingered hands, their tenderness threaded in veins of that same pale gold. It was an oddly bleached metal, and Gallow realized why.

She was wearing melted barrow-wight gold, and Unwinter's parlay would no doubt note it as well.

Puck bowed slightly and grinned. "Then I take my leave."

He's going after Robin. Gallow turned to follow, but the hiss of metal drawn from scabbard halted them both. The marks stung his arms, writhing, and he glanced back to find Unwinter's envoy had drawn. So had Broghan the Black, and the two faced each other while Summer's entire face lit with predatory glee.

"Why, what is this?" she said, very softly. "Do you offer me violence in my own hall, Cailas Redthorn? Yes, I remember you of old. You were a merry lord, once, and fell when the mood struck you."

"You harbor one who is under the hunt, Eakkanthe of Summer." The Unseelie knight let out a chill, disdainful little laugh as a gasp went through the assembly. To use Summer's name so was something only a fullblood highborn would dare. "Your treachery threatens to extinguish all of Danu's children, and I am come to treat with Gallow, not with you."

"To treat with..." Her eyes narrowed, and Jeremiah backed up a step, two, as Puck stepped aside, perhaps recognizing that something deadly was about to occur. "To *treat* with *him*? I am Summer!" The gold-clasped vines shifted, slithering against her mantle, and she took a single step toward the edge of the dais.

"You are weakened," the Unseelie pointed out. "And *he*, lady of Seelie, is who my lord sent me to pass words with, and demand a price from."

Okay, Jeremiah. Think fast. Time to throw a pair of bone dice, and see where their rattle landed. "He wants the Horn." He smoked with sickness and mortal sweat, dirt, ditchwater, and even his armor could not hide the tremor in his hands. He drew the medallion from beneath his chestplate, pushing aside Robin's locket to do so.

The Horn's round othershape glinted, a cold breath exhaling through the room, and several Seelie knights took a step back, recognizing what it was under its seeming. He dropped it back against his chest, patted his armor over the thing's chill-burn, denying the lance its freedom with a gutclenching effort.

Heavy silence greeted the revelation. The Unseelie's blade was crystalline silver—a glassmaster, then. Quick, and deadly. He would be dangerous even if Jeremiah were well-rested and healthy. Gallow took a deep breath. "What is he prepared to offer, Cailas Redthorn?"

"The..." Summer's face lit with predatory glee. "Oh, my Gallow, best of Armormasters, you never disappoint."

Broghan's face filled with thunder. "My Queen—"

"Hush." She floated down a dais step, curled her pale hand about his shoulder. "Come to me, Jeremiah. Bring me your gift."

She thinks I'm bringing it to her? Of course, to Summer, they were all satellites of her sun. It wouldn't occur to her greedy little self that her former Armormaster might have other plans.

He didn't look at the Seelie queen. Now was the moment, and the lance resolved in his hands, a solid bar of moonlight lengthening. The blade flattened, its slightly curved inner edge growing wicked serrations. Metal dulled, and the air of Summer scorched around cold iron. "A gift, Summer? You promised me the Ragged." *Or her life.*

"She still draws breath." Silky, evenly spaced. "What is she to you, when you may be my lord? Come, bring me that trinket."

Loathing filled him to the brim. Did he just have to be poisoned, and inoculated by Daisy's death, to feel no skincrawling sting of desire for the Seelie queen? "What does Unwinter offer?"

Cailas Redthorn's lips skinned back from his teeth. "Foolish Half," he said, very softly. "Do you think you may stand against a Prince of the Blood?"

Fuck this noise. Jeremiah *moved.* The lance pulled at him, filling his veins with sick sweet heat, and the knights of Summer drew as one as if they thought he would attack *her.*

A crystalline scream, a shattering, and a thump. Puck vanished, his spurt of laughter unheard in the sudden noise.

The Unseelie envoy's head hit the tessellated floor. A bright jet of vivid pale ichor fountained from his neck, and his body slumped, twisting inward on itself as the ironblight took hold.

"*Hold!*" Summer cried, and they stilled.

Jeremiah's sides heaved. He finished the movement, the lance's butt smacking the ground at parade rest, and he raised his aching head.

"Fool," Broghan muttered. "You killed an *envoy,* one granted Summer's hospitality. You traitorous, wretched Half dog."

"Shhh." The Queen's fingers tensed, digging in, and though Broghan's face didn't change expression, gems of clear sweat sprang out on his pale brow. Pixies would gather them, if they shook loose. "Gallow, my Gallow, bring me that Horn. When it is placed in my hands, forgiveness shall be yours."

He wet his lips with his dry-leaf tongue and smiled.

"I thought you were beautiful, once." *I sound amazingly steady.* "Then I saw Robin Ragged and knew you were only dust. I was not always Summer, and I *do not serve.*"

It was worth it, he decided, to see the open shock crossing that soft, cruel, beautiful face.

"You scorn me?" Whispering, as if she could not believe it.

"I scorn you," he said, clearly and loud, "for a Half girl truer than cold iron itself, who makes you look the faithless hag you are."

She inhaled, but he was already moving. The doors shattered as he burst through them.

Her scream shook the entirety of Summerhome, from cellar to roof.

"Kill him!"

HOW I DIE

47

It was worse with her eyes closed. It made their voices louder, clearer, and the other sounds, too. The grinding of Daisy's broken teeth. The machine breathing for Mama, in stentorious gasps and heaves. The tinkling of tiny amber shards falling from Sean's naked, lacerated body. Worst of all, Daddy Snowe's footsteps, and the monotonous, terrible cracking of the leather belt.

Robin blundered away, still searching for a wall, any surface she could put her back to. Daddy Snowe kept coming, a slow even tread, not hurrying but nearer and nearer no matter how quickly she moved. *"Whoooo-eeee!"* he yelled. *"Look at me when I'm talkin' to you, girl!"*

She'd stopped making those harsh cawing noises. There was no point. She hawked again; bright blood tinged each wad of phlegm and spit. Had she broken her voice trying to scream? Would the song still work if she had? She only had to open her throat and it would come out, as long as there was breath to fuel it... but she might well tear something and be left mute, or—

"Gotcha!" His hand, cold-fish wet and limp, brushed across

her shoulder, and Robin caw-cried again despite herself. *It's not real, it's not real, it's simply glamour.* She coughed, more blood-flecked spittle flying. Even glamour could kill, if you believed strongly enough. Summer wouldn't lock her in here if the mirrors were full of bannock, ale, and comfortable chairs. *They're all dead. They can't be real.*

And yet. *Mirrors*, those magical things. Every time she found a solid surface and tried to brace herself, it chipped, fracturing, and the reflections became yet more Daisys, yet more Daddy Snowes, all lumbering after her, Mama too slow but her copies the worst because they made that *noise*, the machine she hauled along so she could breathe filling the white-glare room with heavy, hot, rank, foul exhalations.

His soft, persuasive touch again, familiar work-roughened fingers skating down her shoulder. Robin struck out, wildly, her fist hitting his face, snapping his head back. He roared, the old sound of an enraged beast, and she was helpless. Could not even summon a word of chantment, *nothing.* She was no warrior, like Gallow—

A silvery cracking sound. Another shape, broad-shouldered, a gleam of green eyes. The armor, now rent and tattered, his side smoking and dripping bloody pus, the rot exhaling from him. It was Gallow, and she choked.

Not him. Oh God, not him too.

She'd tried to save him. But she was Robin Ragged, and she blighted all she touched, and—

Another shattering crack. Sweet silver and amber tinkling. Her wrist hit something hard and cold; she sucked in a copper-tinged breath and spun.

There. A quivering in midair, a rippling where none should be. She'd finally found a wall.

"*Robiiiiiin,*" Gallow croak-hissed. "*You let me die, Robiiiiiin…*"

She choked. Her throat relaxed. It could cripple her forever, if she let the song loose now.

Robin didn't care. It burst out of her, a wall of golden sound, something tearing wetly in her chest. They clustered around her, the shades of her failures, and right before she threw herself after the song's trailing noise, they screamed, too. Darkness burst around her, the velvet flower of Summer's night, crackling, cascading slivers of stone and glass melting into black curse-birds coasting around her, pecking, their claws dyed bright scarlet. She ran off the edge of the tower's floor, through the hole in the wall, and fell through salt-scouring wind. Tumbling over and over, the sliver-curses puffing into flame, the song dying as she ran out of breath to fuel it. Then there was only the roar of the sea, and she had time to think, *So this is how I die...*

...just before she hit the warm, unforgiving surface of the Dreaming Sea.

NIGHTMARISH GOODWILL
48

He arrived just as the bloody-winking light at the top of the tower turned to pale flame and winked out. From Summerhome, it would be the death of a horizon-riding star, if anyone was watching.

Goodfellow would have wagered, though, that nobody would bother. Not even Summer, her lily-white hands full of other matters and the Jewel on her forehead dangerously dark. Did she guess that some corners of her realm had escaped paleness and fraying because of another influence upon their fabric? What else might the sidhe girl who had taken up First Summer's lovely Jewel have suspicions of?

Could the Tower have consumed the Ragged so quickly? It would be the first disappointment she had given her sire, were that the case.

The courtyard before the tower was sadly neglected, covered with thornvines. Some were blasted, shivering and whispering of the distaste that had blighted them, and Puck clicked his tongue once, shaking his nut-brown head. Such a temper she had, not like First Summer. Pale and deadly patient *that* lady had been, Danu's first-chosen one, until she was betrayed.

And why was he thinking so much upon the past?

Puck sniffed, nostrils widening, and untangled the threads of scent. One in particular—sugared cherries, with a streak of mortal salt and the fabulous, indefinable fragrance-thread of *her*, his own flesh, wayward and rambling—pleased him. She had caused him no little trouble and inconvenience, true—but before that, she had delighted him as few others could, and proven herself the best of daughters. All in all, it was a balance.

And wasn't that so very sidhe of her?

"Oh, my darling," he whispered, "what fine times we shall have, when—"

The sound of breaking interrupted him. The courtyard heaved, and he skipped from stone to stone, avoiding the thrashing of the thornvines. Thick tentacles of spike-laden, juicy green crawled hungrily up the rough bisque sides, and the entire tower shuddered on its foundations.

Cracks racing from the top met the climbing thornvines. Stone-dust puffed out, and the sound was of giant glass plates shattering, over and over. Puck had to hop lively, skipping from foot to foot, to avoid being crushed by masonry grinding itself to finer and finer particles as it slammed the courtyard's face.

His laughter rang amid the crunching and shattering, a noise of nightmarish goodwill. He danced amid the destruction, and when it ended, the Tower was a stump of white rubble, blackened at the top.

There was only one explanation. Its prey had escaped, and wreaked some damage upon it by doing so.

Puck, his sides heaving with deep breaths, laughed fit to die. He clutched his middle and keened, his merriment further blackening questing thorn-tendrils when they drew too close. When the noise finally died, he bowed, sweeping the thick-dusted floor of the courtyard with an imaginary hat, even adding the small flick at the end of the movement that was in fashion among Summer's Court at the present moment.

The bird had flown. If she survived the fall and the Dreaming Sea's cruel, cold, numbing arms, he could collect her later. She had not disappointed, indeed, and now his attention was needed elsewhere.

He straightened, yellowgreen irises flaring with mad joyful light, and stepped...sideways. The Veil closed about him, leaving only the scorch of his eyes on the dust-choked air. It was perhaps a good thing, for as that tear in Summer folded up around itself, there was a faint cough from the wall at the tower's landward side.

Had Puck seen Alastair Crenn's haggard, moss-draped head, his dark eyes gleaming like coals through the damp strands, he might have thought to slay the sidhe who had seen him arrive too late for one of his purposes. Or perhaps not.

Either way, Crenn slid down the other side of the wall and began working along it, pushing his way through the hungry vines.

Sooner or later, he would reach the cliff's edge.

THE GALLOW WHO DID IT
49

Unwinter's Keep turned its back to cliffs falling into the Dreaming Sea. A spine of sharp black mountains marched away from Sea and Keep both, their jagged tops fuming white ash, from dwarven furnace, wyrm-breath, or simply because under the cold exterior stone lay a crimson-hot rage too huge to be fully buried. It was whispered that only Unwinter's will kept his domain—the mountains to the Black Counties, the Dreaming Sea to the Ash Plain and the thorny tangle of the Dak'r Woods—from sliding through the Second Veil into dissolution. The blackstone spires of his Keep flew crimson pennons, and no ash ever dulled its glossy sides.

The palanquin had returned, the bridge-trolls shivering and sweating as they bore its cargo. Inside its velvet-swathed dimness was a paper box, gaily wrapped with silver foil. Carried to the throneroom by two pale, noseless barrow-wights, it was set before the dais. The Throne, its spines tipped with fresh crimson, was not empty, though deep shadow filled its recesses.

An unsound of tearing, the Veil parting, and Puck Goodfellow stepped lightly through. His hair was wildly disarranged, his smile gone, and his leathers had seen hard use, no longer brand-new.

Unwinter's gauntleted fist rose, and the wights stepped back, their pale moon-sickle blades returning to the sheaths. It was unlike the Fatherless to appear so, without the courtesy of visiting Unwinter's bone-frilled High Steward first, and the Lord of the Fell's eye-sparks, crimson orbs strengthening in the cave of his helm, fixed on the visitor.

"I crave pardon, oh Lion of Danu, for appearing thus." Puck bowed, but with none of the fine little movements of Summer's Court fashion. "I hastened to bring you news."

"*Did you, now.*" Unwinter's tone was soft, but so cold. The wights tensed, very much like Unwinter's slim needle-tooth hounds, and elsewhere in the Keep, activity began. It could have been merely a change of the guard, or preparations for a feast.

"Oh, we bear each other no love, but I have done you many a service, lately. Do you know what rests in yon gift, Lord of the Hallow?"

"*I suspect, Fatherless. Her treachery knows no bounds. Once again you come to me, reeking of her perfume.*"

"'Twas not Summer who did this, my lord."

Unwinter's mailed finger twitched. One wight drifted forward, flexed its long strangler's fingers, and lifted the lid from the box. Sealing-chantment broke, and a reek of ironblight rose.

The head of Cailas Redthorn, violet dapples of lightshielding still engraved upon his cheeks, lolled on a purple satin cushion. He was one of the favored, the fullborn highblood who had been with Unwinter since the Sundering and consequently rode as boon companions on night-mare mounts when the hunt called.

"*Who, then?*" Still softly, but the wights both shivered.

Ice crystals decked Puck's hair now, and his ear-tips flicked to rid them of freezing globules. His lashes, weighted with tiny flecks of ice as well, drooped heavily as he blinked. " 'Twas the Gallow who did it, oh Lord of the Hunt. Struck your envoy down in Summer's very hall. Before he did, though, he showed the entire assemblage a wonder."

"*No doubt he did. Why are you here, Fatherless?*"

"To bring thee news." Puck straightened from his bow, his breath flash-freezing and falling tinkling to the blackstone floor. The flames whispered, shifting, in the firepit. "And to offer thee alliance, if you would have it."

"*Why now?*" The mailed finger twitched again, and the wight clapped the lid back on the box. The two picked it up again, reverently, and carried it to the firepit. A heave, and the cleansing flames ate through chantment and paper, sidhe flesh and bone. The thin, bone-white smoke that rose was perfumed with deep, cloying rose-scent, the mark of Cailas's family.

"Summer has taken my little Robin. I bear no deep love for either Court, but I will not brook insult."

"*You never have.*"

The wights vanished, presumably fearing their lord's temper. Puck rested his hands on his boy-slim hips. "Not all of us have your tolerance, gracious one."

Unwinter's short, unamused chuckle shivered the ice, grinding it into finer particles. "*I shall consider us allied, Fatherless, when I ride to war and you and yours ride with me.*"

"And when will that be?"

More laughter, cut off halfway as Unwinter leaned slightly forward. The deep, cloaking shadow broke with glints and glimmers over his fine dwarven-made armor, as fluid as the Gallow's but with no leather sheathing. The Throne twitched, and the blood at its tips was now red ice. "*When I call upon you, free sidhe. Until then, leave me in peace.*"

"As you like." Puck sketched another bow, and as he had arrived, did not bother to walk from the Keep.

He simply stepped through the Veil and was gone.

Unwinter remained very still, the crimson eye-sparks fixed first on leaping crystalline flames, then on the spot where Puck had stood. "*Cailas,*" he said, softly but without the hurtful cold weighting each syllable.

Then, "*Puck.*" His mailed fingers flexed.

Last of all, he settled back and tented those fingers, the mail making a slight chiming as his extra finger twitched. "*Gallow,*" he breathed, and the Keep resounded, from cellar to tallest spire, shuddering as a plucked harpstring.

Unwinter began to laugh.

ANOTHER CASTAWAY
50

The Dreaming Sea touches all shores.
They did not know it, the small group gathered at the bon-fire. Driftwood burned colorful, spit-sparking, and Timmo the Greek had a guitar. Acacia, who worked the ring-tosses, drew her shawl a little tighter. The carnival had closed for the night, Leo had locked the gates himself and given them all a breather. He was in his trailer counting what money they'd managed to bring in on a weekday, and the Ferris wheel was darkened. Some of the lights remained, stars at the top of the bluff.

Joey puffed on a Swisher Sweet and coughed; Marylou pounded him on the back. Guster, broad shoulders straining at his red-checked flannel—he wore it even down south in the worst of the summer circuit—cracked a bit of driftwood in his large capable hands and threw both pieces onto the flames. A burst of sparks went up, and Rick produced a bottle of whiskey.

The Greek picked out a popular tune, one the carnies had put different words to. Guster sang, and so did Acacia, her high, sweet soprano giving the filthy words lilting beauty they perhaps didn't deserve. Marylou passed out the chicken salad sandwiches she'd brought.

Instead of taking one, though, Rick stood up, peering at the sea. "What the fuck is that?"

Acacia rolled her eyes. "How much of that have you had?"

"No, it's a dog." Joey set his Swisher aside to fill his mouth with chicken salad. Marylou made it with little celery bits, but other than that, it was really good.

"Dog, hell. It's the size of a horse." The Greek stood too, stuffing a sandwich half into his mouth and licking at his fingers.

"You're disgusting." Acacia sighed, took a hit off the whiskey, and peered at the water. "Huh. It is a dog. Look at that."

The pale shape darted into the surf, retreated. Did it again.

"Is it playing fetch?"

"At night?"

"Fishing?"

"It's huge. Look at that."

"Weird. Maybe it has rabies?"

"Thanks for that awesome thought, Timmo."

"It's caught something."

"What?"

"Jesus Christ," Joey half-choked, spraying sandwich crumbs. "It's a person!"

They ran for the edge of the earth, and the dog—it was a real monster, probably a Great Dane—leapt into the silver surf again. The water was oddly warm for early spring, but none of them noticed, because the shape was a person, a dark human log rolling amid spume, salt, and sand. It was Acacia who plunged into the water and dragged it closer, the Greek hopping from foot to foot at the very edge of the bubbling brine. Marylou grabbed Acacia's collar as the girl almost went under, her work-roughened hand scraping against soft nape under curling hair, and Guster grabbed Marylou to brace her. Getting closer, Rick got the woman's feet— it was a woman, they could see that now, pale and with a mass of curling hair—and they staggered up onto the sand. The dog danced, making low grinding noises, but it didn't bite or attack.

They carried her to the fire; Joey who turned her onto her side and thumped her back. Acacia shoved him aside, bent and sealed her mouth over the woman's blue lips. Exhaled, hard, fingers clamped on the woman's nose, and Acacia straightened to take a breath.

Amazingly, the woman retched. A jet of seawater burst out of nose and mouth, sinking into the sand. She curled up, coughing still more, and Guster grabbed his work coat. "Get her near the fire!"

She wore black, heavy velvet like Matilda the fortune-teller. She produced an amazing quantity of water with each coughing spasm, and when they ended she drew in heaving, tortuous breaths. The fire snapped and crackled, and if it suddenly gave a much richer golden light, none of them noticed. The dog pressed close, nosing the woman's face as she struggled to breathe. Her hand came up, dead white, and wound in its damp fur. It folded down and began licking her cheeks, almost frantically.

"Is she townie?" Marylou, hugging herself and shivering. The picnic basket had been kicked almost-sideways; Acacia rescued it and stood near the fire, wringing out her long hair.

"Dunno. She doesn't look townie." Guster, solid and phlegmatic as usual, tossed another hunk of driftwood on the fire.

"Can you hear me?" Joey, awkwardly patting at the woman's hand. "You're safe now, you're okay."

The rasping, choked sound might have been a laugh. She retched again and clung to the dog, who whined low in his chest.

"We should take her uphill." Marylou, ever practical. She glanced at the ocean, as if it might vomit up another castaway. "Leo will want to know."

"Should call the cops," Rick piped up. "An ambulance, at least."

The woman shook her head, erupting into motion; the dog growled. Joey let out a surprised little cry and snatched his hand back.

She had deep-blue eyes, and even under the sand, with kelp caught in her draggled hair and her lips livid with drowning cold, she was...pretty.

More than pretty.

She coughed, propping herself against the dog. "No...cops." A husky, almost-ruined voice. "No ambulance. No."

"Easy there." Guster squatted, making his bulk smaller. If he felt the chill, it didn't show. "You almost drowned. Just take it easy."

"No ambulance." She coughed again, and retched, a deep racking sound. "No. Hide. Hide me."

"Oh, shit." Marylou sighed. "Not another one."

Acacia tensed, but she said nothing. Joey glanced from the woman to Acacia, and back.

"You wanted for something?" Rick wrinkled his nose. "Huh?"

She shook her head. "No." Little tracers of steam rose from her cheeks, from the tattered velvet. Underneath, flashes of blue. She still had her shoes on, too—high-quality heels, black and covered with sand. "Not a...a criminal." More coughing, and when she took her fist away from her mouth Marylou glimpsed bright red on her wrinkled-wet white fingers.

Maybe it was that tinge of scarlet that made her decide. "Gus. You want to help me carry her up the hill? And you, ma'am, is your dog friendly?"

"V-very. If you are." She shivered, and the dog—funny, but its eyes looked a little like hers, though only Joey noticed—went back to licking at her with its incredibly long, incredibly pink tongue. "Ugh, stop it."

The dog wriggled. Its tail thumped the sand, flinging up a fan of tiny particles.

"Okay then." Marylou bent down to peer at the woman's face. "Gus?"

He rose, slowly, and sighed. "Leo ain't gonna like this."

"She's a mermaid," Joey said, suddenly, with utter certainty.

"I am not," the woman retorted hotly, in that scraped voice. It was painful to hear the words rasp, and to hear the awful sounds she made when she coughed.

"No siren would admit it, would she." Timmo laughed, but sobered quickly when Marylou shot him a look. He picked up his guitar. "I'll help."

"Me too." Acacia finished wringing out her hair, picked up the picnic basket, and pushed it into Joey's hands. "You carry this. Leo can't be an asshole with everyone watching."

"You're such an optimist." Rick began pouring sand on the fire. "We didn't even get to sing 'Kumbayah.' Shit."

The woman lapsed into silence and was only semiconscious when Marylou and Guster got her on her feet. The dog shook sand over all of them and pranced ahead, as if he knew the way up the hill and into the maze of carnival trailers.

She was bird-thin, and too hot through the wet, steaming velvet. Marylou began muttering about pneumonia and getting some acetaminophen, Joey cadged another half sandwich from the basket and started trying to coax the dog to eat, Guster kept stolidly plodding—he would do anything Marylou asked, really—and Acacia ran ahead, fleet and sure even in the darkness. The fire began to gasp and struggle, but Rick kept at it until only coals remained and decided it was good enough. Their voices had receded, and he didn't like being alone.

Normally, he didn't mind. But for some odd reason, he was almost certain he was being watched.

A POKED ANTHILL
51

Summerhome was a poked anthill, roiling. Gallow stopped at the top of a rise, panting, his hand clapped against his armored side as if it hurt. It didn't, not yet, and his strength was returning. The dwarven healer had done his work well.

You shall find your maiden in a white tower. Well, there were towers and towers, through all the sideways realms. Who knew, or could guess, which one now held Robin? Puck had vanished, and was no doubt searching for her at this very moment. What would he do when he found her? What hold did the Fatherless have on the Ragged? He'd brought her to Summer, perhaps she felt a debt.

That wasn't the real question, though. The question was how Summer had gotten hold of her in the first fucking place. As soon as he thought about it, Jeremiah had the answer.

Crenn. The bastard had probably tricked her, or dragged her, or . . .

"*Hist!*" A low fierce whisper, a broad-shouldered shape. "Gallow, this way!"

He peered into the gloaming. Night had fallen with a vengeance, and riders with torches were spreading from Summerhome.

There was a twitch against Jeremiah's throat—the locket on its gold chain, tugging sharply. In the distance, a silvery hunting-horn cried out. Not one of Unwinter's, but dangerous all the same.

"You." The marks tingled, prickled fiercely. "What do *you* want?"

Puck shook his head, droplets melting from his hair. "Does it matter?"

"Did you find Robin?"

A fraction of a heartbeat's pause. "Not yet. The bird has flown."

Great. What the fuck did *that* mean? Had Robin escaped the tower, or did Puck realize there were many of them, and Summer had not given him enough to track her? "What do you expect *me* to do?" *I'm kind of busy at the moment.*

Hoofbeats, and the stars of torches. They were getting closer. He had to find an exit.

"Gallow-my-glass, I will find her, and you will help." The sapling he stood near shivered, either because of the flatness of his tone—or maybe Puck Goodfellow was trembling. "Can you find her, by track or Sympathy?"

Gallow regarded him, narrowly. "Why? What is your purpose where Robin's concerned?"

"Call me her god*father*." Puck's giggle spiraled up into a gruesome chuckle. "Can you find her, or not?"

I'm weak, even though the lightfoot hasn't deserted me. I'm fast and I'm canny, but they'll find me unless I get the hell out of Summer. "If I said I could?"

"Then I'll help you."

"And if not?"

"I might leave you to make your own way."

Comforting. He took a single step toward the clump of

bushes. "Whenever you start asking after Robin Ragged, Goodfellow, chaos follows. What is she, to you?"

"A girl who should respect her elders, and a sidhe whose voice delights me. One last time, Glass-the-Gallow, hunted of both Courts, will you aid me in finding my wayward daughter?"

Daughter? Jeremiah's mouth closed with a snap. Puck had claimed her as kin before Unwinter, too. Maybe that hadn't been a half-lie or a figure of speech.

With the Fatherless, it was always difficult to tell. *Oh, for God's sake.* What other choice did he have, though? "I will," he said heavily. "I need a quiet place to think, Puck."

"Come along, and quickly." The boy held out his slim brown hand, and Gallow took it. There was something else nagging him, and now that his head was clearer he realized what had been bothering him all along.

Where's his knife, and his pipes?

Puck's chin lifted, his irises firing in the gloom. He exhaled, softly, past his sharp white teeth. "Do you hear that?"

Jeremiah shuddered. In the distance, the ultrasonic cry of silver huntwhistles lifted. Unwinter was not hunting in Summer, but since her borders were so frayed, the sound would rub through, like knives whispering across thick paper.

I have four days. Maybe less, if the antidote stops working.

Jeremiah Gallow took Puck Goodfellow's hand. A sharp tug, a stumble as if he were stepping down into another room, and the hole in the Veil closed behind them just as Summer knights armored in silver, their elfhorses caparisoned in Summer's green, crashed through the thicket, their torches casting a cold, glaring light.

DID YOUR PART
52

There was some commotion, and they carried her to a rickety trailer. The owner of the troupe, a fat balding man with the stub of an unlit cigar stuffed in his mouth, filthy as a dwarf though not nearly as sweet smelling, waved his hands. "For God's sake, we're not a charitable concern! And that dog—"

Said dog, his fine fringed tail lashing, gave a short yipping bark.

Alastair Crenn, seawater in his leathers and slosh-weighting his mortal boots, narrowed his eyes. The sea, both mortal and Dreaming, filled his hair, too. Maybe the salt would kill the moss, maybe not. His throat burned from the gallons he'd swallowed, and his stomach was none too happy with him.

Still, he had managed to find her. Mortal hands had pulled her from the water. He had been left to make his own rescue.

"—Who's going to fucking feed that dog?"

"For God's sake, Leo," the taller woman, also wet clear through, spat. "*I'll* feed him. If you don't have any Tylenol, *shut up.*"

The slighter, shorter girl, her long hair dripping, pushed at a youth with sun-colored hair. "Go get some Tylenol, Joey. Gus?"

"Here." The stolid, muscular man in flannel appeared with an armful of blankets. "I knocked on Geta's door; he's bringing soup."

"What about Marlon?" the girl wanted to know, subtracting the blankets from him with quick efficiency.

Flannel-Man shrugged. "Dead drunk. He took a night off with a vengeance."

"Oh, for God's sake." The owner raised his hands to heaven. "I am *not* running an orphanage or a hospital ward!"

"Leo, if you'd prefer us to call the cops—"

"Don't know why I ever hired you. Troublemaker! That's what you are!" He shook a fat finger, and Crenn tensed, but the generously hipped matron seemed supremely unconcerned.

"You hired me because I'll feed your crew on biscuits and gravy even when there's nothing but dust to eat, and because I put up with *you*. Go count your money; I'll deal with this."

"Come on, old man." A squat, dark-haired troubadour, carrying a guitar, took the owner's arm. "We'll drink. I have some ouzo and some cheese. I'll play you 'Moon River' again."

"I hate that song," the owner muttered. "All right, Marylou, fine. But she works, or she doesn't stay! Just like her damn dog!"

"Leave the dog alone!" she called after him. "And you, Rick, go sit with Marlon."

"Why is that always *my* job?" This man, keeping to the shadows in a way that made Crenn's nose twitch, was already moving to obey.

"Because he's *your* husband," the girl shot after him, and the matron shushed her, taking the blankets.

"If you ever bite your tongue you'll die of poison. Go get cleaned up."

"I got her first." The girl tossed her hair and put her newly freed hands on her hips. There was a feral sharpness to her features that bespoke some manner of sidhe blood in her ancestry, but she smelled purely salt-iron. She hadn't been taken over the border into any sideways realm, and might not ever be; she would most likely die a mortal death if she never manged to breach the Veil. "Come on, Joey. Let's find some goddamn Tylenol."

The dog kept wagging its tail, ears perked. It shook itself, sending sand spraying everywhere, but nobody noticed. The man in flannel waited until the girl and the young lad had vanished, the girl's sharp voice chivvying the boy along, before he looked up at the matron. For an instant, his sad mortal face was alight with a kind of hunger Crenn almost recognized.

"I suppose I'm not coming in tonight," the flannel-clad knight said.

The woman looked down at him, pausing before she spoke. "Not unless you're going to sit up with her."

"I will, and you can sleep."

"Who can sleep with you breathing on them?"

"Come on, Marylou." A softness in his growl of a voice, and her shoulders relaxed.

"Sorry. It's just...Leo. You know."

"Yeah, I know. I'll sit up, you get some sleep. He'll be a bear tomorrow, and who knows what she is?"

"She doesn't smell townie."

"You and your nose. What else does it tell you?" He put a boot on the lowest step into her frail trailer. The whole thing rocked alarmingly. Crenn stilled, his breath turning thief in his throat.

The matron smiled at the flannel-clad man, her expression crossing the border into tenderness without even stopping to show its papers. "Trouble on the wind, Guster. You can come

277

in, until they bring the Tylenol. No telling how she might act if a man's here when she wakes up."

"*If* she does."

"Well, if she doesn't, there'll be a whole new set of problems for Leo to bitch about." Marylou retreated into the trailer, tapping the door with a heel just before it slammed to keep it quiet.

"No, boy," Guster of the Red Flannel said to the dog. "You did your part. Wait out here. Maybe Marylou has a bone in her fridge. I'll check."

Pepperbuckle, as if he understood, plopped down to sit next to the steps, his tongue lolling. The door closed again—softly, so as not to disturb the sleeper within.

Crenn sagged on the roof.

She was alive. They were rough people, but they had given her shelter. In the old days, they would be rewarded with gold or chantment, all he could scrape out of purse or glamour-strength.

Alive. It was up to him to provide the rest, whether she would thank him for it or not. His newly smooth, traitorous cheek twitched a little, and he closed his eyes for a moment. There, on the roof of another shoddy trailer, Alastair Crenn dropped into a doze.

TWO PROBLEMS
53

nother mortal night, another dispirited drizzle of rain. Gallow stumbled, his side aching, and Puck Goodfellow whistled a little, a wandering, tuneless melody. "Just a little further," he crooned, the words threading through the breathy scree of air.

He was, after all, a very musical sidhe. It would make a mad sort of sense if he *was* Robin's father. Daisy had been purely mortal; maybe Puck had left the mother and only thought to return later, when Robin was older?

I was twelve when I was taken, she had told him. She'd never given any indication she viewed Puck as anything other than a question mark. Except...Jeremiah had left her sleeping in his own house, and when he'd seen her again Puck had been with her. Robin, as a sidhe of Summer, had given the invitation to Unwinter to step over the border and cause havoc.

And Puck himself had called her *daughter*.

Puck led him up a long, gentle slope, ducked through a tangle of broken chainlink fencing. A mortal city closed around them, its stink of exhaust and cold iron. Pavement that bruised the feet, concrete walls that closed around the soul. For all that, it was better than Summer, and Jeremiah's shoulders relaxed slightly. It was a relief to tread in familiar surroundings again.

I really do prefer mortals. Mostly. He shook his head, sweat slicking his forehead and his hand clamped to his side. *Think, Jeremiah. Come on.*

Every single turn of goddamn events lately had Puck Goodfellow all over it. Even him leading Jeremiah to Robin at the Rolling Oak, neat as you please, and disappearing when the barrow-wights arrived. Probably leaving Robin in Gallow's care, since she looked so much like Daisy, and . . .

And of course, Puck had forced Robin into extending the invitation into Summer. How long had he been laying his plans? And if he'd planned the breaching of Summer's borders, well, what else had he designed? Had he just seen an opportunity, with the plague running rife among both Summer and Unwinter?

Recognition jolted through Jeremiah. The city was familiar. It was, after all, his own. Summer's Gates moved according to their own whims, slowly but definitely, and they'd been here for some twenty mortal years. In another ten or so, they'd be in another city, and the smaller entrances would follow in their almost-random patterns, branching through the mortal world like secret, sweet-poison veins.

Unwinter, of course, could be reached from anywhere.

Puck nipped into an alley; Jeremiah followed. A fire escape loomed, and they began to climb, Puck hissing as he skipped glove-shod along iron grating. "Just a little more, my fine Gallow. Then we shall see, we shall see."

Where the hell are we? He looked down, saw an alley, then a familiar slice of street. Ninth, with the *shawarma* place he'd eaten at damn near every day while they worked the Claigh Bank Building's upper floors. That had been a hell of a job, and

Clyde the foreman had brought a flask to work for the last week and a half.

Think, Jer. Where are you?

It had to be the Savoigh Limited. He stumbled a little, fetched up against the railing, and the entire iron contraption rattled.

"*Fool!*" Puck hissed. "Come, up to the roof. We may parlay there. Be warned, Gallow-glass, Glass-Gallow, if you cannot find her, I will—"

"A father's care." Jer cleared his throat. The consciousness of danger bloomed along his skin, and the marks tingled. He had in mind a different weapon, though, and his right hand crawled to his throat. "Touching." The proverb rolled from his lips. "*It is a foul father who eats his own.*"

Puck halted. His narrow, supple back was to Jeremiah, and he had the high ground. His head turned slightly, the fluid, terrible movement of sidhe articulation in every joint. It was enough to make you nauseous if you weren't used to it. "You are a canny beast indeed, Half."

"Not as canny as I should be." *I'm slow, I know as much. But I get there.* "You don't mean Robin any good."

"Hers is a fine voice."

She's more than just a voice. "You don't love her."

Puck shrugged, a loose, easy, repulsive motion. "What is love? *You* took the dregs instead of the fine floss, and well my Robin knows it."

Does she? "You left her in the trailer park, *Fatherless*. Not me."

"And I returned; I brought her to Summer." Puck kept climbing, and Jeremiah followed. "'Tis not any concern of yours, *Armormaster*."

The marks tingled on his arms. "There is something that *does* concern me, Puck."

"Oh?" Puck reached the top, clambered lightly over the waist-high barrier to the roof. Jeremiah followed, cautiously, but Puck merely paced across the rooftop to a particular spot, where a slug-opalescent residue of a sidhe death shimmered faintly. The lance solidified in Jeremiah's hands, and the Horn burned cold-furious at his chest. His side burned, too, with a deeper, frost-rimed flame. *I need one of the antidotes, dammit. Which will just leave me with three.*

Sort of ironic, how he wanted to *live* now. He couldn't have been bothered before, but at this particular moment, he found he really, truly did want to survive. No matter what.

He wasn't ready to lie down and show his belly just yet.

The drizzle intensified. A single huntwhistle thrilled into the ultrasonic to the south.

It wasn't one of Summer's.

"Yeah." The lance lengthened, its blade dulling through silver, flushing along the sharpening edge. "Daisy."

Puck spread his narrow hands. "A mortal chit, a pale reflection of my Robin."

"My wife." *You and Summer both told me she went to meet a sidhe the night she died. A straightaway, a dry road, and an oak tree. Robin waited for hours, but Daisy didn't show.*

It was pretty goddamn simple, when you thought about it.

A gleam of yellowgreen irises, an impatient movement. "That does not make us kin, Half. Now, can you find my Robin?"

"I can." *I have the locket.* "Why can't you?"

Puck shook his head. "You have something of hers. Some gift my fine girl gave to thee." His smile widened. He didn't seem particularly concerned by the lance's sudden solidity. "I shall take it from thy corpse, and send thy head to Unwinter."

"There's two problems with that plan."

The boy shrugged, spreading his extra-jointed fingers.

"First, I'm still breathing."

"That can be remedied—"

Jeremiah was already moving, the lance shrieking as it yanked his recalcitrant body through space. A lateral sweep, Puck skipping aside with the eerie blurring speed of the sidhe. More huntwhistles bloomed, north and west; the lance doubled on itself and jerked back, tassels of moonfire blurring off its blunt end. Puck ducked, weaving, and Jeremiah's breath tore in his chest. The burning in his side slowed him, he should have taken an antidote vial before this.

It didn't matter.

Daisy, at the door. *Just a quart of half-n-half, since you like your milk so much.* Her shattered mortal body giving up its soul, the flat, atonal cry of the machines as her heart ceased. Daisy, flinching a little just like Robin did. She rarely spoke about her childhood, and he'd been content to leave it there so he didn't have to talk about his own.

It was the shadow of his own stupidity he chased across the rooftop, the lance warming to its work and humming, its hungry core alive at the prospect of worthy prey.

Puck darted in, trying to get close enough for claws, and had to leap aside, ducking as the lance whickered through space and kissed a lock of his shaggy mane. The hair crisped, puffing up smoke-steam as cold iron blighted it, and Puck snarled, his face losing all its boyish handsomeness. Had Daisy seen that before she died? Pressed against a windshield, it would give any mortal a shock and send them veering off the road.

Puck didn't have his knife. Why? Jeremiah found he didn't care. Here on open ground, with foe finally clearly revealed, all that mattered was the death he would mete out. A last gift, both to Daisy and to Robin.

He hadn't done right by either of them, but God, how he'd *wanted* to.

Puck darted for the edge of the roof, but the lance swept in again. Had the Fatherless still possessed his pipes or his knife, it would have been a much different fight. The battle-madness was on Jeremiah now, and for once he didn't try to control the lance.

Instead, he gave himself up to its hunger, and the Horn was a cold star against his chest.

Sidestep, blade singing, every possible move unreeling inside Gallow's head, all narrowing to a single, undeniable point— Puck faded aside again, but the lance was there, sinking into the boy-sidhe's left arm with a *crunch* that sent tiny cracks spider-webbing out across the rooftop. An HVAC vent a little ways away resounded like a gong, and the iron blade bit deep across Puck's chest, grating on ribs.

The Fatherless screamed, whipped aside like a spider flicked into a candleflame, arms and legs folding in around the wound. Jeremiah panted, his knees buckling, and lunged forward, but Puck was rolling across the rooftop, his passage throwing up dust from the cracking, heaving rooftop, scattering steam from the flashing drizzle and spatters of thick blue-green ichor.

The lance keened, hungry to finish the job, but fire-claws gripped Gallow's side. His breath heaved, and his knees grated against the rooftop. Tried to surge to his feet. Couldn't.

Puck panted, harsh cough-choking breaths. He lay crumpled against the HVAC vent, curled into a tight ball, his yellow-green irises flashing, dimming. "I shall repay thee for this, Gallow." His face, horrifically beautiful, was the last thing his mortal prey would ever see. A hideous blood-freezing grimace, but Jeremiah was past fear now. "Do you hear me? *I shall repay.*"

"Sure you will." Gallow coughed, swallowed blood. *I need one of those goddamn antidotes.* "You fucking sidhe *bastard.*" The lancebutt socked into the rooftop, the entire building shuddering like an unhappy horse. He dragged himself upright and tacked drunkenly for the vent, the lance lengthening. Even if Puck somehow scurried away, the ironblight would give him something to worry about.

He drew the lance back a little. Its tip, leafshaped now, quivered hungrily. "Daisy," he murmured.

"You're not the first to wound me in her name," Puck panted. "Gallow. You think you can kill *me?*"

"Let's find out." The lance lunged forward with a crunch, and Jeremiah Gallow *twisted* it. Blood hot on his lips, dribbling down his chin.

Puck Goodfellow screamed.

The huntwhistles rose again, so close the drizzle flashed into sharp silver ice. The lance shrieked, gulping life into its fiery core. He twisted it again, and the scream rising from the flopping, jerking body pinned to the rooftop pushed his hair back. Windows broke all around, sweet shivers of broken glass, and the building sagged again. Anyone in it probably thought it was an earthquake.

It is.

One last time, Jeremiah Gallow *twisted*, the blade growing serrations, tearing and ripping flesh, tangling in ribs, drinking greedily. Lava filled Gallow's veins. So much power. So *much.*

They boiled over the edge of the rooftop, nightmare steeds

and bright-eyed hounds, a crowd of drow with golden nets, but Gallow was past caring. The poison burned afresh, but he couldn't let go of the lance to dig in his pocket for a vial and let Puck wriggle away just yet.

He jammed the lance further down into the rooftop, and did not need to twist it again. The lance hummed, sucking Puck's dying agonies into its core. Its bearer slumped over its hungry keening, not even bothering to flee.

Jeremiah Gallow was well and truly caught.

THEN LEAVE
54

It was dark, and it reeked of mortals. She floated, somewhere between sleep and waking, restless when voices reached her.

Come home to visit! Whooooo-eeeee! Look at me when I talk to you, girl!

Other voices, swirling. *Oh, my primrose darling...I will have your voice.*

Her own despairing scream, glass shattering, the long fall. Something over her mouth—she struggled, hearing a low faraway grumble, and a hissed word in a strange language.

Her eyelids snapped up, her hands sprang like white birds to defend her, but he batted them aside. "Shhh, pretty girl." Low and husky, another almost-familiar voice. "They're sleeping; let's not wake them."

He was just a shadow, and she lay on a narrow cot in a small tin shell. It was a trailer, but she didn't hear the moan-whisper of wind outside. The shadow had dark eyes and shaggy hair, and terror crawled into her throat like a stone.

"Shhh," he soothed. "You're safe now."

There is no safety. She clung to the thought; it was sanity in the middle of a jumble of broken glass and distorted faces. She blinked, her skin crusted with salt and sand, and he eased his hard-callused hand away. She could breathe again.

"There," he whispered. "They're all sleeping, helped along by chantment. Do you know me?"

She shook her head. Her hair was stiff and heavy, filthy and matted.

The trailer was close and stifling, and there were solid shapes in the kitchenette, slumped against each other on a pair of rickety chairs, their heads together as if they were sharing secrets. Something heavy hung dripping in what had to be a tiny bathroom, and someone had wiped at her face to get the sand off. They'd tried to clean her up, and a woman had made her take two tablets and drink water. What she wanted, though, was milk. There was nothing better, and she craved it, her throat afire. She tasted blood, salt water, rotting ocean—but the stranger smelled oddly familiar. Spice and something wonderful under a tarnish, dampness and black wet earth.

She coughed, rackingly, but the sleeping pair didn't stir. "Robin," she choked. "I'm *Robin*." As if she had just now realized it. Where was her coat? The heavy velvet had weighed her down, but she wanted its comfort now.

"You are." He nodded, a faint gleam of eyes in the dimness. It was so *dark* in here. "And you do not know me?"

If I did, I might not say so. She rubbed at her eyes, wincing a little at the grit. "Who are you?" The words were coated with rust, as if she hadn't used them in a long time.

A gleam of teeth, and she recoiled. He stripped his hair back, and the nightlight's faint glow showed a slice of high cheekbones, the shape of his mouth, dark eyes.

He was beautiful, and her breath caught. He seemed so *familiar*, but the fractured pieces inside her head wouldn't form a constellation.

All the stars of Summer's dusk...Robin-mama, why did you kill me?

A whine from outside. *That* was familiar, too. The hound.

"P-pepper," she breathed. "Pepperbuckle."

"He's outside. Wouldn't you like some free air? And milk. I'll wager you want a draught, to ease your pains."

How do you know? "What does it cost?" It went better when she whispered. And she knew, didn't she, that everything had a price?

He shook his head, his hair falling back down to curtain that sharp handsomeness. It looked like a habitual movement. "You are the creditor, Robin, and I the poor debtor. Have mercy on me, and come outside."

Mercy? What the hell? She found she could move, and propped herself on her elbows. Her feet were bare, and that wasn't right. "My shoes." Two harsh, grating words.

"Here." He held them up—a pair of black heels, scuffed in some places, shining in others. She made a small sound, grabbing for them, but he whisked them away. "Easy, pretty girl."

Why does he call me that? Her heart beat, fast and thin, humming in her wrists and throat and ankles. *Don't trust him.*

But he had her *shoes*. "Give them back."

"I will. Let me help you."

She snatched for her shoes again, and this time he let her take them. She clutched them to her chest, the sharp edges of the heels biting her naked upper arms, and stared distrustfully at him.

He sighed. "We cannot stay here, Robin. It's dangerous."

So are you. Memory teased, turned into a yarn-ball inside her skull. The shivered pieces twitched, and she had the idea she wouldn't like the picture they made when she put them back together. "Then leave," she whispered.

He nodded, once, and gained his feet in a lunge. She shrank

away, against the trailer wall, but he just stared down at her, too tall for the confined space. Her arms hurt, and her throat filled with numbness. She inhaled, as if to scream...

...and the trailer door shut, soft as a whisper. He was gone.

Robin clutched the shoes and closed her eyes. "I am Robin," she whispered. At least she knew that much.

But where am I? Who was that? And what...where...

She slid back down into the bed smelling of mortals—what a funny word, *mortal*—and her entire body turned to lead. Her eyes closed, and she fell back into half-dreaming again, rocking in the narrow cot. It was like her bed at Court.

Court?

But it was gone. She slid back into soft sleep.

Outside, a warm spring night rustled palm trees, and a hound with a redgold coat sniffed carefully at a man's hand. "*You* know me, don't you? I fed you pigeons."

Pepperbuckle nosed the proffered palm, showed his teeth, and backed away a few steps. His haunches thudded down again, and he fixed his intelligent blue gaze on the trailer's door again.

Waiting for his mistress. When the stranger walked away, ducking under lines where washing hung to dry, the hound didn't even twitch.

A FAIR PRICE
55

irens resounded in the distance, mortals scurrying to repair
damage. Full night had fallen, and the drizzle turned to pel-
lets of stinging ice. The deepest pool of shadow, beyond the
hooded slump of the HVAC vent, grew blacker and blacker.
Jeremiah kept the lance steady. The rag of sidhe-flesh, smoking with ironblight, was still screaming, making noises that
could drive a mortal mad. Curse-birds took shape, battering
at Jeremiah's hair and shoulders, spreading out to peck at the
dogs and the armored knights, who simply waved them away
or spoke single soft words of chantment, crunching them into
puffs of noisome smoke.

Gallow stabbed one last time, seeking the heart-knot holding the Fatherless to life. The ironblade found it, flushing forge-
hot, and Goodfellow's screams became choking gurgles.

The clot of shadow behind the vent birthed a slow, mur-
derous gleam, light playing on a serrated blade. It spread,
and became the foxfire limning of dwarven-made armor. A
rider and a high helm, a flowing cloak of motheaten velvet
hanging from spiked shoulders, the rooftop cracking and settling as the cold radiated. Atop the black charger, its massive

head a horrible reflection of a horse's—because no horse had predator's teeth—the bulk of the bloody-eyed lord of the Hunt and the Hallow smoked with ice that fell with tiny musical crashes.

The hounds ringed Jeremiah and his victim. They champed and slavered, but their master's will kept them from darting in to nip at him. The drow kept their distance as well, hissing and shaking their golden nets; the knights simply sat, hands tight on reins and the sparks of their eyes glowing hot. They were every color possible, those glowing eyes, except one.

Only Unwinter bore the bloody gaze.

"*Gallow*," the once-Consort of Summer said, softly. The scar on Jeremiah's side clenched, red-hot, but he kept the lance steady. The Horn grew heavier, its chain cutting cruelly at the back of Gallow's neck. "*I find you at murder again.*"

His mouth decided that he was already dead, so he might as well say what he thought. "Can't get away from it, sir. No man can." *At least, no sidhe can.* He should know, he'd tried.

Unwinter made a low grinding noise. The hounds cringed, and Jeremiah tensed—but it was merely Unwinter laughing.

Glad to know he finds me amusing. He ground the lance-blade, and the violated, Twisted thing under it choked out one last burble of agony and sagged, dissolving into bubbling, silent slime.

Unwinter waited. Patiently. Of course, he had all the time in the world, now.

The lance drank, and drank, until there was nothing left. Finally, Gallow tore the blade free. The blunt end smacked the hillocked, crumbling roof, and he straightened. The Savoigh Limited shuddered, and now he wondered why Puck had led him here, of all places.

He was just trying to tire me out. Then he could, what? Take the Horn, certainly. And probably Robin's locket.

The instant he thought of it, Robin's necklace twitched in his pocket. Was she still alive?

She has to be.

If she wasn't, he would tear apart Hell itself to find her. Though she would probably go straight up to the angels. Maybe they would deal with her more kindly than he had.

He faced Unwinter again, without the thin protection of holy ground. The lance hummed, the sick heat of stolen life coursing up its length and through his hand, up his arm to jolt in his shoulder. The scar ached, burned, and even the unhealthy surging fire of the lance couldn't keep the poison back.

Okay, Jer. Make it good.

He dug under his chestplate. The medallion came out, and Unwinter's crimson eyesparks narrowed. The collected host, crowding the roof, spectral knights and fanged drow, made an uneasy, restless movement.

"*You amuse me,*" Unwinter said, finally. "*Do you still seek to trade my property for your own miserable life?*"

Gallow shook his head. "No. But I'll hand it over without a whisper for your promise."

"*And what promise is that? The Horn is mine.*"

Not right now it isn't. Possession is nine-tenths, motherfucker. "The same as last time. Protect Robin Ragged. Keep her safe, let her live. Revenge any hurt done to her, guard her." The Horn became heavier, unfolding into its other shape. An alien curve of blackened metal polished to high silver where runes of no make mortal or sidhe were hammered into its surface— *starmetal,* the dwarves said, and denied any making of the thing. They said it had simply been dropped whole onto the screaming, shuddering earth before the Sundering, even before Danu's children woke in the forests during the Long Night. Long before the mortals had crawled forth to begin wrenching iron from the depths.

Unwinter made that same grinding noise. "*So much trouble for one little Half bird. Tell me, Gallow, why I should not simply strike you down? You challenged me, you robbed me, you insulted me, and you slew one I held dear.*"

He's not asking about the poison. Jeremiah shrugged. "Because you're not Summer."

One of the drow gasped, as if Jeremiah had screamed an obscenity.

"You're a just lord," Gallow continued. "And I'm dead soon anyway. I might as well get a fair price for my exit."

Unwinter stared at him for a long, empty, cold moment. *Please*, Jeremiah thought.

Please let him be amused.

Finally, the high-crowned helm dipped slightly. Unwinter nodded.

"*Bind him,*" he said. "*Take him to the Keep, deliver him whole and undamaged.*"

Wait, what?

He fought, but the drow were many, their nets tangling, the lance vanishing as chantment sparked in the hair-fine golden strands. They searched him as they cocooned him, and the Horn bit and sparked with cold as they sought to tear it from him. Since they could not, they settled for the next best thing—Robin's locket gleamed, ripped from his neck and sizzling against drow flesh.

"My lord!" the creature cried, and dropped it, chiming, to the ground.

"*Ah.*" Unwinter sounded thoughtful. One of the knights dismounted, carefully tweezed the chain up, and tossed it from hand to hand as if it was too hot to hold. Of course, it was truemetal, and Robin was of Summer.

He struggled as the knight handed it up to his lord, and Unwinter dangled the locket thoughtfully, seeming not to notice the steam that rose from his gauntlet. *"Pretty jesses, for a little bird."* At least Unwinter did sound pleased. Terribly, fully amused.

No! Jeremiah thrashed. It made no difference. His side cramped again, and blood burst between his lips. The Horn tangled in the netting and snarled, its cold breaking through the strands, but more crowded to take their places.

Before the sweating sickness of the poison and the dragging languor of net-chantment robbed him of consciousness, Gallow heard Unwinter's final command.

"Ride in hunt of the Ragged. A prize to whoever catches her alive, and whole!"

THE SAME AT NIGHT
56

Midnight came, and passed. She tossed and turned on a stranger's bed, and little by little woke fully, goose bumps standing out all over her.

What's that?

Now that she'd had a little rest, the pieces inside her head were a little less jumbled. *Robin Ragged.* She pushed herself up on her elbows. *That's who I am. I escaped.* Her breath came smoothly, four in and four out, and her throat was no longer afire. Still, she craved milk. Even skim, that pale ghost, would do. Her shoes, half-tangled in the covers underneath her, jabbed at her ribs, so she drew them out.

This late, the only other breathing noise in the trailer was a mortal woman with a little extra flesh on her rangy bones, propped against the kitchenette's oven. A tiny travel-trailer—Robin looked up. There were no pictures above the cot, but it was eerily familiar just the same. She studied the woman's face in the dim nightlight. Even slack with sleep, she looked determined and no-nonsense, her cap of dark curls not daring to disarrange itself much. She looked a little like a brughnie slumbering at a hearth. All she lacked were bare, horn-clawed feet and a kerchief made of spidersilk.

Robin eased herself up to sitting. Her dress shed sand and guck alike, and the seaweed tangled in her hair had already crisp-dried, falling in flakes as a sidhe's heat and breathing chantment loosened it. *I fell. I was in Summer, I think, and I fell.*

Then what?

She slid off the bed in increments. It didn't creak or whisper, and she worked her feet into her shoes, sighing in relief as the tingle against her toes told her their chantments were still active. The bruises on her legs were glaring and garish, probably from rocks; her arms were scraped and salt-stinging.

A tiny fridge hummed under the kitchenette counter. She eased down onto her knees, glanced at the sleeping woman. Threads of chantment worked over the mortal; she wouldn't wake.

Probably for the best. Robin's head ached, a vise around her temples. She frowned—where had the men gone, both the sleeping one and the other with his glittering eyes?

She decided not to care. Her belt was still fastened at her hips, the knife in its sheath and the pipes—probably ruined, who knew?—in their case as well. She flipped open the top of the case, stuck her pinkie in the largest reed—it met glass, a third of the way down, and she exhaled softly with relief. She couldn't quite think of why that was important, but it was. If she could just get some milk, she could no doubt remember more.

The slice of golden light from the mini fridge showed every wrinkle on the mortal woman's face, the sand still clinging to her capable hands, her workboots grimed with it. The rest of the trailer was spick-and-span; she seemed a neat soul.

There was no milk. No carton of creamer, even. There were, however, two sticks of sun-yellow butter, and Robin wrinkled her nose but took them both. The waxen wrapper on one peeled away just like a banana's skin, and she began to eat. The first few bites were heaven, and she finished the first stick in short order, licking her fingers and scraping her tongue against her top teeth as the grease coated it. At least it was salted; that caused a pleasant sting all the way down. A lump of heat congealed behind her breastbone. It wasn't milk, but it would do.

Nibbling at the other bar, she slid past the sleeping woman, edged into the bathroom. Her velvet coat hung in the tiny shower, sand sluicing from it as Robin brushed her hand along its folds. She shook her hair, too, and whispered a small chantment that worked grit and seaweed free.

The knife gleamed when she eased it from the sheath. In here, the nightlight's glow was like a candle's, and it showed a skinny sidhe girl in the flyspecked mirror, her cheekbones standing out startlingly and buttergrease smeared on her pale lips. She shuddered, and the mirror cracked with a whisper, from one end to the other. Its pieces reflected two Robins, and she shuddered again . . . but nothing else happened.

I have to know. But know what? She stared at the dagger's leafblade, tiny veins in the metal collecting a thick green smear. The edges would be whisper-sharp, even drenched in seawater, and the blade would never rust. The hilt was warm, and fit her hand exactly, even though *his* was shaped differently.

Think, Robin. Think.

It was hard. She took another bite of butter, grimaced a little. A brughnie could probably eat a whole pail of it in one sitting and call for more, but Robin was Half, and didn't have the stomach for so much concentrated fat.

Green venom collected at the knifepoint. She bit her lip,

held her arm over the sink. Carefully, she tilted the blade this way and that, collecting a bead of liquid.

When it broke free, falling, and splashed against her arm she hissed in a breath, expecting pain.

Nothing happened. Puck's poison did not burn her.

She swallowed, hard. *It's true.*

Of course it was true.

She grabbed her hair, held it away from her face, sawed close to the scalp. It fell, drifts of coppergold, probably clogging the sink. Dwarves would pay a high price for it, but a mortal would simply throw it out. She took care not to nick her own skin; her immunity might not extend that far.

She finished the butter and laid the last hank of hair in the small sink. *I should clean up.* Chantment would serve her; she could spend some of her limited, slowly returning strength to erase her traces here. She rolled the hair into a club, whispering the strands together in a mess of stickiness, and clutched it in her palm, squeezing harder and harder. Her arm shook, and when she opened her fingers, fine goldenred ash scattered into the sink.

She shrugged into the velvet coat. Whispered a word at the sand; it rolled itself into a ball, bumped over the doorsill, and continued along her scattered trail. The woman in the chair muttered uneasily, and Robin chewed at her lower lip as she watched the mortal woman's sleep.

It was no use. All she could do was breathe a little goodluck chantment, her fingers leaving a flushed-gold smear against the thinning flesh of the mortal's aging cheek, and hope it was enough. Instinct and common sense demanded she move, get outside, get *away* from these fragile creatures. They had miraculously dragged her from the sea; it would be poor indeed to bring the wrath of either Court upon them.

Thank God Puck's dead. She felt at her left pocket, touching the familiar lump of a small blue plastic ring. Opened the door as the sandball, having dragged bits of kelp and a rather large dustball—Daddy Snowe had called them *ghost turds*—bumbled past her and scattered down the steps.

Look who's come home to visit!

She shuddered. Bits and pieces were coming back, no matter how much she might wish them not to.

Pepperbuckle leapt to his feet, his tail thudding against the side of the trailer with a hollow boom. She shushed him, bent down gingerly, smoothed his head and scrubbed behind his ears. "Good boy," she whispered. The words burned her throat, rasping free with effort. "*Best* boy. I should never have left you."

Except if I hadn't, someone might have killed you too, and all this for nothing. She sighed, and leaned on him. The night was fragrant and warm, and when she peered about she saw palm trees rising over a jumbled collection of trailers, electrical lines strung hither and yon. It looked strangely familiar, the circular bulk of a Ferris wheel rising dead and dark with evil red glimmers along its struts. The sea-sound was almost like a dust-laden wind.

All carnivals looked the same at night. Who knew?

The first thing to do was to leave this place. The butter was a lump high under her breastbone; it didn't soothe her throat the way milk would, but it gave her enough strength for simple chantment and sealed the worst of the agonizing grating when she thought about speaking.

"All right," she whispered, testing the sound. Coughed a little, into her palm.

Pepperbuckle's head came up. He sniffed, deeply, and under her hand his shoulder turned hard as tile. A tremor ran through him, and his irises were now luminescent, a low blue glow.

301

"What is it?" she whispered. "What is it, boy?"

Then she heard.

High silver whistles thrilling in the distance. A ring of them from every direction, piercing the formless mutter of the sea. The goose bumps came back. Robin swayed, closing her eyes.

It would never be over. They would chase until they caught her.

Pepperbuckle growled, and when she opened her eyes, a shadow loomed at the corner of the trailer. Dark eyes gleamed, and terror filled her throat, almost buckled her knees.

"I'm a goddamn fool. I can't leave you," the man said, and beckoned. "Come *on*."

ANY MORE THAN I HATE MYSELF
57

aunt and pale, her eyes huge in a wan little face, Robin ran
between him and the hound, her fingers wound in the creature's ruff and her choking, labored breathing hurting Crenn's
own chest. Either she didn't recognize him, or she was numb
enough to have forgiven him, or she thought he was her best
chance of survival, or...who knew? It didn't matter.

The whistles pierced every corner, a silver net. They'd even
worked around the bluff toward the seashore, and there went
his chances of getting her out of here quietly. He almost wished
he hadn't gone to steal her some milk, thinking she needed rest
and he could at least *begin* to coax her into—

"*Crenn!*" she gasped, in a painful husky whisper. Had she
just now recognized him? She tried to slow down, but her fingers were caught in the dog's fur, and he had her other arm,
dragging her along the beaten-dirt pathway eastward. "You...
you..."

"Save...your breath...for running," he told her. "Don't try
to sing. The weed."

"The *what*?" The words rasped hotly; she almost tripped

over cables carrying electricity to each of the trailers, the two RVs, a field kitchen under a canvas tent. It reminded him of the Hoovervilles, the dust and the desperation, the babies crying and the police descending with their truncheons and shiny badges. The scars were gone, but he still felt them, a river of fire over half his body, the other half cold with the terror of any hunted animal.

They burst onto the dark, shuttered fairway, and Crenn almost thought they had a shot at escaping unseen—until the shadows at the far end, under the Ferris wheel's spidery bulk, birthed a cold gleam and silvershod hoofbeats rang on packed dirt. The rider, a black paper cutout, smoked with *wrongness*, and Robin's despairing, mewling little cry ignited something in Crenn's bones.

Funny, how things became very simple once a man's course was decided. It was the aimlessness of choice that made mischief, among both sidhe and mortals.

"*That way!*" he said, and pushed her. The dog took over, hauling her up a rickety ramp, bursting through a chain stretched between pillars into a dark passageway beyond. A gigantic clown was painted above, its gaping mouth the entryway, its rubber-red lips leering in the low lamplight. FUNHOUSE FUNHOUSE FUNHOUSE, the painted boards cried, and below, IT'S A SCREAM!

No doubt Gallow would do something stupid, like charging the rider with his lance out. He had always been one to rush in blindly, while Alastair hung back to see the shape of the battle before deciding where to intervene. It wasn't cowardice, he told himself for the thousandth time, it was *survival*, and woe to those who did not obey its dictates.

Crenn's hands moved, the curve of wood strapped to his back yanked free, and a word of chantment snapped the bow out, its arms gracefully bending into tension as his fingers felt along fletchings and found the one he wanted.

He nocked and drew back to his ear, the whistle-blast becoming a high keening of *prey found, prey found!*

The needle-tooth hounds would be along any moment now.

Still, he took his time, the world becoming a still small point as if he balanced on a bough in the Marrowdowne, waiting to send a flint-needle bolt through a sparrow's eye. This arrow was fletched heavily, and its head was cold iron; the hoop in Crenn's ear burned as chantment woke, humming.

He loosed.

The night-mare mount's steady jog turned to a confused walk as the rider stiffened, a grotesque choking audible down the dust-trodden length of the fairway. The rider slumped, the arrow a flagpole poking from the jousting helm's eye-bar. Crenn didn't wait to see him hit the ground, just spun and plunged after Robin and the dog.

Complete darkness. Choked cries, shattering glass. A whining bark, and he blundered into a hallway lined with mirrors, faint light from the end reflected over and over. Robin, trying to scream, reeled drunkenly from side to side, her reflections distorted-dancing; he ran into her with an *oof!* that would have been funny if he hadn't heard more urgent silver whistles filtering in from outside.

"Don't look!" he snapped, and grabbed her, earning himself a flurry of blows as she thrashed. Maddened with fear, she even bit him as he hauled her through the hallway, and the flooring underneath shifted treacherously, groaning under Pepperbuckle's weight. They pressed forward in a tangle, and he realized he was cursing, swallowed half an anatomical term a woman should never hear, and got his hand over her eyes. *"Don't look, damn you! Keep moving!"*

Turns in quick succession, and all of a sudden a doorway loomed, the dog leapt and carried it down in a shatter of splinters. Back on the fairway, Robin's eyes tightly closed as she ran, clinging to his hand.

Don't just move, Jeremiah Gallow had always said. *Move and think, that's the ticket.*

As if that bastard had any other setting than just charging in with that goddamn pigsticker of his, confident Alastair would be there in the background to do the hard work so Jer could play the hero.

Well, he's not here now, so I'll have to do both jobs.

Crenn skidded to a stop at the end of the fairway. His ears tingled, perking. They were *loud*, and the hounds were belling furiously now. The dog pressed close, whining, and he calculated its size, and hers.

"Listen." He dropped his bow, caught her face. Her summersky eyes flew open and she stared, witless with terror, perhaps, or just numb. "Listen to me, pretty girl. The dog will take you, I'll hold them. You run, you *stay alive*, and I will find you. I promise."

Her mouth worked for a moment. Her skin was so *soft*. What was she doing tangled up in this?

"I hate you," she whispered under the ultrasonic thrills. Close now, the net tightening, but there was a hole in its knotting, and he was about to send her through it. The dog was fast, and one sidhe with a bow and a habit of hunting could make merry hob of a pursuit. With a little luck, that was.

Or just a little cold calculation, and a willingness to fight dirty.

"I *hate* you," she repeated, and sense flooded her dark-blue eyes. "*I remember what you did!*" Her voice was a husk of itself, broken to pieces.

I did that to her. I dragged her to Summer.

He shook his hair back, stared down at her. "You can't," he told her, "hate me any more than I hate myself, Robin Ragged." He beckoned the hound, who pressed close, shivering and sweating, and lifted her. She grabbed at fur, righted herself, and he'd be damned if the beast didn't bulk up a little, its legs thickening to carry her weight. "Now *run.* I'll find you later."

"I'll kill you," she informed him in a whisper, with the utter calm of despair. Bright blood tinged her lips. "I will rip your heart out with my bare hands, Alastair Crenn."

Looking forward to it, pretty girl. He stepped aside, and the dog jetted forward, a coppergold blur.

Crenn scooped his bow up, closed his eyes, and *listened.*

Hoofbeats. Whistling. The pads of Unwinter's hounds, a frantic baying. The receding soft *thump-thump* of Pepperbuckle's feet. And, to top it all off, the clamor of mortal voices. The carnival folk were beginning to wake to strangeness in their midst.

"Time to hunt," he murmured, and drew another arrow from the quiver by touch. He held it loosely nocked and ran toward the noise.

A BODY TO EXPLAIN
58

In the morning, with the fires under control and everyone finally accounted for, Leo stood, his arms crossed, in front of the blackened skeleton of Marylou the cook's trailer. Marylou, the shawl pulled tight over her shoulders, leaned on Acacia. "They didn't find a body," she said flatly, and shivered. The younger girl braced her, circles under her eyes and a bruise on her cheek. She could have sworn she saw men on horses riding through the chaos of two trailer fires last night, and somehow the funhouse had been broken into. Gus had dragged Marylou out of her trailer; he was at the hospital with smoke inhalation. The only other injury was Kastner the barker's broken leg; he swore to God a man on a black motorcycle had run him down, and that the man had fallen off the chopper with a tomahawk embedded in his skull.

Of course, Kastner had probably been higher than a kite, since his pot habit was rivaled only by Marlon's drinking. Marlon's trailer had burned down, too. He'd just managed to escape, and he was telling everyone who would listen that the bad fairies had been at him.

Marlon was Irish, and was also full of shit.

"*Jesus Christ.*" Leo ran his hand back over his balding head. "*Trouble, Marylou. You and your strays, always trouble.*"

Acacia glared at him, but she was always glaring. If she didn't have such a gift for blinking her big eyes and getting guys to spend a wad at the ring-toss, he'd tell her a thing or two.

Marylou shook her head. "*Next time I'll leave someone to drown. Would you like that?*"

"*Shitfire and save matches.*" He grumbled a bit more, then lapsed into silence, staring at the smoking wreck. The townie fire department had been quick and thorough, and they hadn't even cited him for code violations. They'd been in too much of a hurry, and Leo had greased palms on his way into town, as he did every time. None of the assholes he carted around understood what it took to keep them all moving along, year after year.

Maybe he should retire.

Finally, he clapped his sweat-stained fedora back on. "*Well, at least we don't have a body to explain. There's a dealership over on Sunset. I'll see if they've got something reasonable for you. Marlon can bunk with Timmo, it might even do him some good. Get some coffee going, will you?*"

"*Yes sir.*" Marylou didn't even give him any shit. She just turned around and set off for the cooking tent with Acacia trailing in her wake. The cook limped through a bar of sunlight, her leg a little stiff—she'd have a bruise the size of a cat's head on her thigh later, from banging into the open fridge door as Gus dragged her out—and Leo squinted. For a moment she seemed covered in gold.

The disaster was their last bit of bad luck. The next six months were easy sailing. Nothing broke, Marlon quit drinking, and the take was good and steady. Marylou retired to Florida, Gus went with her, and Leo retired a month later, handing the carnival over to Acacia, who happened to have quite a head for business. When she wasn't glaring or rolling her eyes.

And for the rest of her long, semi-charmed life, Marylou wondered about the girl from the sea, and what had really happened that night. Guster never ventured an opinion, but he did often rib her gently about being lucky.

Especially in love.

A SERVICE TO PERFORM
59

A stone cube. His armor. The Horn at his chest. He wasn't chained, but he lay on the pallet writhing with fever, his side a mass of spiked agony, and it was useless. Everything was useless.

A thrumming ran through the Keep, and shortly afterward the dim torch outside the barred door sputtered. Jeremiah panted, readying himself for the next great gripping cramp.

It didn't come. He held his breath, waiting, until black flowers bloomed over his vision, but it still tarried. A gush of sweat broke out of him, sour and acrid, and he heaved over the side of the cot onto the stone floor strewn with sweetrushes.

By the time the torch brightened, sensing some feral current in the air, he was dozing. He suspected he was very near the end. *Robin. Where is she?*

When the door groaned open and the tall, broad-shouldered sidhe man glided through, Jeremiah could only blink hazily. This sidhe had a shock of matted white thistledown hair, pale ringed fingers, and a dusty black doublet; a plain silver fillet clasped his pale brow. He stepped into the room, avoiding a pool of bile and sick, and regarded Gallow.

Jeremiah blinked, hazily.

"*Can you imagine,*" his visitor said softly, "*feeling this, for an eternity? The Horn you stole, Half, will not let you die.*"

Jeremiah choked on a fresh flood of puke. Tinged with blood, it burned his nose on the way out. The Horn quivered on his chest. Cold, so cold.

The sidhe man's eyes were crimson, from lid to lid. Fine black veins webbed their orbs, and they resembled nothing so much as Summer's ageless black eyes. The same burning presence, the same terrible intensity—even though there was no pupil or iris, you could tell what they had fixed on by the sheer weight of the gaze alone.

Gallow said nothing. There was nothing *to* say, so he didn't even attempt it. One thought burned in the smoking fog his brain had become.

He's here. If he's here... Robin got away.

Two thoughts. *Or she's dead.*

The sidhe spoke again, the effluvia on the floor crackling into ice. "*I shall remove the poison, Half.*" A long, considering pause. "*What do you think of that?*"

Jeremiah's eyes rolled back in his head, and his body convulsed again. Even in extremis, he did not beg for mercy.

Perhaps that was the final deciding factor. Or perhaps Unwinter had decided long ago, and only waited for the correct moment to do as he pleased.

Unwinter bent to the wrecked body on the bed. Here in the bowels of his Keep, the lord of the Hunt pressed one elegant, wasted hand to the former Armormaster's side. Seizures passed through the body below him, hollow, choked screams were lost in the maze of stone corridors that were Unwinter's dungeon.

When it passed, Unwinter straightened, flicking his fingers.

Colorless venom roiled and sent up crackling steam. A very faint smile tilted the sidhe lord's bloodless lips.

"Rest well, Gallow. You have a service to perform, and I wish you whole for it."

The door screamed on dust-caked hinges as it drifted closed, and as Unwinter strode up the hall, he began to laugh. The cold, bitter, sharply musical sound turned the stone passageway briefly into a blizzard, and the torch was snuffed.

In the womblike dark, Jeremiah Gallow fell into a deathly sleep. Above him, Unwinter's Keep loomed, and from its high spires crimson pennants shredded to nothing on a sharp, ice-laden wind. They were replaced by black flags, a sight few sidhe had ever witnessed. Summer could have told them what it meant, or Puck Goodfellow, had either of them been inclined.

The crimson was Unwinter's peace.

The black, though...

The black was *war.*

GLOSSARY

Barrow-wight: Fullblood Unseelie wights whose homes are long "barrows." Gold loses its luster in their presence.

Brughnies: House-sidhe; they delight in cooking and cleaning. A well-ordered kitchen is their joy.

The Fatherless: Robin Goodfellow, also called Puck, the nominal leader of the free sidhe.

Folk: Sidhe, or clan within the sidhe, or generally a group, race, or species.

Ghilliedhu: "Birch-girl"; dryads of the birch clan, held to be great beauties.

Grentooth: A jack-wight, often amphibious, with mossy teeth and a septic bite.

Kelpie: A river sidhe, capable of appearing as a black horse and luring its victims to drowning.

Kobolding: A crafty race of sidhe, often amassing great wealth, living underground. Related to goblins, distantly related to the dwarven clans.

Quirpiece: A silver coin, used to hold a particular chantment.

Realmaker: A sidhe whose chantments do not fade at dawn. Very rare.

Seelie: Sidhe of Summer's Court, or holding fealty to Summer.

Selkie: A sealskin sidhe.

Sidhe: The Fair Folk, the Little People, the Children of Danu.

Sluagh: The ravening horde of the unforgiven dead.

Tainted: Possessing mortal blood.

Twisted: A sidhe altered and mutated, often by proximity to cold iron, unable to use sidhe chantments or glamour.

Unseelie: Sidhe of Unwinter's Court, or holding fealty to Unwinter.

Wight: "Being," or "creature"; used to refer to certain classes of sidhe.

Woodwight: A wight whose home or form is a tree, whose blood is resinous.

ACKNOWLEDGMENTS

Thanks must go to Mark Sanders, whose dream provided the impetus for Gallow's world, and to Mel Sanders for telling me I could certainly write it. Additional thanks must go to Miriam Kriss for encouraging me, to Devi Pillai for putting up with me, and to Lindsey Hall for not strangling me when I change things at the very last moment.

Lastly, as always, thank you, dear Reader. Come a little closer, just around this corner, and let me tell you a story...

extras

orbit

meet the author

Photo credit: Daron Gildrow

LILITH SAINTCROW was born in New Mexico, bounced around the world as an Air Force brat, and fell in love with writing when she was ten years old. She currently lives in Vancouver, Washington.

introducing

If you enjoyed
ROADSIDE MAGIC
look out for

WASTELAND KING

Gallow & Ragged: Book Three

by Lilith Saintcrow

Faint Comfort

1

Gray highway ribboned over tawny hills touched with sage-bush clinging to any scrap of moisture it could find, heat-haze shimmering above sandy slope and concrete alike. The morning sun was a brazen coin hanging above a bleached horizon as if it intended to stay in that spot forever, a bright nail to hang an endless weary day upon. The night's chill had whisked itself away, an escaping guest.

Cars shimmered faraway, announced their presence with a faint drone, and passed with a glare and blare of engine and tire-friction. Most didn't stop, even though two signs, each leaning somewhere between ten and twenty-three degrees away from true, proclaimed LAST GAS FOR 80 MI.

An ancient pair of gas pumps squatted under a rusting roof; they and the convenience store keeping watch over them had been refurbished probably around twenty years prior. Tinny music blatted from old loudspeakers on listing poles, the tired breeze dragging shackles made of paper cups, glittering dust, and a dry, skunky whiff of weedsmoke through umber shade and gold-treacle sunshine.

A burst of static cut through the music just as the slim shade on the north side of the building rippled. A single point of brilliance, lost in the glare of day, dilated, and there was a flutter of russet, of indigo, of cream.

One moment empty, the next, full; a large dog winked into being a split second before a slim female shape appeared, clinging to the canine's back as the Veil between real and more-than-real flexed. The dog staggered, its proud head hanging low, and slumped against the building. The girl slid from its broad back—the thing was *huge*—and her hair was a copper-gold gleam, firing even in the shade. Tattered black velvet clung to her, swirling as it struggled to keep up with the transition, the hood not quite covering her bright hair. She heaved, dryly, a cricketwhisper cough under the tinpan music.

Robin's stomach cramped, unhappy with the seawater she'd swallowed *and* the butter she'd filched. The fuel from the milkfat had already worn off, and her throat was on fire again. Her hands spread against dusty grit; there was a simmering reek from around the corner of the building that shouted *Dumpster*, and the music was a tinkling rendition of a ballad about mothers not letting their children grow up to be cowboys.

Good advice, maybe. But you had to grow up to be something, even if you were a Half, mortal and sidhe in equal measure. It was her mortal part that had trouble blinking through the Veil like this. It was much better to use a proper entrance, or someplace where the lands of the free sidhe overlapped, rubbing through what mortals called "real" like a needle dragged along paper. Creasing, not quite breaking, almost-visible.

Pepperbuckle made a low, unhappy noise. The dog had carried her away from the nighttime carnival, hauling her through folds and pockets, light and shade pressing against Robin's closed eyes in strobe flashes. He'd be weary. They'd run past dawn, the silver huntwhistles further and further behind them.

Concentrate. Four in, four out. The discipline of breath returned. A lifetime's worth of habit helped—if you couldn't breathe, you couldn't sing, and the song was her only defense.

She might have broken her voice, though, by singing with shusweed juice still coating her throat. The prospect was enough to bring a cold sweat out all over her, even though it was a scorching afternoon outside the thin slice of shade where she and Pepperbuckle cowered.

Where are we?

She sniffed, gulping down mortal air full of exhaust and the dry nasal rasp of baking metal and sand. A whiff of something green and living—sagebrush? No hint of anything sidhe except her and the dog, his sides heaving under glossy, red-tipped golden fur. His fine tail drooped a bit, and he eyed her sidelong, his irises bright blue and the pupils uneven orbs. It gave his gaze an uncanny quality.

She'd wrought well. In for a penny, in for a pound, and all the old clichés. There was the large unsound of wind, and a drone that could have been traffic in the very far distance.

327

The music wound down, and another song started. Someone was standing by her man. A wheezing noise was an ancient air-conditioning unit on the roof.

Robin shuddered. She pushed herself upright, making her knees unbend because there was no other choice. Pepperbuckle was depending on her, and while the mortal sun was up, they were safe enough from Unwinter's hunt.

It was some faint comfort that Summer would think Robin either still trapped, or dead.

Don't think about that. Her lips cracked as she parted them. She wanted to say Pepperbuckle's name, stopped herself. She had to shepherd her voice carefully. No more raving at that treacherous bastard Crenn when she had the breath to permit it.

You can't hate me any more than I hate myself, he'd informed her, calmly enough, before slapping Pepperbuckle's haunch to send them away. Why had he bothered to save her, after delivering her to Summer's not-so-tender mercies?

Had he also betrayed Gallow? It was entirely likely. Not that it mattered—Unwinter's poison had most likely finished off her dead sister's husband.

Don't think about that, either. Her head throbbed.

She uncurled, one arm a bar across her midriff to hold her aching belly in. The night was a whirl of impressions, everything inside her skull fracturing like broken—

Mirrors?

She shook her head violently. *Glass,* like broken *glass.* That word wasn't as troubling as the other, the *m*-word, the terrifying idea of a reflection lurching and . . .

Robin's shoulder struck the wall, jolting her back into herself. She glanced around wildly, her shorn hair whipping—it stood out around her head now, the halo giving her a headful of cowlicks. The gold hoops in her ears swung, tapping her cheeks, and she forced herself to straighten again.

A prefabricated concrete wall, either painted a dingy yellow or simply sandblasted to that color, met her. The angle of the shade and the taste of the air said *morning*, and it was going to be a hot day. Pepperbuckle sat down, his sides heaving as he panted, and his teeth gleamed bright white. The scrubland here was full of small, empty hills, and if she peered around the corner she could see ancient cracked pavement and the two gas pumps.

A little *ding* sounded, and her breath stopped as a lean, rangy mortal boy with a certain sullen handsomeness to his sharp face stepped out into the sun. He hunched his shoulders, lit a cigarette, and ambled for the pumps. A red polyester vest proclaimed him as an employee of HAPPY HARRY'S STOP N SIP. Harry was apparently a cartoon beaver, even though such an animal had very likely never been sighted in this part of the country.

Robin exhaled softly. Pumps meant a convenience store. They would have a refrigerator. Very likely, there was milk. The burning in her throat increased a notch as she contemplated this.

She glanced at Pepperbuckle, who hauled himself up wearily and followed as she edged for the back of the building.

She didn't think using the front door would be wise.

Pixies

2

Matt Grogan liked leaning against the pumps and having a smoke, even if the bossman would give him hell about safety. It wasn't like anyone ever used them, despite the fact that they were live. You had to walk inside to pay for what you pumped, and nobody wanted to do that. They wanted the ones with the credit card readers, and they drove straight on to Barton to the shiny stop-and-robs there.

When he came back in, he thought he was dreaming.

Nobody had driven up, but there was a redheaded woman in a black velvet coat in front of the ancient cooler-case, the glass door open and letting out a sourish frigid breeze as she drank from a quart of milk, probably right at its sell-by date. Christ knew no tourist ever bought anything but cigarettes and Doritos, pity buys really so they could use the small, filthy CUSTOM-ERS ONLY bathroom around the side.

Her throat worked in long swallows, her weed-whacker-cut coppery hair glowing under the fluorescents, and she was a stone *fox* even if she was drinking straight out of the carton. Skinny in all the right ways, and wearing a pair of black heels, too.

The only problem was, she was drinking without paying, and right next to her was a huge reddish hound who stared at Matt with husky-blue, intelligent eyes. A dog shouldn't look that damn *thoughtful*, as if it was sizing you up.

"Hey!" Matt's voice broke, too. Cracked right in the middle. Bobby Grogan, the football savior of Barton High and Matt's

older brother, had a nice low voice, but Matt's had just fractured its way all through school, even though he would have
given anything to sound tough just once.

Instead it was *crybaby Matt*, and the only thing worse was
the pity on Bobby's face in the parking lot. *Lay off him, he's my
brother.*

She didn't stop drinking, her eyes closed and her slim throat
moving just like an actress's. She finished off the whole damn
quart, dropped it and gasped, then reached for another.

"Hey!" Matt repeated. "You gonna pay for that?"

Her eyes opened just a little. Dark blue, and she gave him a
single dismissive glance, tearing the top off the carton in one
movement. Milk splashed, and she bent like a ballerina to put it
on the piss-yellow linoleum with little orange sparkles. The dog
dipped his long snout in and began to drink as well.

Oh, man. "You can't just *do* that, man! You gotta pay for it!"

She reached into the case again, little curls of steam rising off
her bare skin as the cooler wheezed. Those two quarts were all
the whole milk they had, so she grabbed the lone container of
half-n-half—ordered weekly because the bossman said offering
free coffee would make someone buy it—and bent back the
cardboard wings to open it. The spout was formed with a neat
little twist of her wrist, and she lifted it to her lips, all while the
dog made a wet bubbling noise that was probably enjoyment.

Oh, hell no. "You can't *do* that!" he outright yelled. "Imma
call the cops, lady! You're gonna get *arrested*!"

The instant he said it, he felt ridiculous.

She drank all the half-n-half and dropped the carton, wiping
at her mouth with the back of her left hand. Then she stared
at Matt, as if he was some sort of bug crawling around in her
Cheerios.

Just like Cindy Parmentier, as a matter of fact, who let Matt feel her up behind the bleachers once but kept asking him to introduce her to Bobby. Then she spread that goddamn rumor about him being a fag, and even Bobby looked at him like he suspected it was true.

The woman's mouth opened slightly. She still said nothing. The dog kept sucking at the opened quart on the floor, but one wary eye was half-open now.

"And you can't have dogs in here! Service animals only!"

She tipped her head back, and for a moment Matt thought she was going to scream. Instead, she laughed, deep rich chuckles spilling out and away bright as gold while he stared at her, spellbound.

When she finished laughing, the dog was licking the floor clean. She wiped away crystal teardrops on her beautiful cheeks and walked right past Matt Grogan. She smelled like spice and fruit, something exotic, a warm draft that made him think of that day behind the bleachers, soft sloping breasts under his fumbling fingers and Cindy Parmentier's quick light breathing.

The dog passed, its tail whacking him a good one across the shins, way harder and bonier than a dog's tail had any right to be. Matt staggered. The door opened, the early-summer heat breathing into the store's cave, and Matt ran after her. "*You didn't pay!*" he yelled, but he slipped on something—it gave a little weird underfoot, like the floor itself was flexing to throw him off.

He went down hard, almost cracking his skull on the racks of nudie mags they couldn't sell inside the Barton city limits. *That* was the real reason this place held on, and once he started working here they started laughing even more.

"Ow!" Matt rolled, thrashing to get back up. Something jabbed at his cheek, and something else at his finger. Tiny, vicious little stings all over him.

332

The bell over the door tinkled again. "Stop that," the voice said, low and sweet as warm caramel, with a hidden fierceness. It made the sweat spring out all over him.

It was a good thing his eyes were closed, or he would have seen the tiny flying things, their faces set in scowling mutiny, their wings fluttering and a deep throbbing blue spreading through the glow surrounding each one, spheres of brilliance bleached by daylight and fluorescent but still bolder, richer than the colors of the tired mortal world.

A low, thunderous growl. It was the dog, and Matt rolled around some more, suddenly terrified. His bladder let go in a warm gush, and the stinging continued.

"I said *stop it*." Everything inside the store rattled. The floor heaved a little again, and that was when he opened his eyes and saw... them. The little naked people, their delicate insect-veined wings, their sharp noses and the wicked merriment of their sweet chiming pinprick voices.

They darted at him, but the woman said "No," again, firmly, even as they piped indignantly at her. "Leave him alone. He's just a kid."

They winked out. The door closed with a whoosh, and he lay there in his own urine, quivering. Her footsteps were light tiptaps on the tarmac outside, before they were swallowed up by the hum of air-conditioning.

And a faint, low, deadly chiming. Little pinpricks of light bloomed around him again, and he began to scream.

Not long afterward Matt Grogan got up, tiny teethmarks pressed into his flesh on his face and hands, and bolted through the door without waiting for it to open, shattering glass into the parking lot. He ran into the sagebrush wilderness, and nobody in Barton ever saw him again.

Mislaid

3

Summerhome rose upon its green hill, its fair flowing pennants in wind-driven tatters. The walls should have been white and green, the towers strong and fair like the slim necks of ghilliedhu girls, and around its pearly swordshapes the green hills and shaded dells should have rippled rich and verdant. The Road should have dipped and swayed easily, describing crest and hollow with a lover's caress; there were many paths, but they all led Home.

The hills and valleys were green and fragrant, copse and meadow drowsing under a golden sun. They were not as rich and fair as they had been before, nor did they recline under their own vivid dreams as in Unwinter's half of the year. The ghilliedhu girls did not dance as they were wont to do from morning to dusk in their damp dells; the pixies did not flit from flower to flower gathering crystal dewdrops. The air shimmered, but not with enticement or promise. Strange patches spread over the landscape of the more-than-real, oddly bleached, as if fraying.

The trees themselves drew back into the hollows, the shade under their branches full of strange whispers, passing rumor from bole to branch.

Rumor—and something else.

Occasionally, a tree would begin to shake. Its spirit, a dryad slim or stocky, hair tangling and fingers knotting, would go into convulsions, black boils bursting from almost-ageless flesh.

First there were the spots and streaks of leprous green, then the blackboil, then the convulsions.

And then, a sidhe died.

Dwarven doors were shut tight, admitting neither friend nor foe, and the free sidhe hid elsewhere, perhaps hoping the cold iron of the mortal world would provide an inoculation just as mortal blood did. Some whispered the plague was an invention of the mortals, jealous of the sidhe's frolicsome immortality, but it was always answered with the lament that no mortal believed in the Good Folk anymore, so that was impossible.

Summerhome's towers were bleached bone, and the greenstone upon them had paled significantly. A pall hung over the heart of Summer, the fount the Folk issued from. The vapor carried an unfamiliar reek of burning, perhaps left over from the disposal of quick-rotting bodies, both from the battle with Unwinter and from the plague itself. Sparse though the latter were, there was no real hope of them abating.

From the sugarwhite shores of the Dreaming Sea to the green stillness of Marrowdowne, from the high moors where the giants strode and those of the trollfolk allied to Summer crouched and ruminated in their slow bass grumbles to the grottos where naiads peered anxiously into still water to reassure themselves that their skin was unmarked, Summer shuddered feverishly.

Inside the Home's high-vaulted halls, brughnies scurried back and forth, but no dryads flocked to carry hair ribbons and little chantment spangles for their betters. The highborn fullbloods, most vulnerable to the plague, kept an unwonted distance from one another, and some had slipped away to other estates and winter homes, no doubt on urgent business.

On a low bench on a high dais, among the repaired columns of Summer's throneroom, she sat, slim and straight and lovely still, her hands clasped tight in her lap. Her mantle was deep green, her shoulders peeking through artful rends in the fabric and glowing nacreous. The Jewel on Summer's forehead glowed, a low dull emerald glare. It was not the hurtful radiance of her former glory, but her golden hair was still long and lustrous, and her smile was still soft and wicked as she viewed the knights arrayed among the forest of fluted columns.

Broghan the Black, the glass badge of Armormaster upon his chest, stood on the third step of the dais. He did not glance at the knight who knelt on the second, a dark-haired lord in full armor chased with glowing sungold. Dwarven work, and very fine; Broghan's own unrelieved black was all the more restrained in comparison.

Or so he wished to think.

The *brun* knight, Summer's current favorite, stared at her slippered feet, waiting for a word.

She did not let him wait long. "Braghn Moran." Soft, so dulcet-sweet, the loveliest of her voices. The air filled with appleblossom-scent, petals showering from above as layers of chantment, applied at festival after festival, woke in response. "A fair lord, and a fell one."

"Your Majesty does me much honor," he murmured in reply. No ripple stirred among the serried ranks, though no doubt a few of them grudged him said honor.

The wiser knew it was only a matter of time. *Fickle as Summer*, some said—though never very loudly. Braghn Moran's lady-love had left Court not long ago, when Summer's gaze had turned upon him.

"Something troubles me, Braghn."

The knight could have observed that there were many troublesome things afoot among the sidhe lately, but he did not—

336

perhaps a mark of wisdom itself. He kept examining the toe of Summer's green velvet slipper, peeking out from under the heavy folds of her mantle. If he compared it with another lady's, none could tell.

"I seek a certain troublesome sprite, and I would have you find him for me."

"Who could not come, when you call?" Broghan the Black commented.

Summer did not spare him so much as a glance. "I believe Puck Goodfellow is leading a certain former Armormaster down many a path."

A rustle now *did* pass through the ranks of Seelie knights.

Gallow. The Half who had committed the unforgivable, who had insulted Summer and all of Seelie to boot.

"You wish me to kill Gallow?" Braghn Moran did not sound as if he considered it much of a challenge.

"No, my dear Braghn. Puck Goodfellow has mislaid his head; it belongs on my mantelpiece where I may gaze upon it. I have had enough of his play at neutrality. If the free sidhe are not with us, they are with Unwinter." Cruel and cold, her beauty, not the visage of the simple maiden she often wore. This was a different face, one haughty and motionless as marble. "And I will not tolerate Unwinter's insolence further."

Braghn Moran rose. He glittered as he stood before Summer, stray gleams of sunshine striking from dwarven-carved lines on breastplate, greaves, armplates. "Yes, my queen."

"Do this, and you shall be my lord." She smiled, softening, a kittenish moue of her glossy carmine lips. Petals showered through the air.

He made no reply, merely turned on his heel. The ranks parted for him, and some may have noticed he did not swear to her before he left, nor did he glance back. His face was set and pale, and when the doors closed behind him Summer's softening smile fled.

"The rest of you," she continued, "are required for other work."

Tension crackled between the floating rosepetals. For Summer to expend her strength on this glamouring, for her to appear thus, was unheard of.

"Jeremiah Gallow, once Armormaster, offends the Summer Queen." Her hands tightened against each other in her lap, each finger tipped with a wicked-sharp crimson nail. "Kill him, and bring Unwinter's Horn to me."

introducing

If you enjoyed
ROADSIDE MAGIC
look out for

BLOOD CALL

by Lilith Saintcrow

*Anna Caldwell has spent the last few days in a blur.
She's seen her brother's dead body, witnessed the shooting of
innocent civilians, and been shot at herself. Now she has nowhere
to turn—and only one person she can possibly call.*

*Since Anna dumped him, it seems waiting is all Josiah Wolfe
has done. Now, she's calling, and she needs his help—or rather,
the "talents" she once ran away from. As a liquidation agent,
Josiah knows everything about getting out of tough situations.
He'll get whatever she's carrying to the proper authorities, then
settle down to making sure she doesn't leave him again.*

*But the story Anna's stumbled into is far bigger than even
Josiah suspects. Anna wants to survive, Josiah wants Anna
back, and the powerful people chasing her want the only thing*

*worth killing for—immortality. An ancient evil has been
trapped, a woman is in danger, and the world is going to see just
how far a liquidation agent will go...*

Chapter One

Thin winter sunlight spilled through a window, a square of
anemic gold on blue carpet. He stared, turning the knife over
in his hands and watching the bright gleam of the blade.

Spent a lot of time doing that, these days. Retirement wasn't
boring—once a man got old enough, he learned to like it when
bullets weren't whizzing overhead.

A faint sound broke thick silence.

He'd fooled himself into thinking he'd heard it so many
times, the actual event was a dreamlike blur. Then the phone
buzzed on his desk again, rattling against the leather cup that
held two pens and a letter opener.

It was *the* phone. He'd had the number transferred to a
newer one, just in case, and the bill was paid automatically
every month from an account that never went dry.

Just in case. It was silly, it was stupid, it was probably a
wrong number. The ID started with *1-89,* and that meant a
pay phone.

Definitely a wrong number. Still... Josiah Wolfe dropped
the knife and snatched up the slim black plastic case, hit TALK
with a sweating finger.

"Hello." No betraying surprise in the word. His hands were
steady. *It's just a wrong number. Someone hit a nine when they*

should have hit a six, a two when they wanted to hit five. Don't give anything away.

Her voice came through. "Jo? Josiah?" A staggering gasp, as if she'd been punched in the stomach.

His knees had turned to water. Sweat sprang out on his lower back, under his arms, in the hollows of his palms. Was he dreaming?

Pinch me. No, don't. Let me sleep. He managed to speak. "Anna." *I still sound calm. Jesus God, thank you.*

Wait. Is she crying?

The thought of her crying made his chest feel hollow and liquid.

"I wasn't..." Another one of those terrible gasps. Was she trying to catch her breath? Drunk? Was that why she was crying? "I wasn't sure you'd answer. Or if the number was even s-still good."

He had to drop down into the chair. His legs wouldn't hold him up. "I told you it would be." *When you left me.* The words burst out, hard little bullets, surprising him. "I keep my promises."

He almost winced as soon as it left his mouth. That was like waving a red flag in front of a bull; she might have a sudden attack of good sense and hang up. *Keep her talking, idiot. Keep her on the line.*

Finally, after three years, Anna had called him.

There is a God. Thank you. Thank you so much.

Another deep ragged inhale, as if bracing herself. She sounded like she'd just paused during a hard workout, sharp low gasps. He heard city noise behind her. Cars, the imperfect roar of traffic, and the sound of cold wind. Where was she?

"I d-didn't know." Her voice broke, and he was now certain she was crying.

Warning bells were ringing. It wasn't like Anna Caldwell to cry, especially on the phone with the man she'd sworn at, slapped, and dropped like a bad habit three years ago when she'd found out what he did for a living. It doubly wasn't like her to be at a pay phone, especially on a winter day that, while sunny, was only in the thirty-degree range. She felt the cold acutely; she slept with a blanket on all but the stickiest of summer nights.

It especially wasn't like her to sound so terrified, she was stuttering.

"I d-d-didn't th-think this n-number would w-w-work, b-but I h-had to…" She broke down again, hitching sobs thin and tinny in his ear.

This isn't good. "Anna. *Anna.*" He used his calm-the-waters voice, nice and low but sharp to grab her attention, cut off the panic. "Where are you, baby? Tell me where you are."

It worked. She took a deep breath, and he could almost see her grabbing for brittle calm, the way she'd done right before she'd walked out on him. That little sound, and her green eyes going cool and distant, her shoulders drawing back—he could picture it clear as day, even now. "I'm on the corner of Maple and Twentieth, in an awful ph-phone booth. I'm cold and I think I'm still wet from the p-pond and I'm scared, and I need your help. I *need* your help."

He was already moving, taking the small pad on his desk and making notes. *Pay phone. Maple and 20th. Pond.* "Stay put. I'm coming to get you."

"I d-didn't know who else to call," she whispered, and the most amazing thing happened.

Josiah began to get a hard-on. He still remembered the way her hair smelled. Still remembered the taste of her sweat, and her low, throaty moan at delicious intervals.

Jesus. Three years, and the woman still managed to turn him on.

"I'm in trouble," she whispered into the phone, as if afraid someone might hear. "Bad t-trouble."

So you called me. "Maple and Twentieth." He was already scooping up his car keys and his black hip-length jacket. His legs shook, but they would carry him. Of all the scenarios he'd played out in his head over the years, he hadn't ever dreamed this one up. "You're outside?" *Idiot. She said a phone booth. You can hear the traffic behind her. Is she at a gas station? Good for a grab, someone could just take her right off the street.* "I'm on my way."

"No!" She practically yelled, and he stopped dead, inhaling sharply and closing his eyes.

Focus, Josiah. Control is everything.

Calm returned, the killing quiet. Anna was in trouble, and he had to be cool and collected. *Get her locale, get in, and retrieve her. It's that simple.* He opened his eyes and got going again, placing each foot with precision.

"No," she repeated, as if he'd argued. "It's not... it's not safe. The Blake, in the foyer. Come in on the... the east side. Through the revolving doors."

The Blake Hotel was less than three blocks from Maple and Twentieth. It had three exits and usually a clutch of tourists taking in the old-fashioned foyer with its crystal chandeliers, ancient wainscoting, and red velvet upholstery. In other words, a security nightmare. He'd done a few jobs in the Blake, none serious. Just deliveries, a long time ago.

Don't foul your own nest was a good maxim to follow.

"It's not safe?" The question was out before he could stop himself. Even worse, it sounded cynical. Condescending. As if he suspected her of setting him up.

Nobody in the gray knew about him and Anna. He'd kept that secret successfully, at least. Of course, in this business, it was hard to be sure.

"I think they're still f-following me." She was whispering again. "If you see someone…oh, God. *God*."

A cool bath of dread began at his nape and slid down his sweating back. *Just what kind of trouble are you in, baby?* He didn't want to waste time asking. "Anna. Calm the fuck down and breathe, I'm coming to get you. The Blake. I'll be there in twenty."

Hitching sobs, again. "I d-didn't know w-who else to—"

Yeah. Who else could you call if you were in trouble? "Get to the Blake, get inside, and put your back to the wall. Warm up. I'm coming to get you." He was already on the stairs on his way to the garage, thankful that it was Hassan's day off and Wilhelmina was in the kitchen; nobody would see him leave. "Hang up and get moving, baby."

"Oh, God…" She sucked in a sharp, hissing breath. "The car. That goddamn black car."

What the hell? "What black car?"

Too late. She'd hung up, or had run out of time on whatever change she'd dropped into the phone. Unless she'd used one of the newer ones with credit card readers. No, she was too smart to do that, if she was in trouble bad enough to call him. She was too goddamn smart for her own good.

The wonder was that she'd found a pay phone at all. They were a vanishing breed.

Great. Now his heart was hammering and he tasted copper, as if he was under fire. He shrugged into his coat and checked his watch, habitually noting the time, and slipped the cell into his left-hand pocket. There were a couple of prepaid ones each in the cars, nice and disposable. His shoes made no noise on the stairs; he avoided the creaky spots out of habit as well. He made it to the garage, chose the blue BMW because it had a 9mm and ammo in the concealed compartment, and it would blend in around the Blake.

He'd never expected her to call.

Then why did you keep the phone, Josiah? The garage door went up, and the engine roused itself like a sleepy cat. Willie's little red sedan, the sleek gleaming SUV, and the dirty, primer-spotted Taurus sat in their accustomed places, watching with blank, dead headlights as he pulled out.

What kind of trouble was she in? Trouble so bad she would call *him,* of all people.

I don't care.

The sun struck him fully, and he slid a pair of shades on. Frost still glimmered in deeper shadows where the light didn't hit until afternoon; the roads would be treacherous. He flipped the radio off and felt the little subconscious *click* inside his head that meant he was thinking clearly again.

She's called me. She needs my help.

All right. This time she's not getting away.

Josiah Wolfe smiled as he drove.

Chapter Two

She'd wanted to warn him about the black cars, but she'd run out of change and she didn't dare use her bank card *or* her beloved iPhone. Who knew what they could trace? They might think she was dead.

I certainly hope *they think I'm dead. Everyone else, too.* Maybe nobody else would...die...if they all thought she was gone.

Anna shivered, glancing nervously at the gas station. She looked like hell; she hadn't combed her hair and she was still wet to the knees from the goddamn pond; her makeup was probably running and blisters were starting inside her shoes. Heels were *not* the best way to escape men with guns and walk for miles, ending up in a phone booth that smelled like someone had used it for a urinal. Vivian at Fillmore West would be furious, thinking Anna wasn't even bothering to show up to her own showing; Tasha would be heartbroken. She'd missed drinks with Robbie and Tor; they would be perplexed and hurt.

Also, she was beginning to run out of ideas.

Not only that, but she'd stood and stared at the phone for a little while, zoning out. The numb, glazed calm echoing inside her head and chest *had* to be shock. Nobody could be as calm as she was right now after seeing what she'd seen.

Eric...oh, Eric...

She pushed the thought away, shoved the door open, and stepped into a light breeze knifing up from the lake's faraway, innocent baby-blue shimmer. Her black canvas purse strap dug into her shoulder; the purse itself was freighted with the files they presumably wanted to kill her for. Pale winter sunlight poured down on a convenience store parking lot, weeds poking up through cracked concrete and graffiti tangling on a wall over a huge Dumpster around the back. The booth was at the very edge of the lot, and she stepped over two broken syringes as her weary body started to shiver again, reminding her that she'd run away from George Moorhouse's lovely split-level wearing only a gray business suit with a thin jacket over a silk shell, a knee-length skirt, and a pair of nylons that were definitely the worse for wear now. She'd had a long black scarf, but she'd lost it in the mad scramble to get *away*, hearing bullets *pockpockpock* into the freezing earth behind her.

A car horn blared. *"Hey, baby! You sellin'?"*

Anna, yanked back into the present, whipped the guy in the chopped-down Cadillac the finger. *I look like a hooker? Or you're just an asshole.* The Caddy zoomed off, the kids inside laughing, and she choked back another black wave of desperation masquerading as hilarity. Little jackasses in mama's car. *What a way to get propositioned.*

She had to wait, shivering and shifting her purse from shoulder to shoulder, for the light at the corner of Fifteenth and Verne; she hadn't told Josiah *exactly* where she was, for no other reason than the instinctive caution of a hunted animal.

I'm doing pretty well. At least I'm still alive. And he might help me.

At the thought of Josiah, she shivered again. She crossed her arms and stared at the red DON'T WALK sign, willing it to change.

For a horrifying second, she'd thought she'd forgotten his number. Then her brain had kicked into gear and she'd dialed, hoping, praying, begging God. After the last four days, she seriously doubted she could do anything else but pray.

I don't have anywhere else to go. And he…knows about this sort of stuff.

That's why you dumped him.

Her stomach growled, reminding her that she hadn't eaten since yesterday afternoon. The wind was going straight up her skirt. She was down to ten dollars in cash and a purse stuffed full of incriminating paperwork she hadn't even had a chance to *look* at yet. Tears burned under her eyelids. *Eric. God, Eric.*

Don't start. You already look strange; you start sobbing on a street corner and someone will call the cops, and you'll be dead before you know it.

A molten tear trickled down her cheek. She swiped it away with the back of her cold hand, swallowing the sudden lump in her throat.

The nightmare rose behind her eyes again, Eric's head tilted back and the gruesome smile of the gash in his throat leering at her, the terrible stink and the *heat*; someone had turned the thermostat up and it had been tropical in the bedroom office. They'd stuffed a ball of paper in his mouth, probably one of the scattered pieces always strewn around his offices like confetti. They had torn his place apart, probably looking for the folders she had in her purse right now.

The files Eric had asked her to keep safe, because he thought his place might be burgled. *One thing, Annie,* he'd said, laying his hand on her shoulder. *If my house is tossed, I'm not calling the police. You get me?*

She came back to herself with another jolt. The DON'T WALK sign was flashing; had she missed it?

Her high heels clattering, Anna bolted across the street and took a right. A stitch slammed up her ribs, forcing her to slow. A short Latino man walking his dog gave her a curious look but stopped outside a bakery, which was sending out a tantalizing smell into the chilly air. It would be break time at work, leaving the desk to Alan so she could run out for her morning latte. Hunger cramped as fiercely as the stitch in her side.

Don't stop, and don't spend any money. If he doesn't show up you're going to need every penny.

Yeah, like ten bucks is going to get me very far.

When she could walk again, she set off toward the Blake. The buildings were getting higher on either side, breaking the force of the wind, but they also blocked the sunlight. There wasn't much of a crowd at this end of Verne Street. Nearer the Blake, there would be well-dressed people out for shopping or the tourist attractions; the museum was up a few blocks and the opera hall a short cab ride away.

Could you hide out in a museum? Now *there* was a thought.

Anna's arm clenched, keeping the black canvas purse tight against her side. She swiped at the icy tears on her cheeks, willing herself to keep moving steadily. *If I could get away from armed men, I can do this. I'm going to make them pay, dammit.*

She had never even *dreamed* she would ever dial Josiah's number again. She racked her brain for alternatives one last time as she walked, her heels clicking against the pavement and her teeth clenched to stop them from chattering, her head held high.

There was nothing else she could do. Eric and George had both warned her not to go to the cops, and she didn't know anyone else who was likely to have even an *idea* of how to handle this. She was a temp; nobody at the office would miss her or think anything of her sudden absence. Her few friends and fellow artists were good people, but you couldn't ask someone whose last installation had been all Plexiglas cocks and red Jell-O vulvas to risk taking a bullet over this. Tasha would hide her, but how could Anna ask her best friend to take that sort of risk?

There was no one, now.

Nobody except the man she'd walked out on. Less than a week before their planned Las Vegas elopement, as a matter of fact. She had gone on with her life and her art, and done her best to forget him.

No matter how much it hurt.

Her hair fell in her face, tendrils of dark brown she wished she'd had a chance to dye. Maybe blond. She'd look bimbolicious as a blonde, but it might be enough to throw someone off.

The walloping unreality of the last four days hit her again. *I've called Josiah.*

He'd sounded unsurprised. Calm, as usual. *I'm coming to get you.* As if she'd been stranded at a bar or with a flat tire somewhere. Even, casual, and completely confident.

For a killer, she supposed, an ex-girlfriend calling at ten in the morning with a crazy story and a hysterical demand for help must be small potatoes.

Can you just focus on getting to the goddamn hotel? You don't have anyone else you can trust right now. Tasha knew a woodcarver who happened to be a cop; she'd probably want to go to him—and end up shot.

Don't trust the police, Eric and George had both said.

Anna walked along at a good clip, each step hammering into her sore ankle, her busted-up knee—scraped from falling into the ornamental pool; she'd erased most of the skin on her kneecap with that move, but it had saved her head from being turned into hamburger—her aching hips, and finishing up by stabbing into her lower back with a bar of fire. As she got closer to the hotel, crossing Verne Street and cutting up Eighteenth, she started running her fingers back through her hair, trying to straighten it. Maybe she had a comb in her purse?

She wasn't going to be able to talk her way past the doorman. Which was why she'd asked Josiah to come in the east door; she could catch him on the street outside if she was lucky.

I wish I could take my nylons off. That would be even colder, though. She shivered at the thought.

The crowd thickened. One of the great things about living in the city was the way everyone minded their own business—or at least, pretended to. She got a few curious looks, but not many. At least she didn't have blood or muck splashed on her; she had avoided the worst of the gunk in the pool and a scrubbing with paper towels in the gas station restroom had worked whatever wonder it could.

She no longer looked like Anna Caldwell, secretary by day and mild-mannered freelance artist. No, she probably looked like a mad Lady Macbeth.

Or just possibly like a woman on the run in a nightmare that just kept getting worse.

Go figure; she was running for her life and worrying about if she should have tried to find a comb in the restroom, too.

She sped up. Her heels clickety-clacked, traffic buzzed, and her head began to feel too big for her narrow stem of a neck.

Don't you dare pass out.

She finally glimpsed, with a swimming delirious relief that bordered on the crazed, the carved white marble facade of the Blake rising up, catching a reflection of morning light from the mirrored skyscraper opposite and glowing like heaven's doors. Anna let out a little sigh, chopped into bits by her chattering teeth. She must have been walking without paying attention, because her cheeks were still icy-wet and she didn't remember the blocks between here and the bakery.

Wake up. Look around, look for that goddamn black car. She clutched her purse to her side and clamped her teeth together. Stared at the hotel up the street. This was the south side; she would have to cross the street twice and go around the corner to get to where she could see the revolving door.

What if he'd gotten here before her? Or not come at all?

She almost moaned in dismay. Just because his cell phone number was still good didn't mean that he'd forgiven her for walking out on him, or for what she'd called him the last time she saw him, or...

Though she was perfectly justified, she reminded herself. Perfectly.

Oh, God. I'm going crazy. Please help me.

She swiped at her frozen cheeks with her jacket sleeve, shivering so hard she imagined her hands blurring like a cartoon character's. She had to get inside, one way or another. If she stayed on the street she'd freeze to death.

Josiah. The thought of him, tall and dark-haired and utterly imperturbable, was oddly comforting. Like putting her head down on his shoulder and being certain she was safe; a feeling she hadn't had since before that last, volcanic fight.

He'd said he was coming to get her. She certainly hoped so, because she was out of options. Her last great idea had ended up with Eric's editor shot and Anna herself running for her life. She had precious little left to lose.

I'm just going to have to hope he still feels something for me. She swayed, a funny feeling of her head getting too big and stuffed with cotton wool making the world blur. The cold was working its way in through her skin; she was almost too tired to shiver. *I can pay him, I've got savings left over from Mom's inheritance. That's what he always worked for before, money. And lots of it, if his apartment was any indication.*

She flinched at the turn her thoughts were taking, and almost tripped. Her left foot slid oddly inside her shoe. Something warm trickled down her heel.

I am a total fucking mess.

Her vision blurred. Eric's throat with its horrible necklace of a bloody smile rose in front of her again. She cast a nervous glance at the milling crowd on the sidewalks, the cars crawling through downtown traffic, and took hold of her rapidly thinning courage with both mental hands.

Get into the hotel. Have a goddamn nervous breakdown later.